CC

Omnibus Vol 1

THE FATE OF THE STARVISTA 4

The second of the StarVista 4 Saga

A Science Fiction novel

By Paul Money

Cover artwork (2023):
Principal Designer ASP
Based on ideas by Paul Money

@ Mary McIntyre

Shutterstock.com
@ Catmando
@ Andreiuc88
@ Dave Wetzel
@ Algol
@ Kinga

COPYRIGHT NOTICE

Astrospace Publications
18 College Park, Horncastle, Lincolnshire LN9 6RE
www.astrospace.co.uk

Copyright © Paul Money
November 2023
All rights reserved.

The right of Paul Money to be identified as the author of
this work has been asserted by him in accordance with
the Copyright, Designs and Patents Act 1988 (UK).

All the characters in the story are fictional
and any resemblance to real persons either
living or dead is purely coincidental.

No part of this novel may be reproduced in any
form other than that which it was purchased and
without the written permission of the author.

This novel is licensed for your personal enjoyment
only and may not be re-sold or given away to other
people in either this or any other format.

Language: UK English

ACKNOWLEDGEMENTS

The author would like to acknowledge the support and help of his wife, Lorraine who patiently listened to the idea and subsequent development of this Sci Fi novel and gave invaluable advice, encouragement and editing ideas as the story evolved.

He would also like to thank the following for their advice, informed opinion and wisdom as this novel took shape.

Gill Hart
Julian Onions
Mary McIntyre
Peter Rea
Peter Williamson

PREFACE

Andrew James Hansone, AJ to his close friends, grew up with an obsession about finding the lost star passenger cruiser 'StarVista 4' after watching a docudrama about the fate of the ship when he was just a twelve year old.

After discovering fame and fortune designing and building starships, he joins the crew of the EXSSV Erebus to solve the mystery once and for all.

But with past history between himself and Captain Eric Andersohn along with an obsessed chief engineer, little does he realise how dangerous a mission it is.

All completely unaware that the Azaline Empirate is almost ready to strike at the primary worlds of the Galactic Arm Association ...

Join AJ as he sets out to discover The Fate of the StarVista 4.

PROLOGUE

2505 AC

Andrew J Hansone, AJ to close friends, sat in the shuttle contemplating everything that had led up to this moment.

This moment.

He was en route to the EXploration Space Salvage Vessel, EXSSV Erebus and he couldn't help wondering what he'd do if this gamble went wrong, for that was surely what it was, a gamble. His passion, some would say obsession after watching an episode of 'Wonders of the ever-changing Universe' hosted by his favourite holovid star, Sir Harley Ryker-Smyth, had haunted him ever since he'd first come across the episode, around twenty-four years earlier.

Back then as a twelve year old, he'd been confined to his room and for a large part of a week, to his bed, after he and fellow school children, including his 'beloved' sister, Carla, had contracted an almost long forgotten virus that in theory had been consigned to the history books.

One night, he'd been bored and came across a channel showing old episodes of 'Wonders of the ...' and the one he stumbled upon, covered the mystery of the disappearance of the star passenger cruise ship StarVista 4.

He fondly remembered how it started ...

The programme titles flashed by then the

narrator, none other than the famous explorer Sir Harley Ryker-Smyth began telling the tale. AJ had chuckled at the old fashioned and almost hardly ever heard of Sir moniker, but loved the opening 3D holographic fly around of the vast StarVista 4 interstellar cruise liner.

Sir Harley also looked the part of an ancient explorer with his old-fashioned black waistcoat, cream frilled shirt, very large flowery bow tie and black neat fitting trousers. The moustache also made him look distinctive, especially as few men or women grew them anymore. Apparently long ago it was quite fashionable.

Sir Harley began ...

"Hello fellow explorers, it is I, Sir Harley Ryker-Smyth, yes he of the fame of charting the jagged scars of Eldered Five, exploring the savage jungles of Alteran Twelve and escaping from the ravenous hordes of Scorios. Tonight on 'Mysteries of the ever-changing Universe' I'll be taking a look at one of the most mysterious and strange happenings of the last one hundred years that is still forcing us to ask the question: Whatever befell the StarVista 4 with its two thousand passengers and seven hundred crew."

As he spoke, a holographic replica of the StarVista 4 swung around his body as if in orbit, just as he finished talking, he grabbed it out of the air and held it dramatically toward the viewer.

Yes, AJ had been totally hooked on the story as Sir Harley explored the many theories as to why such an amazing ship had met its end. Sir Harley built it up until at the end of the episode, he had concluded the authorities had been right all along and the ship had not vanished into the ether but had suffered an unfortunate crash into an unknown icy moon.

It still puzzled AJ however, that the ship had been given permission to travel to the edge of Galactic Arm Association space to a planet in the relatively unexplored Cantrara system, a gas giant planet which was said to have the most fabulous and extraordinary ring system.

If that were the case, why wasn't a science vessel sent well beforehand? Sir Harley may have followed the official line, but AJ was left with questions unanswered, and those questions stayed with him to this very day.

It had spurred him on to study engineering, advanced spaceflight propulsion and much more besides. He was now considered the foremost starship engineer and designer, with his own company worth a planet sized fortune.

Admittedly his three failed marriages took a lot of that fortune and he felt a little apprehension knowing who the captain of the Erebus was as the shuttle made final approach.

His old school and university best friend, Eric Andersohn whose sister had been AJ's third wife. But it had been a couple of years since the divorce and as he had designed the EXSSV ship for a specific purpose, he had no choice but to hire it for the momentous task ahead, regardless of his connection to the captain.

AJ saw the space port looming ever larger and off, docked to one side, he could see the Erebus: he braced himself for the task ahead …

PART I

2505 AC

The EXSSV Erebus

1: A WARM, AND NOT
SO WARM, WELCOME

"Come in, sit down and make yourself comfortable."

The captain of the EXSSV Erebus motioned to the fair-haired man as he entered, who in turn grimaced and put his hands on his hips.

"Is that how you greet an old friend then Eric?" the newcomer asked. Captain Eric Andersohn stood impassively, watching as the newcomer walked round and stood in front of him, holding his hand out in greeting.

"You don't change a bit, do you AJ," Eric shook hands then both embraced warmly before parting as Eric thumped AJ on the shoulder. "Andrew James Hansone, the old whizz kid from school who always drove everyone round the bend with tales of mystery and suspense. None of us ever thought that you could make a fortune, own your own company, several hundred patents for advanced engineering, design and build spaceships blah, blah, blah ...

DON'T mention or bring up recent family events, I don't want to discuss them as this is work, not play. But I do want to know what the hell are you doing on my old rust bucket out here at StarPort Eldered Five?"

AJ wandered over to the large view port and gazed out at the crescent illuminated planet they were currently orbiting. It was a breath-taking sight, the night side sprinkled with city lights just barely visible as per the planet's night light pollution laws.

Vibrant greens and deep browns were just visible on the day side of the planet.

StarPort Eldered Five was a vast orbital complex serving the needs of the Galactic Arm Association Security Services, Commercial Exploration Sector and Intergalactic Leisure Conglomerate. Thank heaven no one had decided to use it as an acronym: GAASSCESILC would have been an unspeakable mouthful!

"Suit yourself. I wouldn't call the Erebus a rust bucket. If I recall correctly, the EXSSV Erebus is the largest, most advanced exploration and salvage ship ever built and is only four years old. Pretty young compared with many ships of the GAA. I couldn't have hired a better ship if I'd tried.

The fact that I was the one who designed it and had it built by Hansone Industries is beside the point. Pity the GAA decided they wanted it for themselves as I was planning on keeping it as it is a great ship. Mind you, I'm not sure about her captain ..."

"Cheeky sod," replied Eric. "Who was it that recovered the mining ship Carson's Mother from the gravity well of X477-213? Yeah, MY ship! You've got the best ship and captain. Time to spill on why you are here and why I've been told, nay ordered, to do everything, I mean, EVERYTHING, you ask?" Eric was stern, his face hinted he wasn't really annoyed, but certainly curious at the situation he found himself in.

AJ smiled, swiped the air before him and a holoscreen appeared. He swiped a couple more times then motioned to Eric.

"Remember me always going on about this?" he swiped to play and the original docudrama he had cherished since a young boy, began to play.

Eric shook his head, knowing AJ would not have hired the Erebus if he had not discovered something. His heart sank a little as he realised where their ultimate destination was likely to be.

He didn't relish the prospect.

AJ fast forwarded through some of the more over the top ideas the programme had explored then played the segment he had always been fascinated and puzzled by …

"Hello and on with our next possible explanation for the fate of StarVista 4, I'm your host, Sir Harley Ryker-Smyth here on 'Mysteries of the ever-changing Universe'."

Eric in the meantime just shook his head and grumbled something as if in pain.

Sir Harley continued unabated …

"We've looked at the more extreme theories but now let us explore something that has been put forward by Astrophysicist Armandan Zolic of the Alteran Science Foundation. He has extensively studied what little data we have about the final

moments of the StarVista 4 from the standard engineering data all star cruisers have to transmit when carrying fee paying luxury passengers.

Remember the official explanation from the StarVista corporation and the GAA? StarVista 4 was the first passenger ship to be allowed to add the Cantrara system to its itinerary. Why?

Well, it was the discovery a decade or more earlier, of the amazing and unique multi-inclined rings of the largest planet, Tianca, that captured the imagination and lured people into wanting to see them for themselves.

Perhaps the granting of that application was the first step towards the doomed fate of the StarVista 4.

Records show that StarVista 4 arrived in orbit at Tianca on time and it was only a matter of less than two hours later that signals appeared to abruptly cease from the ship. Astrophysicist Zolic noted that the signal did not actually abruptly cease but faded over a matter of seconds, something not in line with the official explanation of a catastrophic crash into an unknown icy moon.

So, what do the authorities say happened? The official line is that this was a relatively unexplored system and not all moons, minor objects or even the full extent of the ring system was known or mapped in sufficient detail. It was postulated that, until it had been fully explored, no one should have granted public access to the StarVista corporation on grounds of safety and that StarVista 4 is proof of *the foolishness of their being allowed to go.*

StarVista 4 is believed to have crashed into an undiscovered moon of Tianca with the loss of all hands. This moon was only a few miles in size, comparable indeed with the size of StarVista 4 itself so ..."

The holovid was cut short by Eric's frustrated hand gesture through the view, disrupting it.

"I KNOW all that, this is a waste of my time and ships resources."

"ERIC, bear with me. Do you think I'd be here, hiring you if something new hadn't cropped up?"

The captain frowned and walked round to his seat and sat down a little heavily, knowing only too well he was going to have to play along with his old school friends' wild fantasies and theories. Especially as he was expected to give his full cooperation. He shook his head but looked up and waved for Andrew to continue playing the holovid and as AJ swiped the air in a particular way, it resumed playing ...

"... so it does indeed seem plausible BUT, surely a large sophisticated ship like that would have detected such a moon on approach? It seems baffling that the StarVista 4 did not at least do its own quick survey to ensure the safety of its passengers. Something that is considered standard procedure when entering any system. This aspect has always been brushed aside, a little too quickly if you ask my good self.

However, since the official investigation, the system has been off limits to all activities, 'to show respect for the loss of so many lives' yet this smacks of a cover up. The ring system itself was blamed for causing a strange flux of highly charged particles that could disrupt ships systems making it a dangerous place to visit, so it is a world kept out of the public gaze.

That has not stopped many investigators from seeking new answers until someone could go back and actually explore the forbidden site. Come back after the break and discover the shocking news that another ship did indeed meet its end in the same system twenty-five years later, but until recently this was kept from public knowledge ..."

AJ skipped over the break since he now had the skills to circumvent them compared with when he was twelve, but paused as Eric once again voiced dissent.

"But we know all this, that small scout ship was hired to snoop around and got too close to the ring system. The pilot was killed, and they found her in the wreckage."

AJ smiled grimly and raised his right eyebrow a little.

"Ahh, you remember it well. And that's what the programme also says. I'll not bother showing you that segment then. Indeed, the programme went on to basically follow the official line that it was an accident."

"EXACTLY!"

"But I now know different."

Andrew filled in Eric with what he was privy to, leaving Eric stunned but with a great deal of concern.

"Well, I'll be dragged across the hull in my shorts without a spacesuit. I think we should at least inform the senior officers of your findings, but hold back on telling the rest of the crew until we approach Cantrara. Agreed?"

"Yes, I'll accept that. Lead on Captain."

#

The officer's briefing room was more like an oversized cupboard than an official meeting place for the top people of the ship to convene. AJ was sure he'd designed it with more space but said nothing.

With seven people in the room, it was decidedly crowded. Eric pressed the intercom to order chimes to bring everyone to attention.

"At ease everyone. Some of you will no doubt recognize my guest, but for the rest may I introduce Dr Andrew J Hansone, Engineer of the highest order of the Alteran Academy, Engineer with first class distinction from the Santa Alto Engineering University, founder and owner of Hansone Industries, and better than all that, a good old friend of mine from our school days."

"Less of the old, Captain!" AJ smiled at Eric who just shook his head as a sign of despair at his friend.

"Dr Hansone has hired the ship and is along for the ride so to speak, but more importantly he is also here to brief you on our current assignment and oversee operations at our intended destination. Over to you Dr Hansone."

AJ stepped forward now assuming a serious tone.

"I am sure many, if not all of you, remember the story of the StarVista 4 lost with all hands back in 2405. This year marks the centenary of that tragic disaster and we have been given permission to go to the Cantrara system."

There were general murmurs of shock and surprise from the five officers, AJ waited for them to settle down again.

"As you should know, the official explanation was one of a tragic accident when the ship crashed into an uncharted icy moon on the outskirts of the extensive ring system of the gas giant planet, Tianca.

It was a lie. A deception, call it what you will, it was done to protect the public at large and deflect interest from the system. To what end however is still a mystery."

Again, the officers responded with surprise and much muttering but at least one, a female with an engineering insignia on her shoulder patch nodded slightly as if it confirmed her own suspicions. Her action was not lost on AJ, but he carried on.

"There were rumours that in fact the ship had somehow become suspended between space and time, indeed Astrophysicist Armandan Zolic of the Alteran Science Foundation postulated such back in 2429. That led of course to the then popular theory that the ship was trapped, and the passengers and crew were somehow alive, but, with the Cantrara system closed off, no one could confirm Astrophysicist Zolic's theory.

He was in fact vilified and went into hiding due to the backlash from the remaining relatives of the two thousand seven hundred who never returned from that voyage. When he passed away, interest in his 'outlandish ideas' waned, and he and his theories were generally forgotten.

In the meantime, you may well be aware that there were also rumours that a small scout class ship from Alteran, piloted by Quaal Eliif slipped into the system to try to prove Zolic's theory the following year in 2430. Again, the official line was that she was reckless and got too close to the ring system and her ship was subsequently destroyed, adding to the calls to reinforce the ban on travellers to Tianca and place the system off limits as a sign of respect for all those lost lives.

Now, you are all under oath and what I am about to tell you is strictly on a need-to-know basis and not for public discussion. That understood?"

Everyone nodded as they waited with bated breath for AJ to continue.

"My services have been hired by the Galactic Arm Association Security Ministry to check out Tianca for the first time since 2460 as they believe the StarVista 4 is indeed in suspended space as postulated by Astrophysicist Zolic."

A hand was hesitantly raised, AJ recognised it was the engineering officer, perhaps just a few years younger than himself and he motioned to her to speak.

"But I've never heard of anything happening in 2460, what source have we got this from?"

"The highest, direct from the GAA Security Ministry itself. Indeed, it was because I have always been fascinated by the StarVista 4 since a twelve-year-old, that they came to me. For years, I followed up in my spare time Astrophysicist Zolic's theory and was able to confirm that Quaal Eliif had indeed travelled to Tianca and got past the security measures.

We were led to believe that she died when the scout ship was destroyed and there was wreckage recovered including remains that were identified as hers genetically. That much is true.

However, something bothered me and did so even as a teenager. Pretty much all Alteran scout ships of that era and design had TWO crew, a captain, in this case Quaal Eliif and a science/

engineering officer, Quaal Elaaf ..."

"Ahh, yes, in some cases the Alteran culture uses the last name to denote rank *and* their gender so Quaal Elaaf would have been a lower ranking male of the species.

Plus, he was related to the captain as both are Quaal," offered Tracheria. AJ recognised the officer as a native of Eldered Five that he had specifically requested for the mission. Fortunately, he had already been assigned to the Erebus for its last two missions out of Eldered Five starport. It was clear Tracheria would be a useful asset and was already an integral part of the command officer staff.

"Yes, good to see we have a navigation and ring specialist on board; glad to see you Tracheria, you come highly recommended.

So, the question I have had since a boy has been, what happened to the second Alteran on board the scout ship? And why was that bit of information never released to the public? I don't want to sound as if I am a nutter, but the information was suppressed, so why, if there is nothing to hide?

Recently I was given privileged access to the short salvage mission that recovered Quaal Eliif's remains and there were definitely no signs or mention of Quaal Elaaf.

What happened to his body? Not only that, not quite all of the scout ship was salvaged. Indeed, records show that only several small sections were recovered, so what became of the rest of the ship?"

The engineer looked as if she wanted to say something, and AJ motioned to her.

"How has this gone on with no one else's knowledge? You can't hide an entire star liner for this long without something turning up?"

"And you are? Captain Andersohn may have introduced me to you all but he isn't good at introducing his officers is he!" AJ turned and winked at Eric who just scowled back at him.

"Chief Engineer Andrica Parsons, sir."

Eric grimaced then indicated to the other three officers: "Comms officer Liqxal, chief salvage officer Craysol and medical officer Dr Magda Delfinch."

"Very good. Well, my digging into the details caught someone's attention, as I discovered through my contacts that the GAA Security Ministry had dispatched a ship to Cantrara back in 2460. It was the GAA security ship Zal and I have been given access to their classified records. Specialists had worked on an advanced version of Zolic's theory that every few years the StarVista 4 reappears for a few hours.

The Zal arrived, waited for a few weeks centred on their estimate of when it would reappear, but nothing happened. It was eventually concluded that it had been a fool's errand and the StarVista 4 did not appear on a regular basis after all, and they were wrong in their calculations.

Of note is that two people who lost loved ones on the StarVista 4 were on board that mission but didn't see anything, or at least never reported anything officially. I'm guessing they were under oath not to divulge anything to the public.

However, I believe they were wrong on a multitude of levels. I am hoping we will have better luck. although, I don't believe in luck as I have taken into account more variables and better data than even they were privy to.

Within less than a day of our arrival we should know if I am correct or not. We may well finally discover what happened to the StarVista 4, its passengers and crew and the fate of Cherice Richmond, the youngest person ever to be allowed to travel on such a long duration voyage."

Andrica felt a shiver go down her spine at the thought of being on the team that solved the mystery and could only look at Dr Hansone with awe.

As it happened, she was fully aware of who he was and she hated to admit it, but she was quite a fan, okay, almost a stalker, but of course she would never admit that to anyone ...

AJ looked round the officers and smiled.

"Well, if there are no more questions? No? Good. That is all for the time being ladies and gentlemen so for now I will leave you with the good captain as I have work to do. By my calculation we have a seven-week trip ahead of us, and that's if the good captain here takes the quickest route!" AJ threw a quick cheeky grin towards Eric who just shook his head.

As AJ turned and left, Captain Andersohn could see his chief engineer was dying to speak to AJ and he nodded to her to follow as he dismissed everyone.

Trying to make it look calm and a non-event, Andrica caught up with AJ and coughed lightly for his attention. He stopped and turned but had clearly been in deep thought and appeared a little annoyed at being disturbed.

"Er, sorry sir, I, well, I erm," she flustered and dried up.

"Whatever you have to say, get on with it as I have work to do before we arrive at the Cantrara system."

His abrupt, almost rude attitude, was completely at odds with how he had been in the briefing. Especially as it would be several weeks before they got to the system so there couldn't really be that much of a rush.

Andrica hesitated but then found her voice.

"Sorry sir, Captain Andersohn asked me to liaise with you on your research so I would be familiar with, and up to speed on, what to expect when we arrive."

She wasn't exactly lying as she knew that being the chief engineer on the ship, she would be expected to know everything, considering this could now be a proper salvage attempt.

AJ looked at her and frowned.

"No, I don't need anyone to baby sit. This is going to be a potentially difficult encounter as it is, and I don't need another engineer second guessing what I have worked on for the last few decades. I will be there and so your job is to make sure the Erebus is up to the task and operating at full capacity and efficiency."

With that AJ turned abruptly and walked down the corridor back in deep thought before turning into another corridor to go to his cabin. Andrica stood confounded and angry at the same time.

"Well, the miserable so and so ..." she too turned round and headed off back to engineering, furious with herself for not standing her ground and letting herself get a little star struck.

Of course, she couldn't let on that for several years she had been a very keen fan of Dr Hansone, to the point, some would say, of obsession ...

2: FROSTY THEN
A THAW

Over the next four days AJ stayed in his cabin as the EXSSV Erebus entered hyperspace and made several course corrections to put them on target for the distant Cantrara system. Cantrara was on the outer edge of the Orion arm some four thousand light years from Earth and three thousand light years from the GAA capital system of Zianca.

It would still take them several weeks and at least three hyperjumps to get to the last way station before they had to use the ship's own hyperengines to travel the last thirty, empty, light years.

Cantrara was certainly a distant system and one that had always puzzled AJ as to why, even with its fame, it had been added to the StarVista 4's voyage, what would become it's final fateful journey. A bit out of the way, he thought for the umpteenth time since he was a twelve-year-old. He shook his head and put down the old-fashioned sheaf of papers with calculations spread all over them as his personal com link chimed for attention. He saw the name pop up briefly, smiled a little and opened the vid channel on his wall comm.

"OK big Sis, what gives?"

"Oiy, less of the big, I'm down three stone since I last saw you, so less of the cheek," the middle-aged woman looked at him and made a face. "And my name is Carla so use it when you greet your wonderful sister."

"Still the usual bossy self then eh sis… Carla!" he quickly corrected himself and she narrowed her eyebrows at him whilst eyeing him.

"You put on weight?" she cheekily asked.

"It's the camera angle, I'm still only a slim kid you know."

"Scrawney more like, you should get a good meal down you like my George." AJ had a brief flashback of the last time he had seen George and mentally shuddered at his size.

"No comment. Regarding your darling hubby that is. Anyhow, what's with the call - everything OK with the kids, Mom and Pop?"

"Ahh, nothing a good talking to won't cure, that's the kids, not Mom and Dad, although they could probably do with one too. By the way, Shelly is now at the Alteran Uni whilst Goron has decided he wants to be an actor. I despair I tell you, but he is rock solid, and we can't sway him, so I guess when he is poor and comes to us for aid we'll probably have to bail him out as all good parents do."

"Let him be, you know I've always said everyone should follow their dreams. Look what could have happened if Mom and Dad had really had their way. I'd be a bloody pen pusher sitting

22

in an office somewhere on a backwater planet!"

"And yet look where your choices have got you, your own company and highly successful too I'll admit but, at what cost? Three, I said three, failed commitments - sorry, I always struggle to use the word marriage when it comes to you. You don't half pick 'em don't you!"

"Look, Melanie, Ho la Sanlk and Carmen are in the past and we learn by our mistakes. How was I to know they were only after my fortune and not my handsome rugged body."

"Oh, good grief I feel sick now and I won't get that image out of my mind for weeks. You've scarred me for life, boy!"

"Less of the boy, cheeky! Anyhow, you don't make such long-distance calls for no reason, Mom and Dad OK?"

"Yeah, just that they've decided to move again for the fifth time in four years. Guess where they're looking at now? Scorios! Scorios I tell you! It'd take me weeks and a small fortune to visit from our home here on Kileska three. I don't understand why they want to move from Alteran. They have a great place, get on well with the Alterans and have done very well out there. But no, they want more they say. Can you have a word with them?"

"Why? It's not up to us to order them about or dictate what they do, let them get on with it and live for goodness' sake! Perhaps it's a giant hint that they're trying to get further away from you and George!"

"Hah, miserable so and so, I knew it'd be useless asking you. I'll be ..."

Just then there was a soft chiming at the door.

"Hold fire, I have someone wanting to come in. Must be important so I have to go. Nice chatting with you sis but gotta go, work you know and all that, bye ..."

AJ cut the connection just as he thought Carla was about to swear. She could be rather pushy at times and always wanted to control their parents which did annoy AJ.

He swiped his hand towards the door, and it slid open to reveal the captain.

"Oh, Eric, everything OK and on course?"

"Yes, no concerns regarding the ship and we will reach the Cantrara system in just five weeks' time as I had indeed planned on a fast route. It will then be around six hours to home in on Tianca then you can feed us the closely guarded coordinates you seem so eager to keep to yourself."

"OK, so what's with the visit?"

"Give her a break."

"Sorry?"

"My chief engineer, Parsons. You are supposed to be liaising with her on my orders and you've done nothing but avoid her. I don't care that you're the one that's hired the Erebus. On this ship, I am the captain and I expect you to be cordial and work with my people and that means Parsons as well.

So don't bullshit me, I want my crew in tip top condition and fully conversant with what we are aiming to be doing at the Cantrara system. Is that understood?"

AJ looked down at the side of his chair then picked up a sheaf of paper he'd missed earlier as he tried to avoid looking directly at the captain.

"I guess so *Mr Captain Sir*. Now if you will, I have some simulations to run and refine before we reach the initial orbital position."

He turned and, placing the papers on the desk, began to study them, deliberately ignoring Eric, who scowled then headed out. For a brief moment he thought of calling Carla back but then decided against it as she'd only pressurise him to speak to their parents.

It was up to them to do what was best for themselves and not for him or Carla to dictate to them what they should and shouldn't do. Mind you it would be a big upheaval for them, and quite amusing if they did want more space between themselves and his sister, or rather her awful husband, he mused.

Half hour later AJ grimaced finding he couldn't concentrate on the matter at hand. Shoving the sheets out of the way he stood up, striding out of his room with a new purpose.

#

"Check the manifold one more time, I want this ship perfect when we arrive at our destination. Is that clear Jaal?"

"Yes Sir." the young engineer took the hand scanner from Chief Engineer Parsons and left, heading out of the engineering bay just as AJ walked in. AJ hesitated then marched forward and stopped in front of Andrica, blocking her exit. She looked at him warily.

"Yes, Dr Hansone?"

AJ looked at her then smiled a little and relaxed. He swiped at the air in front of them and the ship immediately configured a holoscreen to hover in front of them.

"Open up your holoscreen."

She did as she was told and as they stood there, her holoscreen appeared next to his. AJ touched an icon on his screen then swiped it over to hers."

"You have the next twenty hours to devour that info and know it off by heart. Don't look at me like that, this is not what I like to do or share but seems I don't have a choice in the matter according to his royal highness, the captain."

He said 'captain' a little more harshly that he'd intended but waited for her reaction.

"But, but, I can't leave my station on engineering for that long. The captain would have me walking the hull in my underwear." For a brief moment AJ started to dwell on that thought then stopped himself daydreaming as

Andrica sussed what he'd been thinking and gave him a stern look.

AJ continued, "Well, considering you'd be dead within moments of that first step, I wouldn't worry about having to do that. I will take up your duties as there is nothing more I can do with the data at this early stage of our flight. It will make a change and perhaps keep me from worrying about the upcoming encounter."

"But you don't know this ship, I've spent four years as the chief here since it's inaugural flight and I still find out things that I can do to push it harder."

"Well, that is one worry you don't have to think about. Listen. I know we got off on the wrong foot but the last thing I needed was some fan fawning over my work. This is too important to me. Literally a lifelong ambition to finally solve this mystery, plus, I always work alone." he narrowed his eyes as he looked straight at her.

"This is a Ziancan designed and operated ship, yes?"

Andrica nodded affirmatively.

"Wrong. I designed this ship seven years before they launched the Erebus. I sent the designs to the Ziancans and naturally Hansone Industries built it for them. Then the next thing I know the GAA Security Ministry have assumed charge of the ship and we were frozen out due to 'matters of a security nature'. I've studied and quadruple checked the schematics, and it is my design down to the last quantum weld.

So, I know this ship and its systems inside and out, probably better than you do. Plus, I specifically asked for the Erebus as part of the reason I designed her was for just this purpose."

AJ hesitated before carrying on. "Listen. Parsons, if you have any questions, ask. I've looked at your career record and perhaps I've been a bit judgemental, but as you can now imagine, I feel happier letting you into what some of my friends call my inner core. Go through what I've given you and then meet me at my quarters and we can go over the plans for the possible rendezvous with the StarVista 4."

She nodded, smiled, swiped the holoscreen off then left engineering to go to her cabin. She had a lot of catching up to do. She was also close to doing a quick dance down the corridor once out of view from Dr Hansone but thought better of it.

#

Seven hours later, bleary eyed, Andrica knocked on the door.

"Enter."

The door parted silently and, as she went in, she saw AJ sat at a desk working on a screen. He just put out a hand and indicated to the small chair off to one side and she slumped down into it.

"No plan? You mean to say you don't actually have a plan for when we get there? And I thought you were in engineering doing my duty shift? Jaal told me you'd come back to your cabin almost straight after I left! I'll get shot!" she added caustically.

AJ casually turned in his chair to face her.

"Firstly, hello to you too and, in my professional judgement, Jaal is extremely competent, so I asked the captain if he was OK with Jaal performing the duty and, guess what, he was. Secondly, how can you plan for something when you really don't have any idea of what will happen?" he shot back at her, and Andrica looked furiously at him and stood up with her hands on her hips.

"Does Captain Andersohn know any of this?" she demanded, pointing at the array of paper notes strewn all over AJ's desk, in her sternest tone.

"Of course, he knows. Well, no actually. I lied. Tell me what you would do when we get there?"

"Whatever we do, the captain has to be informed and approve of everything. No question about it and don't argue any other way. Anyhow, we'd monitor the expected coordinates you hopefully will have finally supplied by then, until something either happens or doesn't as the case may be."

"And?"

"Well, if nothing happens then we'd head back to Eldered Five I guess."

"But that's the simple option. How long do you wait? Minutes, hours, days or maybe even months?"

"Well, I don't know I ..."

"Exactly! If we don't know a time frame, we could be chasing phantoms for evermore. But, and here's the good news, I reckon I have figured out why the rendezvous in 2460 failed and why I think we will succeed. I didn't give you all the data, just the official material, sorry I misled you, but I wanted you to come here and question me."

Andrica scrunched her face up and felt her annoyance begin to turn into anger. "Why? What are you after from me?" she stood looking puzzled and annoyed at the same time, although secretly she was quite taken with the idea that he might be interested in her ...

"I don't like upcoming 'would be expert engineers' second guessing my every move and getting it horribly wrong. But I *do* want smart engineers by my side to make sure what we do is right.

Which are you?"

She knew this was a make-or-break point.

"If you so much as leave me out of the loop and give me poor data again, then I don't care who the hell you are I will kick your sorry ass all the way back to Eldered, by heck I will."

AJ sat impassively then smiled broadly and

laughed.

"I daren't ask where this 'heck' is but, good, right answer. OK Eric, I'm happy now." Andrica stared in shock and annoyance as the captain came from the side bedroom and smiled at her.

"Nice one Andrica. I said you'd stand up to him instead of just fawning over him and his so-called fame. Glad you did so too as I now get five thousand Alteran credits from him."

"I don't get it - have you two been playing me?"

AJ smiled at her warmly for the first time she could remember since they met.

"Not quite. I've had my fill of those who fall short of expectation and, with the mission in hand, I needed to make sure you were not 'star struck'. I have to say however that when we first met last week you did seem a bit in awe of me and I couldn't have that. Eric believed in you so you will have to excuse us, but needs must. I am sorry Andrica, may I call you Andrica when we are not on the bridge or in engineering?"

"Er, yes, yes of course." Andrica was still reeling a little over the last few minutes.

"Good, let us get down to business then. Andrica did you notice anything about the data I did give you?"

"Well, apart from the fact it didn't take me a fraction of the time you said it would then … Oh …" she stood deep in thought for a moment. "Where was the station keeping data from when they arrived to just before they vanished?"

"Exactly. I now have that data, as that puzzled me too. Now for most intents and purposes the initial data shows them stationary once they arrived and that is how it remained until poof! They vanished. But I dug up the secondary and some would call minor data stream from the engines, and they show a very tiny extra motion begin an hour or so after they arrived in orbit about Tianca.

Compared with their normal station keeping motion, say with the planet's rotation period, this was barely above the noise level of the data. But look here ..." he swiped at his holoscreen and zoomed into the graph then pointed to an almost level line along the graph until like all the other data it suddenly stopped.

Almost level line ...

"They were moving really slowly but under their own power." muttered Andrica.

"Yes, my conclusion as well, yet all the official records state they were approaching the station keeping position with the planet to give the passengers the best view of the multi-rings of Tianca when they supposedly struck an unknown icy moon or moonlet."

"But why didn't anyone else pick up on this?" interrupted Eric as this was new information to him too.

"The so-called low-level data was just deemed irrelevant and just stored away until I poked around too much. I gather my persistence annoyed several in the GAA Security Ministry, but they eventually conceded that I had worked out they were not looking in the right place, or for that matter at the right time."

"The right time?" Eric was puzzled.

"Ahh, I reckon I get it." Andrica looked thoughtfully at them both and noted the look of expectancy in AJ's eyes. "It's not just that they moved slightly but that was then ... by now, over 100 years later that small discrepancy would be huge and so even when they searched for it back in 2460 the offset would still have built up over those intervening fifty-five years and been quite large, enough for them to have missed it."

"Nice one Andrica. Except for one other thing everyone missed, and nobody thought to take into account," he stopped, knowing the tactic was working to build up the anticipation.

Andrica couldn't wait.

"Stop it - get to the point!"

"How many moons are there in orbit around Tianca?" he asked, pretty sure they'd know the answer. Eric beat Andrica to it.

"Forty-three at the last count according to the info in the GAA database. But that was from that 2460 survey mission now you've given me access to it - have you found another?"

"No, but the nearest but one to the multi-inclined rings system is twice the size of Earth's Ganymede, it's informally called Zospher. That's not just one heck of a moon but a planetary sized body almost two thirds the size of our Earth that also exerts a gravitational tug of war between it and a small moon that lies closest to the rings, Qifp.

Every fifty-two of our days they line up and gravitationally tug at the orbital location of the StarVista 4 when it first arrived at Tianca and so anything in that small zone gets a nudge and causes precession round the orbital plane.

I believe I have worked out the variables enough to give us a better chance of finding the ship. I'm not convinced that it actually vanished, but everyone has been looking in the wrong place all this time …"

"Well, you two seem to be singing from the same song sheet. If it is all the same to you, I am needed on the bridge, so I'll leave you to carry on the good work." Eric knew when he was getting out of his depth, he turned and left as Andrica stood watching him go.

"You mean no one bothered to do several orbits to see if there was anything further along their supposed orbit?"

"Yes and no. From the records of the Ziancan security ship Zal, they did explore round the supposed orbit. But what they didn't know was that orbital tug of war would have made the orbit slightly more elliptical and eccentric. I've estimated it is slightly further out and is further round from its original stated orbital location."

Andrica nodded thoughtfully then looked at him quizzically.

"So ... I sort of passed then?"

"Yes, for now, so don't go making me change my mind. Tell me Andrica, have you ever read the diary of Cherice Richmond?"

"Actually no, I've seen the film 'A very long way from Home' that was based on the diary, made me cry buckets at the end, but I've not read the actual diaries. Why? Have you got them?"

"What do you think? I'm probably one of two foremost experts on the subject and the other one is dead! I have to admit I've seen that film hundreds of times and yes, it gets to me too. A bit farfetched and over the top if you ask me but the lead actress was good." AJ reached under the table to his battered docu-case and pulled out an old-fashioned book and handed it to her. "Look after this, it is one of the most precious things I have, so I mean it, be careful.

It's the collected diary notes of Cherice Richmond of the StarVista 4, published about seventy years ago and I cherish it like no other book. So, look after it you hear! Have a read through the diary and then you might get an inkling of why this feels so important to me.

Cherice had no idea her diary messages sent to her brother would become so famous. Reading them you get a real feel for the voyage as seen through the eyes of an eight-year-old. For me it brought it home that these were real people from a large proportion of the GAA systems who, through presumably no fault of their own, were lost, never to return to their loved ones."

Andrica held the book gingerly in both hands and the enormity of the trust AJ had just given her with the book struck home.

"Can I ask you something a little personal?" Andrica cautiously asked.

AJ was puzzled but nodded.

"Why is it that I feel some tension between you and Captain Andersohn? I thought you were old school chums but sometimes it feels like there's an icy wind blowing between you."

AJ screwed up his face then relaxed a little.

"Let's just say we have history of sorts that we can't avoid. Now, don't ask again unless you want our relationship to go backwards, OK?"

She nodded, mulling over what he might mean by saying a relationship or whether she was just letting her own imagination get carried away. Andrica turned and left him to go back to analysing his calculations once more, but she knew that at some point she'd find out what he meant as she already knew of the nature of Dr Hansone and her captain's relationship.

Something else was also bothering her at the back of her mind, who was the dead foremost expert on what happened to the StarVista 4?

3: CONFESSIONS
OF SORTS

AJ stood outside the door staring at the words adorning it:

Captain's cabin: Eric E Andersohn.

After a few moments pondering if he should walk away, he sighed, knowing they had to clear up a few things. Eric had been quite firm when he first boarded about not bringing up family matters, but it had to be done. He lightly knocked on the captain's door and when there was no immediate answer he almost turned away, but then it opened as silently as did all the rest of the doors on board the ship. Well, at least that was how it was supposed to be, and he almost chuckled at the thought of when he had worked on the schematics of the prototype ship, now the Erebus, all those years ago.

He never forgot the smallest of details when designing ships, but it still bugged him that his original design had been for the Hansone Exploration Space Salvage Ship until it had been taken out of his hands and given a new name. Still, Erebus was an Earth name from a ship from an era long ago, so he didn't really mind the new name.

Just the fact his pride and joy had been

taken from him once he'd completed the design. He shook his head and put those thoughts behind him as he stepped into the room. AJ's eyes adjusted as he remembered Eric Andersohn tended to prefer low level lighting and a little solitude when on a mission. Quite the opposite to his sister, mused AJ.

"And to what do I owe this little visit, as if I couldn't guess? You've been avoiding me most of the time and always making excuses to get back to your calculations." Eric's voice wafted through from his bedroom. AJ stood near the captain's work desk admiring how neat it was, unlike his own.

"Thought we ought to have a sit down and a frank discussion, seeing as last time before this mission really got underway was a bit awkward. You agree?"

Eric walked into the room and stood in front of AJ. "What? About the last time we were in a room together or about what we may be getting into on this mission?"

"You know what I mean. Hell, Eric, you know damn well it wasn't me who cheated on her. Didn't you have any inkling that Carmen was having an affair? You know I resisted her advances after Uni and it wasn't until after Melanie, then Ho la Sanlk left me that you re-introduced me to your sister.

Did you know she was seeing someone behind my back?" he threw accusingly at the captain, a little more angrily than he'd meant. His quarrel wasn't with Eric, but with Carmen, Eric's sister and AJ's ex. The feelings were still raw.

"No, well, if we must have this conversation, well, I had an inkling that something was not right. Several times she called me, and I was able to work out she wasn't where she said she was. She denied it of course and when I pressed the point then she'd say something odd like, 'don't tell you as she wanted things to be a surprise'.

When we met up after such occasions, you never ever mentioned having anything surprising happen, but let's not forget you can be a bit of a jerk when it comes to women.

You let yourself get too wrapped up in your work and this, this obsession with the StarVista 4. It's definitely unhealthy AJ and you don't see how it gets in the way until it is too late."

AJ sat down looking glum but thoughtful.

"I did love her, she wanted for nothing; she spent a small fortune, and I didn't object. It was she who gave up her own work, I didn't force her to. I was happy she had something to do that didn't seem to conflict with my own work and yes, some do call it my obsession. It is more than a hobby to me. Guess few will ever really understand."

"You're too right there. Listen, for what it's worth I did give her a good telling off too but, well to be honest, by then she didn't give a damn as she'd managed to get a settlement out of your lawyers. Pretty poor bunch if you ask me - should have sued them for what she got out of you. But this obsession gave her the ammunition she needed."

"That didn't give her the right to go off with someone else just months after we got married, if you ask me." AJ paused in deep thought before continuing. "Do you keep in touch?" he asked warily as he tried to change tack.

"A little, but as I defended you, I'm not exactly the favourite brother for the last few years so we keep it professional and are polite. Well, she is family after all."

"And to you so was I for a time ..."

"Yeah, it's been a pretty awful affair really hasn't it. Look AJ, it was difficult for both of us, but I never ever blamed you despite this fixation of yours. Once I and Samuel found out, we both said our piece to Carmen but in the end it all fell on deaf ears."

Eric extended his hand out gingerly. "Bygones be bygones and all that?"

AJ smiled, stood up and instead gave Eric a hug and Eric reciprocated like it was old times.

"How is your brother anyway?"

"Oh, he and Christopher moved to one of the Ziancan planets, I can't even pronounce the name of it. They're happily married or at least the Ziancan version of it. More than can be said for you eh." Eric lightly thumped AJ on his shoulder.

"Yeah, pile it on won't you! And what about you? At our wedding, you had a plus one, an Alteran if I remember rightly. Anything happen?"

"Nah. It was just for show so that I was with someone. Would you believe it, they hooked up with the chef doing your reception!"

"Ouch! Sorry I asked. Listen, your Chief Engineer ..." AJ began but Eric gave him a withering look.

"Now don't you go chasing Parsons, I need her in top condition for the ship - she's pretty smart as I think you've figured out, so don't go messing it up!"

"No, you daft bugger, OK she's all right I guess and quite pretty but I meant to say she is quite perceptive and knows something was amiss between us. I'll give her a brief synopsis, so the air is clear, and she's not tempted to ask questions, OK?"

"OK, but remember, she's quite a fan of yours so she must have twigged we were related through marriage."

AJ, however, shook his head.

"You're forgetting that Carmen had been married before so Andrica may not know her maiden name ..."

"Good point. Good luck but remember - no distracting her. Until at least our job is done. But remember, she's a tough cookie, and happily independent so don't push it!"

AJ grinned.

"Erebus, eh? Did you name it?" he asked knowing Eric loved ancient history, especially that of the Earth.

"Err, no actually. Old whats-her-name, oh, on the tip of my tongue, short, quite intense at times, always has to be in charge ..."

"Sounds like Carmen and my sister then to a tee!"

"Don't be daft, ahh, Admiral Dahl-a szay, you remember, the Bilastron who was two years above us at Uni! Quite deep into Terran history and had been reading about how Sir John Franklin led an ill-fated expedition in those old wooden sailing ships to find a way through the ice in the northern reaches of our Earth. The Northwest Passage if I recall."

"So?"

"He had two ships, Erebus and Terror, both were lost with all hands, as was Franklin. The ships were eventually found far from where they were expected in the first decades of the twenty first century. Quite remarkable that they were found at all. The Admiral felt a rescue salvage ship called Terror in human language quite inappropriate so instead it was called Erebus."

"Sounds like the Admiral wasn't the only one fascinated by the story!" quipped AJ and Eric looked at him sternly.

"Less of the cheek, we all have to have our

hobbies, some even have an obsession …"

"Touche', dear brother-in-law."

"Not since you and Carmen got divorced. But old friendships don't die. Now be off with you as this was supposed to be a rest period for me, and I've had precious little of that since you stepped through the door."

"OK, Captain. By your command!" AJ quickly slipped out the door as Eric waved for him to leave and give him peace.

#

AJ stood in front of her as she checked the hyperfield manifolds and found himself smiling at her resourcefulness.

"So, you're telling me you knew all along?" he asked. Andrica just carried on working and somewhat unladylike, snorted.

"Told you I was a fan of yours. Can't keep something like that secret from someone like me. I've known almost since you separated. Now we are being frank with each other, I have to admit, I pushed to get the position of Chief Engineer on the Erebus knowing full well that your brother-in-law was the captain.

I figured that there was always a chance you two would meet up at some point and therefore I'd finally get to meet you, but then of course you separated from Carmen, so I realised it was doubtful you'd ever have a reason to be on board this ship.

Lucky for me I also love the job, more than my sad affliction with following your career, so I set my life on working towards a new goal. I want to be the captain of my own ship one day, so I work damn hard all the time. Then of course who should step onboard just a few weeks back - you!"

"I'm flattered, I think."

AJ eyed her up warily then just shook his head, amused at the thought she'd definitely been obsessed with him but hoped, as he left her to her work, that the obsession was over. Mind you, he wondered, it was amusing to think that not even his three exes had bothered to do any research on him, and he couldn't help feel a little flattered at the thought of Andrica admiring him from afar.

As he left, Andrica waited then slapped herself on the forehead for admitting everything to him and berated herself as she hoped it would not affect their working relationship as they now approached the Cantrara system with the chance of actually solving the fate of the StarVista 4.

She had of course partly held back on a few things, she still had everything she had ever collected about the famous Andrew James Hansone, but she couldn't bring herself to admit that to him now could she ...

#

AJ stepped into the recreation level and saw who was in there, alone.

"Good to see very little has been changed from my original designs, Eric."

"I wouldn't know, this is what I was given when I was asked to become the captain of the Erebus. Come on AJ, this is the recreation level - I didn't expect to ever see you in here!"

"Eric Estobahn Andersohn, don't you be so cheeky!"

"And don't you ever use my middle name again, you know I hate it!"

"Still touchy about that I see! I never did understand why you hated it so much."

"You mean I never told you?"

"Are you daft or what? Of course not, otherwise I wouldn't have asked."

"Estobahn was my favourite uncle, used to tell me, Sammy and Carmy all sorts of stories when we were kids growing up. I was named after my grandfather, Eric, and my middle name was from my uncle. We all adored him.

Until that is he was recruited into the GAA Security service and after that he changed. We rarely saw him, when we did, he couldn't tell us where he'd been or what he was doing. He seemed sad but he must have been good at his job as we always got amazing presents from him.

Then one day we were told we'd never see him again as he was a wanted man. Seems like he was responsible for some bad thing that had happened on a remote outpost. A hundred and forty-three died due to something he forgot to do."

"When was this, I never knew you had an uncle Estobahn!"

"I barely knew you as we were only in our early teens when you and I began to hang out. He'd already been disgraced by then, so it became a family secret. I gather that mom and dad debated as to changing my middle name but as everyone knew me as Eric, it seemed pointless to go through the bureaucracy.

He vanished and we've not seen him since and don't know if he is alive or dead."

"Oh Eric! I'm so sorry."

"Gottcha! You'll believe anything I tell you won't you!"

"You little bugger!"

"Oh, your face! Sorry but you were so hooked on the fib that I couldn't stop! I just don't like the name, that's all!"

"Remind me not to play any serious games with you. Probably why I nearly always lost at chess against you!"

"Yep! Anyway, why are you down here?"

"Well, I did design this ship and I made sure there was a great badminton sim that I could play if I ever was on board."

"I'll give you a game then."

#

18,905 light years away, on the other side of the Galactic Arm Association on a small planet hardly anyone ever bothered about …

"Excellency, I have news of an unexpected nature that may expose our mighty endeavours to the Galactic Arm Association."

"Come forward, you are?"

"Excellency, Triaq, sixth of Arana."

"Very well Triaq, sixth of Arana, speak."

"The Galactic Arm Association Security Service has assigned a ship, the Erebus, to investigate the disappearance of the passenger liner, StarVista 4. It is now enroute to the Cantrara system and should arrive in two of their weeks' time."

"This is surprising news. I thought they had given up after their other ship found nothing in the system. Why now after all these years?"

"I understand that in the terran time keeping, one hundred of their years has almost elapsed. That time frame has some meaning to them."

"Odd, weak and futile. Inform our transfer station at Tianca that they will be having visitors and to take stealth action. We are close to being ready to strike and nothing should change our plans.

Do we have an asset in place?"

"Yes, your excellency."

"Good. As there has not been any sightings of that passenger ship or our Builder ship since the start then I expect the Erebus will be on a fool's errand and return empty handed. For now, tell our asset to do nothing to draw attention to themselves."

"Yes, your excellency."

"And Triaq, sixth of Arana …"

"Yes, your excellency."

"No further bad news, understood?"

"Yes, your excellency."

Triaq, sixth of Arana bowed, turned and walked out of the room before allowing herself to start to tremble with fear. She remembered her mother, Corafa, first of Arana and shuddered at her eventual fate at the claws of his excellency …

4: THE LOST
STAR PORTS

AJ approached the door to the ship's cafeteria but just stopped short as he heard his name mentioned by someone inside followed by several guffaws from those inside having lunch. He listened in whilst keeping an eye out for anyone else coming to get their lunch.

"I'm telling you, it's a wild horse trip and he's barking mad."

"Shut up Cooper, he's highly thought of across the GAA and everyone knows he has this obsession with that lost ship. We all have to have a hobby after all."

"Oh Simonds, you a fan then of his? Been following his career, have we?" shot back Cooper.

"Nah, I have a hobby, guess you just sit in your cabin and have a play eh?" Simonds regretted that barb instantly. "Sorry!"

"Nothing wrong with what I do in my own cabin. I like re-enacting old battles. Very instructive I can tell you. The detail nowadays of the 3d models is amazing and so lifelike. Pity I don't have a bigger cabin but back home I have a large hall that would impress anyone, I can tell you.

Anyhow, I still think we're on a wild goose chase!"

"Hah! I thought you'd got it wrong earlier." Qhrik joined in. "I always think human sayings are somewhat quaint. Oh, that's my hobby if you can call it that, I like to collect odd human sayings and quotes."

"You mean like, 'Hey, I don't agree with the official line, so I'll make up my own ideas, hire a ship and go off into the wide blue yonder to seek out the so-called truth," butted in Dryak.

"The Truth is out there …" said Qhrik, triumphantly just as the door opened and AJ stepped into the room.

The silence was so thick you could have cut it with a knife.

"As it happens Dryak, I do actually agree with both you and Cooper." AJ let them stew as he walked up to the self-serve unit and selected his meal options then waited but turned to face them.

"What's the matter? Cat got your tongues? There's one for you Qhrik.

Listen. I may seem mad to you but remember one thing. I've hired the Erebus and so it is I who is paying your salaries. And for what it's worth, I'd rather have people question me than tip toe around me, so do feel free to question me as to why I think I have a better chance of success instead of moaning behind my back. Agreed?"

In unison: "Yes sir."

Cooper fidgeted. "Sir? Not going to tell the captain, are you?"

"Good grief no, this is between us. Give me your loyalty and trust and I will keep an eye out for you. Any problems?"

"No sir. I'm, I'm sorry for earlier." Cooper looked genuinely sorry, and AJ just smiled.

"Apologies accepted. Now, you folks haven't yet been filled in on what I think may have happened so now is a good time to let you know.

I've been through the crew details and so if in the extremely slightest chance we do actually find the StarVista 4 then there'll be two search teams, Paalk, Cooper and Dryak, you'll be with me and Chelex, Qhrik and Simonds will be part of the second team along with Dr Delfinch and Chief Engineer Parsons. Incidentally, where is Chelex?"

"Bit of a loner sir and prefers to stay in her cabin, rarely eats with the rest of us. Yet she's pretty good when we're working together."

"OK. Oh, my meal is ready, may I join you?"

"Yes sir. Are you able to tell us more about the mission then?"

"Indeed. I'll just get my meal and we can get to know each other better. I need a crew who will trust me, and I hope that's all of you."

Despite no alcohol they all raised their cups to that sentiment.

#

"Dr Hansone, please report to the bridge."

Comms officer, Liqxal announced as Eric studied Tracheria's plotted course and nodded in approval.

Four minutes later AJ arrived wondering if something was wrong.

"AJ, Trachy here has plotted the final course from our current path to Cantrara system. Thought you'd be interested to know we will pass eight light years out from the Viliak system."

"Ahh, you know me too well Eric. Can we do a slow flyby of the old station?"

"Exactly what I was thinking although there is not much left of it. I gather it has been well and truly scavenged for whatever could be taken. Anyhow, thought you'd want to do that. OK Trachy you were right, course accepted. We'll be there in about three days' time at present course and speed. The hyperway is less crowded since the mid 24 hundreds."

"Yes, another mystery never explained properly. The Viliak star was relatively stable so there was no reason to expect such an outbreak of powerful solar storms," added AJ.

Tracheria checked his data on the system. "Interesting, Viliak collapsed rapidly and changed into a neutron star blowing off most of its outer layers into space."

"Exactly, it was a blue giant and astrophysicists still argue about it as there was only a few years warning something was amiss with the star," added Eric but AJ was looking thoughtful.

"You know, now I think about it, Falaise-c-puc did the same thing a couple of years after the StarVista 4 visited its star port. In that case the system was lightly inhabited, and the binary singularities were predicted to merge so that system was evacuated, and the star port closed down.

The astrophysicists of the time initially thought it would be fifteen to twenty terran years before it became too dangerous so didn't expect it to only take three years. StarVista 4 was the last official passenger cruise ship to dock there as a tourist destination. Falaise-c-puc star port was closed down a year later once those remaining had been evacuated."

Liqxal frowned, "So, two major star ports towards this outer extension of the GAA effectively were put out of commission?"

AJ nodded. "Well, I guess you could say that, although Falaise-c-puc is still considered a natural event but it has to be said, Viliak is the real oddity. That's an interesting and slightly worrying observation of yours, Liqxal."

"Now, we can't let our imaginations get away from us like that. Next you'll be saying some malevolent force is at work!"

"That's true captain. But Liqxal has a point. However, this outer region of GAA space is sparsely populated with few habitable planets and we're getting closer to the arms estimated edge. The gap between systems tends to be larger so it would be odd if something was untoward out here."

"Perhaps that's the point?" Liqxal observed and they went quiet as that sunk in.

"We'll know soon enough. Anyhow, anyone seen Chief Parsons?" AJ wondered.

"Overseeing Jaal as he is the newest of our crew but seems to be a pretty good engineer in his own right, but Parsons is like you, wants perfection from everybody!" quipped Eric.

AJ just took it in his stride as he left the bridge to seek Parsons out.

#

The Erebus left the primary Hyperway the next day before reaching the Viliak system via its own hyperengines. Entering the system they began the approach to the abandoned star port.

"Tracheria to Captain Andersohn, Dr Hansone and Chief Parsons, we are on approach and just a few hours from Viliak."

He'd barely got the words out and switched comms back to Liqxal when AJ, Andrica and Eric entered the bridge with Eric taking his command chair.

"Quite a nebula now isn't it?" remarked Eric as they slowed to sub hyper velocity and the view became normal on the screen. Faint twisted wisps of nebulosity lay ahead of them with the neutron star at the centre. Like most nebula, however, as you approached closer the more tenuous it became.

Liqxal suddenly became very attentive to his comms link and looked disturbed.

"Captain, I'm receiving comms from ahead. It's the GAA defence ship 'Cargeon' and it's urgent, I have their captain for you."

"Strange, why are they out here? Put it up, Liqxal."

"This is the EXSSV 'Erebus', Captain Eric Andersohn here. May we be of assistance?"

A Bilastron face appeared on screen with captain's insignia on their shoulder.

"Erebus, this system is off limits to civilian ships, explain your purpose here?"

Eric turned to AJ, "Friendly aren't they! Didn't even introduce themselves," he turned back to the screen.

"Come now Captain, we're GAA security registered and have an agent on board. Also, it would be good to know who I'm addressing?"

The Bilastron didn't change but stared at them. "Ral-cal-quir, captain of the Cargeon. I am sorry but our orders are clear, no unauthorised ship is allowed in this system and checking your security clearance, it isn't high enough.

I understand why you may be puzzled but I assure you all I can say is that we are undertaking fleet trials in the outer reaches of the nebula, but cannot divulge any more. Please be on your way."

AJ moved into view so captain Ral-cal-quir could see him.

"Apologies captain, as you say I don't have that kind of clearance and it was a whim of mine to see the system in the flesh so to speak. We will be on our way and apologise again for disturbing you."

Without waiting for a reply, the Cargeon changed course and headed back into the nebula as Tracheria altered course to take the Erebus out and back to the Hyperway.

Liqxal confirmed the comms link had been terminated as AJ looked around at everyone.

"That's really odd. My clearance, which includes this ship and all on board, is at the highest level so captain Ral-cal-quir is wrong."

"Well, I don't fancy going up against a defence ship like that. Perhaps it's a mistake but it's not like we really need to see the old station. Perhaps they're really using it for the trials, so let's put this behind us and resume course for Cantrara."

"You're right, of course, but something is off. Still, onwards as you say Eric, on to Cantrara! Meanwhile, I'll be in my quarters for a few hours if that's alright with you Captain?"

Eric just shook his head and waved at AJ to depart, suspecting he knew what his former brother-in-law was up to.

#

"Private encrypted channel please Liqxal." AJ wasn't going to waste any time.

He heard the familiar sound as the channel was activated and inputted his security code and details of the call's recipient. He knew that it would take several minutes to be routed through the correct channels and a short while later a familiar face appeared on the screen, the head of the GAA security ministry who had authorised the current mission.

"This had better be good AJ!"

"Yes sir, something interesting occurred a short while ago. Just to confirm my clearance is at the highest level or we'd not be talking now, correct?"

"Indeed. Speak your mind although I know you'd never hold back."

"You are familiar with the last voyage of the StarVista 4 and that one of its final stops before the Cantrara system was Viliak, Spaceport Shalaiq?"

"Yes, you've told me enough times! Go on."

"It was naturally abandoned when the parent star, Viliak, became unstable and collapsed into a neutron star. Somewhat odd at the time, but the station was evacuated and has been left abandoned all these years. So as our course would take us close enough, we took a detour for old times' sake and to satisfy my own curiosity. But we were turned away by the GAA defence ship 'Cargeon', by Captain Ral-cal-quir, a Bilastron. We were informed a secret GAA military exercise was underway using the Viliak Nebula and was off limits to us. Know anything about it?"

The Security head looked puzzled and furrowed her brow.

"No, your clearance should not have been ignored. Very odd. Leave it with me AJ. This isn't good as I'm always informed of such activities. Keep this between ourselves for now and let me know if anything else strange occurs. I can't say anything yet, but I do keep getting spurious reports from across the GAA, although nothing conclusive. This is just one more instance and I don't like it."

"Indeed. Erebus out."

AJ cut the comms and sat pondering what his long-time friend had said. Something was going on as he had also caught oddities in his comms traffic as if someone was possibly listening in. He doubted it was Liqxal as that would be too obvious, so AJ resolved to be on his guard.

#

Meanwhile, inside the young Viliak nebula.

"Sir, they are heading away and have not attempted to communicate with their superiors."

"Good. Our ploy worked. However, I am still concerned that this waystation is not protected enough by the nebulosity."

"Are you questioning the wisdom of the Excellency?"

"Of course not. I am merely concerned about our extended stay here. With thirty ships hidden here, the longer we stay, the more chances someone from the GAA may become suspicious that ships are being warned away."

"That is only the second one in fifty of their terran years. This is a sparsely populated sector of the GAA, that is why the Excellency chose this sector. You would be wise to keep your thoughts to yourself."

"Understood."

5: ARRIVAL AT TIANCA

"Dr Hansone and Chief Engineer Parsons to the Bridge please. We're on final approach and need the closely guarded coordinates you have been holding on to." Captain Andersohn's voice rang out over their personal comms and six minutes later they appeared on the bridge within moments of each other.

"Glad you could finally make it to the party." offered Eric slightly sarcastically but then turned to his navigator. "OK Tracheria, status report?"

"On approach at one third Hyper, two hours from initial standard orbital insertion," the officer replied.

"OK, Dr Hansone, please give Mr Tracheria the final coordinates for us to make what could be an historic rendezvous with a lost ship or not as the case may be ..."

AJ nodded but didn't rise to the sarcastic barb and walked over to Tracheria's station, Tracheria in turn left his seat for AJ to take his place. AJ worked quickly with the console but could feel all eyes were on him burning into his back, at least that's what it felt like. Nothing like a bit of pressure, he mused, as he finished up.

"Coordinates set and locked in. We will swing by the small moon, Qifp then I make it just short of a ten-minute coast into position where Mr Tracheria can synchronise us with the orbital rate of the planet."

"Where will the large moon be?" queried Andrica and AJ turned to face her.

"Almost on the other side of Tianca so we won't get to see it."

"Shame, a large moon like that should have an atmosphere so would have been good to have done a quick survey of it."

"May I remind you, we are here for a purpose, Chief Parsons." AJ shot back, a little annoyed that Andrica seemed to think the trip was a little 'jolly'.

"Yes, of course Sir." she looked at the captain who just smiled at her curiosity but nodded in agreement with AJ.

"Everyone look sharp. If all goes well then history is about to be made, or not ..." said the captain as AJ released the seat back to Tracheria and the lieutenant resumed his post. AJ noted a particular console, causally made his way to it and stood aside it whilst watching the forward viewscreen.

Eric spotted this and pushed himself out of his command chair and walked back to where AJ stood. Both of them being watched by Chief Parsons who was intrigued. Eric leaned into AJ.

"Andrica tells me it was you who designed this ship and your company built it for the GAA."

AJ looked at the captain warily. "And ...?"

"This damned console does bugger all! Care to explain? No one will give me an answer ever since I took command and I generally forgot about it, but you've just deliberately walked over to it. Spill!"

"Not now, it's not for general use, only for if the ship is used for its other role as an exploration ship. If I tell you though to reach under, find and press the raised button, then do it without question. OK?"

Captain Eric Andersohn frowned and shook his head in bewilderment but then nodded and took up position next to his own seat, but didn't sit.

The best, largest and most recent salvage ship of the Galactic Arm Association, the EXSSV Erebus performed flawlessly under the deft control of Lieutenant Tracheria and, as the minutes ticked by, Tianca and its ring system drew closer with each passing moment.

The small moon Qifp slid by looking battered and scarred by tens of thousands of crater impacts, suggesting a very old and undisturbed surface for perhaps millions of years. Then it was left behind as an ever diminishing oddly shaped slim crescent.

Comms officer, Liqxal, for a second, thought he picked up a fleeting signal, but it was borderline detectable and quickly gone, so he just shook his head and monitored the frequencies he knew would have been used by the StarVista 4 all those years ago.

Finally, as the majestic multi ringed planet

Tianca loomed large …

Five were now one, not that anyone's attention was on them …

"Orbital coordinate rendezvous completed Captain. We are now at the coordinates supplied by Dr Hansone and in synchronous orbit with Tianca."

By now Captain Andersohn had taken his seat again and leaned forward.

"Very good Mr Tracheria. Well Dr Hansone, AJ, we are here, now what? Why can't I see the ship on the screens?" asked Eric as he swung round in his command chair.

"I'm a little puzzled if I'm honest. Everything, I took everything into account. Where is she?" AJ was puzzled and a little disheartened and disappointed as he stared at the viewscreen.

"Your educated guess is as good as mine. I thought that as we approached, we would have spotted a ship that size from before we swung by Qifp so where is the StarVista 4?" Eric again asked.

"Captain, may Tracheria scan across the spectrum?" AJ asked looking downhearted as Andrica and the rest of the bridge crew looked on, not knowing what to think.

Was this whole trip a fool's errand? Andrica thought, which was what everyone had to be thinking.

"Already on it Sir, full scan of the orbital co-ord's out to a five thousand miles radius centred on them shows nothing at all." Tracheria stated, noting the frown on Dr Hansone's face.

Andrica, however, had a thought. "Perhaps we should do a full orbit of the planet and continue the scans until we arrive back at the original coordinates?"

AJ looked sceptical but Captain Andesohn nodded.

"If Dr Hansone doesn't object, it could do no harm." AJ just nodded silently as Captain Andersohn nodded to Tracheria. He adjusted the orbital vectors but didn't execute the order as he looked over to AJ, who just shook his head and came to a decision.

"Tell you what, just hold position here for a couple of hours whilst I recheck my calculations. Chief Parsons, care to help me see if I made an error?"

"Yes sir." she replied, a little too eagerly as Andrica looked to the captain and he flicked his head towards the door to say, go.

AJ and Andrica hurriedly left as Eric Andersohn seriously began to wonder if the GAA Security Ministry had yet again slipped up in indulging his friends desire to find out about the StarVista 4, to indulge his childhood fantasy that the lost ship could indeed be found ….

#

They both sat on AJ's bed looking tired after

staring at screens for almost twenty minutes with equations and graphs beginning to blur and merge into one almighty mess.

"I don't see any mistake, do you?" he asked, and she just shook her head, looking glum.

"I have to agree with how it is all summed up, the ship should be there. Perhaps there is some small variable that didn't seem important but has a greater effect than you predicted?"

AJ shrugged and shook his head in dismay. "I have spent years working on these equations and running endless simulations."

"Just a thought but didn't Tracheria say there was nothing in the orbital position at all, no debris or small mini moons?" Andrica offered.

"Yes, nothing on his scans ... But hang on, that also means that if the official line was true then there would still be some debris detectable along the original path the SV4 took, plus the odd bit of debris from the Alteran scout ship.

Yet there is nothing."

"Which is just as odd. I don't know what to make of it ..." Andrica said as her voice trailed away, tired. AJ leaned over and touched his comms.

"Captain, we've done our checks but still arrived at the same conclusion. Advise Chief Parsons suggestion of a full orbit scanning along the orbital plane Zed minus and plus fifteen degrees, just to be sure."

Captain Andersohn's voice came over.

"Very well, I'll inform you if anything crops up," comms switched off, AJ lay his head down on his pillow, tired and bewildered. He looked over at Andrica.

"It'll be at least fifteen hours to do a full orbit about this gas giant. Have you ever seen the docudrama that set me off on this crazy hunt?"

"Well at last you admit it is crazy after all. No, apart from the movie I only heard about the StarVista 4 in history class when I was at the engineering academy on Alteran. Yes, I studied at the same place as you. The professors cited you as one of the most intellectually stimulating of all their students, also one of the most interruptive as well."

"Ha! Glad I made a mark then. You know that for most of the time I failed most of my classes?"

"Sorry? What?" she sat up leaning on one elbow in shock.

"Sooo, you didn't find out all there is about me after all! I was bored. The professors were so dull that I did most of my learning in my own time. I often deliberately failed the mid-term exams just to get a reaction out of them.

It was the end of year exams where I always hit the top spot and showed them up by passing with flying colours. But it wasn't down to them. Having said that there were a couple of profs who did encourage me but overall, I often felt held back.

It was in my last year when I filed my first

patents, you ought to have seen old Bixalac'z's face when I did that and proved a long-cherished theory, he always championed, was no longer valid."

"Sounds like you were quite a handful then." Andrica carefully said not sure how he'd react.

AJ smiled.

"You could say that. Anyway, here you go, watch the docudrama and digest it in full like I did as a twelve-year-old. I'll snooze here as I know it off by heart."

AJ swiped up the large ceiling holoscreen and as familiar words began to sound out across the room he dozed off, Andrica shook her head.

Here she was, on his bed, lying next to probably the best engineering mind of recent times and he goes to sleep!

The programme though caught her attention as Sir Harley Riker-Smyth began ...

"Hello fellow explorers, it is I, Sir Harley Ryker-Smyth, yes he of the fame of charting the jagged scars of Eldered Five, exploring the savage jungles of Alteran Twelve and escaping from the ravenous hordes of Scorios. Tonight on 'Mysteries of the ever-changing Universe' ...

\#

She knew it, she'd held out almost until the end but had finally dropped into a deep sleep as her mind reeled with images, conspiracies and official explanations covered in the docudrama. Andrica awoke and shook her head to clear it as she realised AJ was not on the bed.

The shower was running in the on-suite facility, so she turned over away from the door as she heard the water stop, the air vac run for a few moments then soft padding of AJ's feet come towards the door.

"What's up, not seen someone after a shower then Parsons?" he asked mischievously. She didn't turn round.

"Cheeky. I was raised good and proper I'll have you know."

"That's good to know. By the way I have got my shorts on, so you needn't be embarrassed, or for that matter, disappointed ..."

Andrica slowly turned over and lay on the bed. She had to admit to herself she was disappointed, he did have his shorts on. However, he was true to his word, and she grimaced a little inside. Still, she tried to hide the fact that she was admiring his body as well as trying to look uninterested in him at the same time.

A tall order really.

"OK, fun is over, you get a shower too, put your clothes in the cleaner, they will be done in a few moments then you can join me in the other room. We've been asleep for almost five hours so we must have needed it. And no, I was a gentleman, always have been, always will be. Despite what the media may say!"

AJ left the room and closed the door behind him, so she had privacy.

"Gentleman my foot, that's not what the unofficial biographers say, especially about your three failed marriages. Oh well, guess I'm not that attractive." Andrica muttered to herself as she began to strip off for the shower.

A muffled voice called out from the other room.

"What's was that?"

"Nothing, I won't be long, promise."

Ten minutes later, her clothes clean and shower done, she joined AJ, noting he had five holoscreens up, several with pictures of Cherice Richmond in various poses, taken when she was making her holo messages to her brother Daniel. Not surprisingly there were sheaves of old-fashioned paper littering a table too.

Paper... how quaint, she mused.

"So, what did you think?"

"Oh, the docudrama. Yes 'drama' sums it up doesn't it! How did that trash inspire you to search for the SV4, I'll never know. As for that 'Sir' Harley what's is name, well, what a drama queen."

"I met him you know; he was one hundred and fifty-three when he died, and I met him a couple of years before he passed. Had a four-hour chat that was supposed to have been just an hour but once we started discussing the StarVista 4, you couldn't shut him up. Really nice person actually.

Did you know that most of his so-called amazing adventures were nothing of the sort? His agent blew them out of all proportions from trivial incidents that no-one would have bothered with.

It worked as he ended up both famous and rich, yet no one ever wanted to challenge him about his so-called adventures. At least not whilst he was alive. I gather there is a docudrama being made about him that is, well let's just say it isn't very flattering to him, which is a shame really.

Anyhow, thoughts on the prog, did you spot anything that I might have missed as I was smitten with the whole mystery aspect of it?"

"Methinks it was not the ship you were smitten with ..." he didn't take the bait so she continued. "No, nothing stands out. As we both now know, someone clearly suspects something was afoot but if Armandan Zolic was right and your calculations correct then I'd have expected us to have spotted the ship when we arrived."

She paused, not sure if he would take her next comments well. "Seriously, hear me out for a moment. Do you not think that we may have been on a fool's errand and maybe you were wrong after all?"

She waited for the argument, but it didn't come. AJ looked down at the floor in contemplation.

"Oh, I've always had doubts plague me, even now. I have considered that possibility over and over but even after all this time, there would have been a tiny bit of debris left if they had crashed as per the official conclusion. Indeed, the Alteran scout ship debris would still be detectable so ..." he was interrupted by Andrica as she had a thought.

"We were discussing that before, odd, Tracheria said there was no debris of any kind at all didn't he? There should have been some, where is it?"

"I don't know." AJ shook his head, at a loss.

"Something else bothers me," Andrica continued as her thoughts ran ahead and became verbalised. "There is little about the first rescue mission to find out what happened - surely if something on that scale goes missing then everyone will be rushing to find out what happened?"

"Well, they did. When there was no word from the SV4 that it was heading back, someone noticed the engineering data had stopped suddenly and then all hell broke loose. However, the authorities on Viliak were wary of causing trouble, if in fact it was a mistake, a simple engineering or comms blip as an explanation.

So, they dispatched a small scout ship, one of the fastest they had, to check if the StarVista 4 needed help.

They couldn't find any trace of the ship despite its size so then over a hundred ships of various sizes raced to the Cantrara system to affect a rescue and to search more widely. They couldn't find anything, that's when the GAA Security Authority stepped in, and things went a little quiet.

As the GAA began to investigate, they in turn could not find any trace of the ship either and to avoid embarrassment, they concocted the story that the ship had been lost with all hands. It naturally caused some problems as many simply didn't believe the official line. Cherice's diary messages to her brother also added fuel to the fire as they became popular with the conspiracy theorists. Oh Cherice, you were so young and innocent and should never have been on that voyage ..."

Andrica stared at him as something deep in her conscious mind clicked.

"And there you have it."

"What?" AJ was puzzled at this sudden change of tack.

"Why your marriages failed. I've seen that look before. Without realising it, you were infatuated with Cherice Richmond even though deep down you knew it was impossible!"

"Don't be stupid!" AJ fumbled as he tried to

think of a counter reply. "She...she was just a child and that was over a hundred years ago! How ... What a stupid thing to say!"

"No, not stupid. You say you saw this docudrama when you were twelve. The images that were often shown, showed her aged eight as she is, for all intents and purposes, forever going to be that age. So when you saw the docudrama at twelve, it's easy to forget that by that time she would have been *eighty four* if she'd have lived.

I'm pretty good at sussing these things out. You fell for her image without realising it way back then when you were young and first saw her on that documentary. Didn't you?"

AJ floundered as emotions rushed around in his head and for once he was at a loss for words. He'd been caught out, his guard down he'd never ever thought about it like that.

"Go on AJ, admit it, there's nothing to be ashamed of, it was what used to be called 'puppy love'. We all have such a phase, but I suspect it never left you even though deep down you knew it was impossible. I bet that each of your wives never lived up to what you deep in your subconscious thought Cherice might have been like had she lived to adulthood ..."

"I ...I ..." he looked up at Andrica not knowing what to say as she moved forward and held him in her arms.

"It's okay. Really. It is nothing to be ashamed of. I had a crush on a famous person who was only a little older than myself. But I've finally got over it." she winked at him mischievously.

AJ looked into her eyes.

"No, you haven't. But you are right. I've not thought about it like that but now it does make sense."

"A bit like orbital elements, eh?"

"Sorry, what? I don't get ... Say that again?"

"Orbital elements? Oh my, no, it can't be that simple, can it?" she stammered as they both stared into each other's eyes, minds working frantically.

"You said it would be something simple, so simple we'd overlook it. Check the dates of the most recent orbital elements of the two moons, Zospher and Qifp." said AJ as Andrica swiped up a holoscreen and began to search the orbital databases available.

"Damn! 2460!" she exclaimed with disappointment. She was interrupted by a shudder to the ship then both their personal comms chimed frantically. AJ answered his first.

"Dr Hansone here, what the hell was that?"

"AJ, you'd better get up here pronto."

"You've found her Eric?"

"Sort of. Just get both your asses up to the bridge, OK?!"

They were already rushing out the door before the comms ended, completely missing the fact that Eric knew Andrica was also in AJ's quarters.

#

"Oh....wow!" Andrew James Hansone was for once in his life, lost for words, almost. The huge ship filled the view screen on the bridge as he stood on one side of Captain Andersohn with Andrica on the other side open mouthed looking on at the view.

"You felt that gravity disturbance? That was when it appeared out of nowhere. Tell me this, clever clogs, how does a ship just appear like that?"

"Bloody good question … Tracheria, what shape is she in and are there any life signs?"

Tracheria was already running scans and checks, then turned round, somewhat puzzled.

"The StarVista 4 appears to be fully functional. However, I am not detecting any life signs." he hesitated then continued. "Well, actually the bio scanners keep giving random readings so I really can't say for definite until I can reset them and scan again."

AJ shook his head. "I wouldn't expect any after this length of time, a hundred years, the ships supplies could only have lasted eighteen months to three years absolute max if they rationed everything before running out. I performed loads of sims covering all their options."

Eric turned to AJ.

"As soon as we saw her, we hove too and matched orbit. She appeared exactly at the coordinates you specified. Just lucky that I had asked Tracheria to move us slightly away into an elliptical orbit instead. Otherwise, we would have been in the same spot and I dare not think of the consequences if that had happened.

So, Dr Hansone, you were right about the position, care to explain how she can just appear like that?"

"Armandan Zolic was right, the ship must have been in some form of suspended space. It's like that glimpse out of the corner of your eye that something is there but when you turn and look there is nothing. I didn't add in his data as the theory was considered too far out for a ship the size of the StarVista 4 to just vanish then reappear at random."

"I just feel for the passengers and crew, must have been awful not being able to escape or get word out to rescue them." Andrica sighed and joined Tracheria as he worked at the controls.

"Captain, I've re-scanned and there appears to be no life signs of any description. The environment around the StarVista 4 appears stable at the moment."

Captain Eric Andersohn knew he now had a dilemma. He turned to the comms officer, Liqxal.

"Any communication at all from them?"

"No sir, I've monitored all modern and past

frequencies and there is nothing, not even a mayday call or for that matter engineering data."

"Try hailing them again a few times just to be on the safe side."

"Aye sir." Liqxal lightly taped away at the comms. "StarVista Four, this is the EXSSV 'Erebus' on your starboard bow, please respond." Liqxal repeated himself a couple more times, each time listening in, but the comms were quiet apart from a few static bursts. Liqxal did the human equivalent of a shrug. Eric looked thoughtful, taking in what Liqxal had said.

"Shame, seems the ships systems are working. Sad as it may be, but I think we have to conclude they did all perish. Considering the time that has passed by, I actually thought if we did find it then there would possibly be descendants if they'd worked out how to prolong their food and consumables production.

Looks like I was mistaken. We will set up a small shrine in the recreation room for anyone who wishes to conduct contemplation time for their memory.

In the meantime, Dr Hansone, I congratulate you on helping us make history. Shall we move in and attempt to dock?"

"Yes Captain, I expect the best docking port on the StarVista 4 will be docking port five on their starboard hull from the look of her position relative to us. Docking port three may have been compromised due to the Alteran Scout ship if our historical data is correct. Can you zoom in on that particular docking port, I'm curious as to the extent of the damage."

"Very good." Eric nodded at Tracheria and the screen homed in and zoomed into a close up of the docking port. The rim of a possible docking extension appeared locked around the docking port and Andrica glanced at AJ and he nodded.

"Well, that confirms that, the Alteran scout ship did indeed dock but something catastrophic happened to it. Looks like a little debris drifting close to the ship and some of the docking port of the scout ship is still attached, so why we didn't detect any debris on approach is anyone's guess."

Eric stared at the screen then indicated to Tracheria to zoom back out. "Liqxal, inform Chief Craysol we will use our primary docking port and coordinate with Mr Tracheria to bring us alongside and lock position with the ship. Parsons, you and Dr Hansone will lead the salvage team and go on board. Mr Tracheria, are there signs of a breathable atmosphere over there?"

"Yes sir, normal atmosphere, surprisingly clean and breathable according to the scans."

"Good. Parsons, choose six other crew as part of your team, take chief medical officer Delfinch as well and when we have secured dock, I'll give you the all clear to board."

AJ coughed for attention. "Apologies captain but I have already selected the salvage crew and they are awaiting orders as to which docking port to muster at."

"Very well. Once on board I want you and Dr Hansone to ascertain the state of the ship and decide if it can still be flown. I'd like to fly it back, if we can, under its own steam so to speak. I have to say I can't wait to see the looks on certain faces when we arrive back at StarPort Eldered Five with this beauty."

"You and me too. Why a doctor with us?" replied AJ, puzzled.

"Well, there is the salvage team - don't know what you might encounter so better to be safe. It's also protocol, and you know how I always like to follow protocol!"

Andrica turned, heading for the exit. She paused and looked back at the captain.

"Silly question. How do we know the ship won't disappear with us on board?" AJ looked her straight in the eye and answered instead.

"We don't, but I reckon the captain here will soon shout if anything starts to happen. Can you run fast?"

"Ha! You won't see me for dust if that happens." she replied and they both headed out chuckling to themselves.

6: ON BOARD THE STARVISTA 4

"This is the captain speaking. All hands be on standby, we have docked and secured a firm connection with the StarVista 4. I want all stations alert for any signs of possible trouble. Salvage party, you are go for ingress. Good luck."

The intercom fell silent, and AJ looked at Andrica in her salvage suit.

"Not very sexy, is it?" he quipped and she just thumped him on the arm to the stifled amusement of the other salvage crew as AJ winced, then tapped his comms.

"Charming, I'm sure. OK, you hearing and seeing the feeds, Captain?"

"Loud and clear so cut the chit chat and let's do the job at hand. Both holo drones are now locked on to you and will follow your every step."

"OK." AJ stepped forward to the docking port door and pressed for it to open. It did so to reveal the other end of the intermediate docking corridor and they all entered. He sealed the Erebus door behind them, and they carefully walked along with their magnetized boots holding firm as they proceeded towards the docking port of the StarVista 4 at the other end. Its control panel appeared powered up, a good sign AJ noted through the translucent Erebus docking hatch.

AJ tapped on the panel and the secondary Erebus hatch opened and they stepped through to face the outer StarVista 4 docking hatch.

"Lucky, I studied the schematics and committed them to memory," he said out loud as they reached it, and he pressed the panel in a sequence he had longed to press for the last few decades since becoming hooked on the ship's fate.

It opened, and they stepped through one by one before AJ closed the outer StarVista 4 door.

"OK we are in the decom safety chamber. Console shows everything nominal, and atmosphere equalised so no problem there but everyone keep your suit helmet on until we can be sure there is no contamination. I don't like to bring this up, but it is important as two thousand, seven hundred people died on this ship and the ship's systems may not have coped with such an atmospheric contamination on that scale."

Andrica felt a hand tap her on her shoulder from behind. She turned and realised who it was.

"You mean there could be rotten bodies on board?"

"Possibly Chelex, but I suspect that they will have turned to dust by now so don't worry about it."

"Which is why I wonder about my being here with you instead of in my medical bay," chimed in Dr Delfinch.

"Protocol, Magda, protocol." reminded Andrica.

Meanwhile, Chelex didn't look too convinced, but AJ just watched Delfinch with a wry smile on his face.

"Doctor, once we are happy the ship is indeed stable then we'll need to access the ships medical records. See if there are any clues in them as to the fate of the passengers and crew."

He turned and faced the hatch again. "OK, Erebus, we are going in." He pressed the inner hatch sequence he knew off by heart since a teenager and the inner door slid open.

Stepping into the wide embarkation area of the StarVista 4, for a moment AJ welled up with emotion. His voice struggled as Andrica again touched his arm and smiled at him through her tinted visor. The twelve-year-old boy inside him was leaping for joy as it dawned on him.

This was it.

He'd done it.

He'd found the StarVista 4!

Regaining his composure, he realised Eric was asking him if he was all right.

"Yes, Captain, just a bout of nostalgia and pride that's all. One thing to note straight off, the ship is clean, I mean, well kept and almost clinically clean but there are no signs of pax or crew. Chelex, is the atmosphere contaminated?"

"Surprisingly not sir, it is as good to breathe as the air inside the Erebus, perhaps a little better!"

"Odd. Very well." AJ uncoupled his helmet, attached it to his belt buckle and took a breath. Breathing out he smiled and nodded to the others who did likewise. They looked around, puzzled. Captain Andersohn said what they were all thinking.

"Where are all the bodies? No automation cleaning system could surely have cleared everyone's remains away so spotlessly."

"Hate to disagree Captain but the StarVista corporation were immensely proud of how clean their ships were so perhaps it shouldn't really surprise us at all." butted in AJ.

Andrica stepped forward looking round then faced the team.

"Or they faced the end together in one place on the ship?"

"Not possible, with two thousand passengers, not forgetting seven hundred crew, there would be nowhere for all of them to muster in one place. Not even the entertainment theatre could hold that many.

That's why they had several observation decks for when the ship arrived at its various destinations so that everyone could get good views, and remember, that would only apply to the passengers, not the crew."

"Of course, for all we know, they may have eventually opted to simply step out of the airlock if they felt there was no future for them ..."

offered Magda and Andrica along with the others just gave her a look of surprise that she would think of such a thing.

"What? I'm just saying what no one else will."

Eric's voice cut in.

"Proceed with caution. Dr Hansone, I suggest splitting into your two teams, one to go to the bridge, the other to scout back towards the engineering department."

"Agreed, Andrica, you and the Doctor take Chelex, Qhrik and Simonds as outlined in our planning meeting and head to the bridge, the rest of you with me. We'll head aft towards the engineering section. I'd like to check over the engines.

If possible, it would be good to see if we can indeed fly the old gal back to Eldered Five and give the good Captain his wish. Can you imagine the looks we'll get when we arrive at the Star Port with this ship!"

Eric's chuckle came over loud and clear, but he said nothing.

"OK everyone, I reckon we can dispense with the safety suits, you agree Delfinch?"

"Agreed, if the ship is in this good a condition with such clean air, then I don't see a problem. There are no indications of contaminants or any signs of bacterial infection or virus according to my scans."

AJ nodded and smiled and they all took off the cumbersome suits, pleased they were unnecessary as they stashed them next to the airlock.

"Everyone, proceed with caution. Andrica, keep comms open and we'll see what the rest of the ship looks like. Any sign of trouble then shout."

Andrica nodded and her team headed off towards the right as Paalk, Hooper and Dryak followed AJ in the opposite direction. Without hesitation one of the holo drones took up its position with Andrica's team as the other joined AJ's.

They set off, marvelling at how clean everything looked.

#

Team Hansone:

"Dr Hansone, you don't think it was a hoax, do you? I mean this is spotless, it's like the ship has never had anyone aboard!" asked Paalk inquisitively.

"I know what you mean, but no, too many families were devastated at the news. At the time it was, and in fact still is, the greatest loss of life on a peace faring spaceship.

Trust me, I've gone over everything time and time again since I was a boy, and it still makes me want to cry at all those who lost loved ones - what was that?" AJ suddenly asked, but the others just looked at each other, perplexed.

"Captain, we're on the second starboard observation deck. Did the drone pick up anything unusual?"

"No, everything nominal. Why?" replied Eric, his voice a little tinny over the comms.

"Oh, well, nothing, must be my excitement of finally being here. I've always had a good imagination. We're continuing heading towards the back and will be in the central link corridor in a few minutes. Over."

The Erebus Bridge

Captain Andersohn turned to Liqxal and indicated to mute the comms. He turned to Tracheria.

"Tracheria, just play back Hansone's drone in slo-mo from two minutes ago."

"Aye Sir."

The screen zipped backwards then stopped and Tracheria began to move forward several frames per second. The team on screen looked a little comical as they moved in a jolting fashion.

Eric saw something.

"Back up for ten seconds then step through them again a single frame at a time and enhance the frames fifty percent contrast."

Tracheria did so then they all just stared at the screen in shock.

"Liqxal, check the passenger database …"

Team Hansone - Private channel, AJ

"AJ, can you hear me?"

AJ was walking and the captain had timed it just right as he was a little ahead of the rest and out of earshot for a moment. AJ tapped his comms lightly to make the call private.

"Go ahead Eric, what is it - can't be good if it is on this channel."

"Do you believe in ghosts?"

"Sorry? Don't be silly. You know I don't and I know what you're going to say about my distant relation and I never like to talk about him!"

"Listen up. We've double and triple checked it but twelve frames, I tell you in all honesty, shows a faint impression of a little girl and we've confirmed her identity. I think you probably know everything there is to know about that pax."

"Cherice ... Cherice Richmond? She was the youngest on board. Her father and mother were Carl and Natalie, the newly appointed ambassadors to Zianca.

Ghosts? Huh! Don't believe in them. Could be an effect of the suspended space. Maybe we are seeing echoes of the past when they were trapped here?"

"Look let's just keep quiet and see what develops but keep your eyes peeled OK? And take care ..."

"OK Eric, thanks for that - I don't normally get spooked but thanks a lot!"

AJ cut the link but was now uneasy. Memories

of family tales of a ghost hunter way back in the family tree pre catastrophe times, always annoyed him. He was a scientist, engineer by trade and had never seen a single ghost. All had been explained as tricks of the light or a trick of memory, so he dismissed the thought and waved to the team to follow him to the crew access corridor.

In designing the StarVista passenger star liners, the designers had incorporated corridors that only the crew had access to. This enabled them to carry out the general operation of the ship without interfering with the passenger's enjoyment of the voyage.

It was one of the reasons why they were so successful as the crew were only seen when they were needed and made the whole operation slick and well oiled.

AJ indicated to Dryak and she opened the access door then she seemed to hesitate.

"You OK Dryak?"

"Er, yes, silly, just felt cold as if something had gone straight through me - you know the old saying humans and Ziancans have, as if someone walked on my grave," she laughed but not very convincingly and AJ kept his composure.

"Now everyone, let's not have our imaginations getting the better of us. We have a job to do," he checked the corridor ID. "Yep, Deck 2 C5. Take the left route for about ten paces then there should be a quick access travelator which should cut our walking time down to a tenth if it is still working."

They stepped through and very quickly discovered the travelator wasn't working, so at walking pace, they headed astern.

Team Parsons

"So, what do you make of the lack of bodies then Doc?" Andrica asked. She knew that Chief medical officer Doctor Magda Delfinch was not happy about being on board. She didn't blame her but in the end they all had a job to do, and the doctor could access and understand the medical records better than anyone else.

"I don't agree with Dr Hansone. The clean-up systems couldn't have done such a thorough job as this even after a hundred earth years.

Guess I'll know more when we get to the bridge, and I can access the ships systems. Tell you what, it's spooky."

"Now don't get like that I nee ..." Andrica blinked and Delfinch as well as Qhrik stopped dead in their tracks as Simonds and Chelax bumped into them from behind and looked at the other three puzzled.

"Err, Captain, did you get that just now. Tell me you did?"

"Liqxal here, the captain is talking to Dr Hansone. I'd best let him talk to you. Oh, he's coming online now."

"Go ahead Parsons."

"I repeat, did the drone get footage of what just happened."

"Give us a second, Liqxal is running it now, oh … I see. Dr Hansone and his team have experienced something similar. He believes you may be experiencing echoes of the past due to the suspended space effect."

"OK, can we just confirm what three of us saw then? A faint outline of a Ziancan crew member flitted by and appeared to enter the nearest room."

Eric came back online. "Copy that, we have no idea how frequently you will see these echo's so just push on and the drone will record whatever it is you are seeing, and we will try to identify the Ziancan. Erebus out."

Andrica looked into Delfinch's eyes and her look in return spoke for them all.

"Ghosts …" Delfinch said quietly. "That's all I need to make my day."

They pressed on forward. Suddenly …

"Did you all hear that?" asked Andrica as she looked around at everyone in her party.

"Sounded like faint whispering but I couldn't make out any words. I really don't like this Chief." said Simonds just as Chelax cut in.

"There! Did you hear that? Sounded like someone was asking if they saw something odd pass them …"

They all looked round but could see nothing. Andrica could feel the tension rising.

"OK. Everyone, enough! We have a job to do so from now on ignore things unless you seriously think they are going to compromise the team and the mission.

We're still a couple of decks away from the bridge so let's just try to ignore the effect and try to concentrate on the job at hand. Understood?"

A muttered chorus of half-hearted agreements didn't exactly fill Andrica with confidence but she turned and headed towards what she knew was the travelift to the upper decks and on to the Bridge.

Team Hansone:

AJ and his team had also begun to experience faint voices as well as a couple of times when they felt like they were being watched.

Paalk suddenly let out a yelp and the team turned quickly to face her. White faced she was trembling.

"Something touched me from behind. It felt like a finger jabbing at me …"

The shock had clearly been great as she had changed sex from male to female. This was something AJ always had difficulty understanding, at least the evolutionary reasons why Paalk's species, the Tuuu-rak did this.

"Captain, did the drone get anything?"

"We're analysing now. Will get back to you. Are you at engineering yet?

"One more deck to go when Paalk is settled."

AJ shot him/her a glance and he/she composed herself and nodded.

"OK everyone, let's go," he turned and took a few steps up to the door and opened it then stepped back alarmed.

"What the hell!" he exclaimed as the team for a split moment saw several Ziancans step through the door before fading.

What was just as disconcerting was that it seemed the Ziancans had spotted them too and were also expressing shock before they faded from view.

Eric came over the comms. "AJ, do you wish to continue or return to the Erebus?"

AJ looked round at the rest of his team but stood firm.

"We continue. We have a mystery to solve and we can't do it back on the Erebus."

"Very well but be advised Andrica's team is experiencing similar effects and according to Tracheria they are becoming more frequent."

"Understood."

AJ motioned to the rest, they proceeded through the door and down the corridor before descending via a travelift. Then into the crew corridor again before arriving outside engineering having had two more 'ghostly' encounters. They nervously entered, not knowing what to expect but all seemed normal, nothing out of the ordinary whatsoever.

"Eric, engineering looks much as we

expected, deserted and in an almost pristine condition. At first glance as I approach the control console, everything appears nominal," he paused as he began to run his hand scanner over the engine bay.

"Anyone feel that? A slight vibration? Seemed to pass through the ship. Andrica, did your team experience anything like that just now?" Andrica came over loud and clear.

"What's that? Yes, really strange. I recommend we get done quickly then get back to the Erebus, I don't like it."

"Agreed, scan is almos …" he didn't finish as a distortion swept over the team and he stood there in shock …

Team Parsons

"Eric, we're entering the bridge now. Looks spick and span. Clean as everywhere else we've been. Too clean if you ask me. Everything appears fully functional however." Andrica and Magda felts a cold wave pass over or through them and Chelix just stared at them and pointed past them towards the door they'd just come through.

"A, a Bilastron just walked through you two and left the bridge!"

"But there's no one here Chelix."

"I don't care. I saw them!"

"Hang on, AJ is calling.

"Yes, really strange. I recommend we get done

quickly then get back to the Erebus, I don't like it." Andrica said. Qhrik reached the navigation post as the wave swept over them and for a split second everything was too bright for their eyes, but as the scene settled down, she heard Qhrik scream out and she looked on in horror …

The Bridge of the Erebus

"CAPTAIN! Something is happening - we've got a massive gravitational disturbance centred several kilometres the other side of the StarVista 4 and …" Tracheria didn't finish as the wave rippled over them and alarm klaxons sprung to life all over the Erebus.

Captain Andersohn, Liqxal and Tracheria all stared at the view screen. Eric Andersohn summed up what they were all thinking…

"Where the hell is the StarVista 4?"

For a few seconds no one else spoke. Then Chief Craysol came over the intercom.

"Captain, the SV4, it, it's gone! But here's the rub, we're still docked to it! We're docked to something the right mass and gradational pull of the ship, but it isn't there!"

"Craysol, check the docking port - carefully! Liqxal, are all comms down between us and the salvage party including their drones?"

Liqxal looked round at the sensors." Nothing coming through Captain, just static on all frequencies. I'll try them again. 'Erebus to Dr Hansone, do you read me, over?'"

Static.

"Erebus to Dr Hansone, do you read me?"

Nothing.

"Erebus to Chief Parsons, do you read me, over?"

Just static noise and Liqxal glanced at the captain shaking her head with nothing else to say. Suddenly Craysol's voice came over the intercom.

"Captain, you'd better get down here ..."

Andersohn looked at the other two on the bridge with concern then jumped out of his seat and raced for the door.

Just minutes later he joined Craysol at the end of the docking tunnel and saw for himself why he had called.

The Erebus docking tunnel outer hatch was open ...looking into space with stars but then Craysol pushed a finger at where the StarVista 4's hatch should be and space rippled and his finger started to disappear. He jerked it back and looked as the 'space' returned to normal.

Captain Eric Andersohn looked on and scratched his very short stubby ginger beard.

"What have we got ourselves into? Seal our hatch and keep a beady eye on it. Let me know if anything else odd happens."

Eric turned and headed back to the bridge with a cold feeling in his heart as he heard Craysol mutter.

"What could be odder than an entire ship just

vanishing, yet still be there!"

Eric had to agree with him …

PART 2

One hundred years earlier

2404 to 2405 AD

The last voyage of the StarVista 4

7: A HISTORY LESSON

The StarVista 4.

Constructed at the Tzilliacx orbital construction shipyard over three terran years from 2380 to 2383 and built by the StarVista Interstellar Corporation, owned and operated by a Ziancan consortium and run by, Crylliac Zelt, the CEO.

The first three StarVista cruise liners were built between 2369 to 2374 and were fully operational and, with their success, the order had gone out for three more. A further three were planned once StarVista 6 had been commissioned and had undertaken several cruises of increasing length. StarVista 1 to 3 used an older design of engine but StarVista 4, 5 and 6 would have a newer improved and more efficient design of Hyperengine.

Back to StarVista 4. Technically it should have been designated the StarVista 5 but, when the original StarVista 4 was launched and was undergoing its star trials, a serious malfunction in its new engines left it stranded for over three terran weeks. As the engineers raced to work out and fix the problem, what should have been StarVista 5 was kept at its space dock awaiting shakedown trial runs and once the problem had been identified, its engines were modified accordingly.

As the last three ships had not yet been given their official designations, the fifth ship to be built, became the fourth ship of the fleet to be officially commissioned and operational and was named StarVista 4. Meanwhile the fourth ship was brought back to space dock for lengthy repairs and so it ended up the last of the fleet to become operational. Thus, the final one to be built, StarVista 6, became StarVista 5 and the original StarVista 4 was re designated StarVista 6. Confused? So are space flight historians at times!

Due to the problems that became apparent with the original StarVista 4, the StarVista Interstellar Corporation cancelled the order for the remaining three vessels, so instead of nine flying their colours and plying their trade, just six made up the fleet. However, officially, all six passenger cruisers performed flawlessly once in service and the company began to consider renewing the contracts for the final three ships to bring their fleet up to what some in the Ziancan culture considered a lucky number of nine.

StarVistas 1 to 3 flew short duration cruises of up to two terran months and operated between the eighteen primary GAA civilisations, whilst StarVistas 5 and 6 were given longer duration routes of up to five months. StarVista 4 was the exception as it had proved to be a particularly fine ship and in several trial runs, had been able to conduct eight-month voyages, with the option of up to twelve months or one terran year of operations, with a four month service break between cruises for essential servicing and maintenance.

And so, it was the StarVista 4 that was chosen to undertake what on the surface appeared to be a standard long duration cruise of eight months out to close to the edge of the established worlds.

Its fate had been decided without anyone in the GAA knowing that it, and a little girl's diary of the last voyage, would become famous ...

#

Intercepted communication from the 'Builder ship' translated from the Azline language: Timeframe ~ 2404 AC Earth time.

She studied the translated report of the intercepted transmission with concern. Something was afoot; it puzzled and somewhat unnerved her that recognising that a long forgotten ancient language had resurfaced after thousands of years. The question was, who could she trust considering what was contained in the transmission? She read it once again ...

"We have achieved our objective and all intelligence officers have been successfully placed in situ within

the infernal GAA. Our long-term plan is now in place as we infiltrate deep into the higher authorities ready for when the fleet emerges in twelve azroc cycles (~ 100 years Earth time).

The 'seeding' of the nano construction ring system that will provide the building blocks of the fleet and the galactic transfer system are in place around an unremarkable star system right on the outer edge of the GAA territory.

It is a system they have shown little interest in, based on our agents' initial reports. Only one uncrewed probe has passed through the system several of their time frames ago and its studies have largely been ignored, categorizing the system as unremarkable, warranting little additional study. This works in our favour.

Our initial primary intelligence agent is making plans to return to the system and rendezvous with us for the return trip back to home world. We understand that an unarmed ship, the StarVista 4, will be redirected to the system the GAA calls 'Cantrara' so we may have to deal with it when it arrives, unless our agent can contrive to escape without giving us away.

Azline Empire - forever!

#

Intercepted communication:

Timeframe ~ 2405 AD Earth time:

additional report.

We are at status alert! Well before any ship is supposed to arrive at this system, a private GAA ship has arrived unexpectedly, and we are having to take evasive action to remain hidden. We have some offensive capability, but we are a Builder ship by design and would not normally be involved in any offensive action.

We have moved to the smaller of the closest moons to the largest gas giant planet of this system, known by the GAA as Tianca around which we have seeded the construction ring system. This is ready to build our fleet but we cannot allow this GAA ship to leave if it discovers the true nature of the rings.

She read this latest report and sighed. So far no one had taken notice of her, and she was old and tired. It was always easy to ignore the ramblings of an elder states person, but she was Pallr tsk Pinolver XIX, the head of state for Cep'll and the GAA should be taking notice. Little did she know someone *was* taking notice but was keeping quiet and that sadly Pallr tsk Pinolver XIX would soon be dead ...

#

Timeframe ~ 2405 AD Earth time: additional report #2

We survived but at great cost. The intruder ship destroyed itself as we attempted to capture it and we are heavily damaged with our ability to move the ship severely compromised, but we have some slight forward motion and have moved a little closer to the smallest moon to keep our presence hidden.

Unfortunately, since the death of the only one who had taken notice of the growing threat, no one else in the GAA officially was intercepting the transmissions.

But someone else was …

8: STARVISTA 4 2405 AC
Enter Mr Roberts

Isaac Roberts sat in his cabin contemplating the last few days since he surreptitiously boarded the StarVista 4 at Falaise-c-puc star port. He wondered if the small homing transmitter was still working as it was attached to the Lucky 7 privateer ship that delivered him to the star port. He had surreptitiously attached it close to the outer hatch just as he boarded so with luck, they had not detected it.

He knew their newfound status of being 'legitimate' would soon expire, after all they had been wanted across large swathes of the GAA and they couldn't let that go unanswered.

He did hope that it would be Captain Rii's ship, the GAA Defence ship Cazalee, that would get the honour of capturing them, unaware they were being tracked. They had been after the privateer for several years but somehow the Lucky 7 had always managed to slip through their grasp, hence their captain renaming the ship 'Lucky 7'.

Hopefully not this time.

Anyway, back to the StarVista 4 and why someone had given them permission to add the unexplored system of Cantrara to their itinerary. Although he had just begun his subtle investigations, so far it seemed the crew were in the dark about the reasons and were just glad they were getting a hefty bonus for it. Something that should have raised concerns, but then a bonus is a bonus and a large incentive just to go with the flow.

The passenger he had swapped with bore an uncanny resemblance to himself, probably why he was chosen. That and the fact the passenger was called Ignacio Robertz so it had been pretty easy for Isaac to change the logs and ID to his own ID.

The Bioscan chip had been harder, but he'd cloned Ignacio's chip as he briefly passed the unsuspecting Robertz as he left the StarVista 4 using the instructions the security ministry had sent him.

Everyone had a price, Roberts mused, everyone had a price. Ignacio, however, did have one drawback, he was fond of his tipple.

He was in effect an alcoholic. This was however a bonus for Isaac as one of the advantages he had was a genetic fault that somehow meant he could down a substantial amount without becoming drunk and losing control. He'd used it many times to good effect in his work, putting targets at ease as they became inebriated whilst he acted the part and took his time to get information out of them.

Occasionally, a cover for something more sinister, depending on what was required

It had infuriated his slightly younger brother, David as the genetic defect didn't extend to him, so Isaac could always drink him under the table until David got wise to it.

David.

Roberts became quiet as he thought about his brother. Married and happily settled down as an advisor to the Alteran embassy, his brother was quite lucky. Due to Roberts work he could not discuss anything with his family and it often meant he missed family events.

Including sadly, his parents' funeral when they'd been killed in a shuttle accident just a few years earlier at Zianca.

David and his family had ostracised him for missing their funerals, but he'd been deep undercover and ordered not to attend. They just thought he was out of line for not being with family and friends. It killed Isaac deep inside.

Enough self-pity, he thought and decided to check out more of the StarVista 4. He manipulated the small number of prosthetics he had needed to make the transformation into Ignacio, planning to slowly lose them bit by bit so that he could relax more in his role. In his experience, almost no-one noticed in the past so why would they this time? Exiting his room, he headed out knowing where his first stop should be according to the info given to him about Ignacio and his habits.

#

"Ahh, Mr Robertz, a little later than usual. Are you feeling well?"

Roberts eyed up the bartender and noted his name badge.

"Well, breakfast for some reason didn't quite agree with me this morning which is unusual, but I'm sure my favourite tipple will put things right, Anatonyp."

Anatonyp smiled and prepared the drink which Roberts wasn't too keen on, but to keep up appearances he accepted it with good grace.

"So, bartenders always hear what really goes on behind the scenes, what's with this little excursion to, what's it called again … Tianca?"

"I have no idea what you are talking about. Tianca? Where's that?"

Roberts momentarily froze as he realised, he might be the only one on board at the moment that actually knew they were going to have an extra stop added to the voyage.

"Ahh, no idea, heard someone mention it but to be fair, I wasn't paying full attention. My mistake."

Anatonyp eyed him up. Robertz had a slightly odd accent and usually grabbed his drink and wandered off. He seemed to be a loner and Anatonyp had never seen him engage much with fellow passengers let alone strike up a conversation with him.

Having thought all that, he also remembered there were two thousand passengers on board, and not all frequented the bars, especially if you were from Tragz where any alcohol is poisonous or Ziancan such as himself, where it has to be severely diluted to be safe.

On the latter score he remembered the tragedy of the three Ziancans left behind on Etel Six by their mischievous young colleagues two terran months earlier. One had died, the other two only just survived and their colleagues had been arrested and had been dropped off at Igrocl. If it hadn't had been for Anatonyp noticing two of the stranded Ziancans missing from their usual short but regular stays at his bar, then it would have been much, much worse.

So Anatonyp had an eye for the unusual hence feeling a little uneasy with 'Mr Robertz', when he spotted something on his console for the latest transaction. Time to call security chief Zacklin …

#

A short while later security chief Zacqlin arrived with a companion and sidled up to Roberts.

"Mr Ignacio Robertz?" he asked carefully as Roberts just looked straight at him without a flicker of emotion.

"Well, yes, sort of. Ahh, I get it. Three years ago, I changed my name to Isaac Roberts."

"So, care to explain why our records show ..." Zaclin faltered and stared at his screen.

"I bet it's changed recently, hasn't it? My details I mean. I realised a few days ago that the system had reverted to my old name, so I contacted my booking agent to ask what was going on and they confirmed they'd had a glitch and had reinstalled their back up.

Seems there are quite a few of their customers who have had the same trouble, mainly those who have had official changes to, let's say their marital status, and now many have found themselves in just this same predicament. Sorry for the hassle but I thought it had been sorted behind the scenes so to speak."

Zaclin looked at Anatonyp then back at Roberts.

"Yes, I see now there is a small note of apology from your agent explaining just that. My apologies. You understand we have to be vigilant."

"Quite right too and no apology needed. Glad to have cleared it up."

Zaclin again looked at Anatonyp with a slightly annoyed look, but Anatonyp just performed the Ziancan equivalent of a human shrug.

"I'm sorry too Mr Roberts. I noticed the discrepancy, but I see that it has cleared itself on my system, so I too apologise and to you Chief Zaclin.

"No harm done, I see it as an extra exercise to keep us on our, what's the human term?"

"Toes," offered Roberts and Zaclin smiled, nodded at Anatonyp then with his companion, left the bar.

Roberts smiled at Anatonyp and finished his drink before leaving the barperson to wonder if he'd really made a mistake.

#

Roberts embarked upon the travelator until he reached the exit marked 'Observation Deck B' and tapped for it to slow down and let him off.

He was becoming familiar with the layout and there were a lot of similarities with a previous mission on board the StarVista 1 a few years back. SV4 was slightly larger than the first of the StarVista passenger ships but they generally had the same layout when it came to facilities. One slight indulgence he always undertook on such ships was an occasional visit to an observation deck just to watch the stars to help him relax and so he happily stood and enhanced the view before him.

There were a small number of passengers enjoying the view, but he was lost in his own thoughts as he tried to identify the brighter stars despite them being stretched out as short multi coloured streaks. He mentally chuckled at all the old films he'd seen where the starlight was streaked out fully from front to back, the reality was completely different.

"Do you like counting stars too?" came a little voice slightly behind and to his right side. He looked round then down slightly to see a quite young human girl looking at him and smiling.

"Err, yes, I do actually. I find it quite relaxing." he replied.

"That's good as I like doing it too. I try to count as many as I can, but I prefer to do it when we're much slower, the streaks can make me feel funny sometimes."

"Hmn. Not heard of anyone suffering like that when looking out an observation deck but guess there is always one, eh?"

She wasn't sure what he meant by that, did he mean she was special or that something was wrong with her? It had to be the first ...

"I'm Cherice, what's your name?"

"Quite bold for a little one. I'm Mr Roberts. Where are your parents or guardian and how come you are even on this voyage?"

Roberts knew the answers of course but wanted to hear it from her own lips.

"Oh, I have the freedom of the ship, you can check with the captain as she's my friend, Captain Xaoping Shoo, or shopping shoe, as I often say to my brother in my messages to him.

So as long as I keep to the passenger sections of the ship, then I can explore freely. My parents are the new ambassadors to Zianca and got special permission for me to come with them on this cruise before they take up their new jobs. My brother, Danny, is at university and studying hard so couldn't come and I do miss him as he always looks out for me. But here I feel safe."

"Well, that is good to hear, err, Cherice did you say?"

"Cherice Richmond, at your service. One day I might become a starship pilot, or then again perhaps a starship doctor, or chief engineer, or…"

"Yes, yes, I get it. You have lots of opportunities for when you grow up but let me ask you this … are you having fun?"

Cherice stood and frowned.

"Well, yes, I guess so. My toys didn't arrive and seem to be on their own journey. I sort of miss them, but I've made lots of friends onboard and my friend Lariq has lots of games for us to play so, yes, I'm having fun. How about you?"

Roberts had to chuckle as he honestly couldn't remember the last time he had proper innocent fun.

"Just now, meeting you."

Cherice beamed.

"I'm glad. I had best go now, I'm sure Lariq or my parents may be wondering where I am as I hadn't planned on coming to this deck, so bye bye Mr Robertz."

Cherice did a little wave then walked away and around the corner before it hit him …

She'd emphasised the letter 'z' at the end of

his name instead of an 's'.

Now he was intrigued and waited for a few minutes before setting off in her direction.

#

He stood perplexed. She had disappeared! He walked further along the connecting corridor. He was nowhere near her parents' accommodation, but Roberts wasn't sure where Cherice had been going.

"BOO!"

Came the voice from behind him and Roberts had to work hard to stifle his instinctive response to pull out his gun. He looked at Cherice who was now in a fit of giggles and gasping for breath at how funny he looked.

"Gottcha!" she said triumphantly and Roberts bowed before her.

"So, now perhaps we can add being a spy to your list of jobs, or perhaps being a comedian or escape artist?" Roberts retorted but couldn't help but smile at her ingenuity.

"Ooo, a spy ... I like that one."

"Well, I can't help you there with any of them," he said lying about the first, "but I have to say, this has been a nice distraction from the usual boring day after day antics on this ship. Bye bye Miss Cherice."

With that he turned and walked away around the corner out of view. Cherice squinted and looked in deep thought and began to follow him.

"BOO!"

She very nearly jumped out of her skin as Mr Roberts howled with laughter.

Then stopped himself as Lariq raced round the corner and confronted him. Lariq tapped Cherice on the back to see if she was alright.

"Cherice is this man upsetting you?" he asked worriedly.

Cherice was laughing now and waved at him as she calmed down.

"No Lariq, Mr Robertz and I have been playing hide and seek and he found me quicker than I thought he would. Isn't the right Mr Robertz?"

Roberts nodded and smiled at Lariq who just studied him with disdain.

"I am surprised Mr Robertz, I thought you normally like to be in one of the bars?"

"Not all the time and I discovered that Miss Cherice here likes counting stars as do I. Nice to have met you Cherice and now I am heading back to my room as I have had quite enough excitement for today. I may even ask for room service …" he finished pointedly at Lariq and then walked off leaving them to start giggling.

Lariq stood and shook his head as best he could. "Strange person. Odd how after all this time he's only just met you!"

"Indeed," said Cherice as she thought about it. "Race you back to my room!" without waiting for a reply she was off in an instant with Lariq caught by surprise.

Meanwhile, Roberts was deep in thought.

Careless.

He'd dropped his guard a little just because he had indeed enjoyed that bit of fun with Cherice. But she was a canny one for sure, the way she had looked at him a few times, as if, as if she knew he wasn't the original Mr Robertz.

That pronunciation with the z again jarred at him. Best keep on his guard, he thought, whenever he found himself in her vicinity.

9: THWARTED AGAIN

She carefully prepared everything for another attempt.

Sicanrinka had tried to damage the ships hypermanifold in engineering just a few weeks earlier, but something had gone wrong and only slight damage had ensued. The StarVista 4 was still following its itinerary and she knew it wouldn't be long before the captain would be informed they were having an additional special stop to the voyage.

This time she would succeed. Previously she had only intended enough damage for the ship to stop at their next star port but now …

Now it would have to be a more powerful explosion, not enough to seriously damage the ship, or for that matter hurt the majority of the passengers, which could cause the authorities to investigate quickly, perhaps exposing everything that had been prepared and planned.

Doing it to engineering again would also be too risky so she had identified several targets, the primary one she preferred was the hydroponics section. With that out of action their own strict rules would mean they had to stop the voyage at the next available star port, but when to do it, that was the question.

She wandered over to the display and tapped to bring up the itinerary, pondering the upcoming events and star port stopovers, when she saw something that fitted the bill.

The Gala.

Pretty much everyone, certainly the majority of the passengers and a third of the crew would be either in attendance in the large central amphitheatre or attending holographically as this was considered one of the highlights of such voyages.

And so, it was decided.

#

Gala day

Mr Roberts had kept up the pretence that he enjoyed spending a lot of time at the main bar, mainly so that he could torment Anatonyp, but he made sure people knew he wouldn't be attending such a frivolous event as the gala so he had an excuse for not being interested.

But a few days earlier he had spotted something when he hacked into the ship's systems and gained access to the engineering logs.

Something had happened just after the ship had left Igrocl, on day 130 of the voyage. Chief Engineer Coaraskk had noted an 'accident' in engineering which briefly hospitalised three of his colleagues but had not done significant damage to affect the ship.

He smelled a rat.

Coaraskk had hinted at, but couldn't confirm, sabotage and no remains of a device had been discovered. Yet there was no explanation as to why the hypermanifolds had been damaged as no-one was in that compartment at the time.

Roberts didn't like it. There was also a person he'd taken an instinctive dislike to.

The Haverian reporter, Sicanrinka.

His training was screaming at him that something was off with her. Oddly, he'd even caught little Cherice keeping an occasional eye on her and that in itself had caught his attention. That young girl was really quite canny but the word on the quiet was she would be one of the performers at the Gala herself so at least he didn't have to keep an eye out for her.

So, it was no surprise that Roberts succeeded in putting a small bug on Sicanrinka as they passed that morning at Anatonyp's bar.

He knew she was in cabin C2001 so when his tracker alerted him, she was on the move he began to follow at a very discreet distance. Engineering, that was his bet as he pretty much now suspected the so-called accident was sabotage.

Keeping his distance, he became puzzled when Sicanrinka took a totally different route, well away from engineering. Not only that, but she also headed down several levels so he had to keep up in order not to lose her.

Hydroponics? He watched as she made sure no one was around then she tapped her wrist and …

… faded from view.

'Explains a few things' Roberts mused but decided to stay put until she reappeared. The door opened and a crew member walked out but paused just outside the door looking puzzled before shaking their head and walking away.

Roberts knew what Sicanrinka had done as he did the same thing on various missions requiring a stealth mode. She'd taken advantage of the door opening to slip past the crew member. They'd have felt a light brush of air pass them but, seeing nothing, would pass it off as just one of those things.

Roberts thought about entering but knew he could accidentally run into her and the game would be up. Ten minutes later the door opened but no-one came out. Or so it seemed, but he knew Sicanrinka had left. He quickly tapped a sleeve button and he too faded from view.

It wasn't common tech, not publicly available due to various security laws in the GAA. Sicanrinka became visible just then, as if it was and she just walked away, passing Roberts by a metre as he held his breath. Luckily, he'd made sure he'd sanitised his breath after attending the bar earlier, but he held his breath anyway.

Sicanrinka continued out of view and Roberts dashed over to the hydroponics door.

Looking around making sure there was no one coming, he whipped out a small device and accessed the door controls allowing it to open and he slipped inside.

Keeping his screen active just in case someone did enter, he flipped open a small scanner and began to check the vast interior. A visual check would have taken hours but quickly it detected an anomaly near a primary control panel and he made his way over to it.

A small, cloaked device. Explosive and deadly. A bit overboard but would definitely cause the meltdown of the system and loss of one of the main sources of fresh food.

He scanned it, nothing ordinary about it and in his view so different that it had to be from someone outside the GAA. That was bad. But he had to take a gamble. It didn't look like something that would be triggered by trying to remove it, seemed a little too light for that.

Taking a deep breath, he pried it off the control panel watching it like a hawk, but the odd display seemed to keep on working although he couldn't work out the language it was using.

In no time, he was about to exit when the door opened, and another crew member entered. Roberts dashed out of the door before it could close leaving the crewperson looking perplexed at the slight rush of air next to them.

Now for the tricky part. He studied the device and noted a small, recessed panel so he took a gamble and opened it.

This was almost too easy, but he disconnected the power cell; the display went blank and he waited for the explosion.

Still alive! He knew he'd have never got it to an airlock in time and someone would have noticed the silent explosion on the ship's monitors, so this time he had been very lucky, and so had the StarVista 4!

As he headed back, he briefly wondered how little Cherice was getting on performing in the Gala. He shook his head. Why was he bothered? Perhaps she had managed to worm her way into his subconscious with her air of innocence and yet, he knew she was savvier than she let on, considering her age.

Question was … what would Sicanrinka's next move be when her bomb failed to explode?

10: THE DIARIES

Cherice Richmond, aged eight and several months, sat cross legged on the soft cushions on the floor of her room and pondered her ongoing diary of her adventures on the StarVista 4.

She used her shorter diary messages to send to her brother, Danny, throughout the voyage but often added more in this secondary diary for research when she would begin attendance at the Ziancan school and their eagerly awaited report of her adventures.

She was aware that once her parents, Carl and Natalie, OK, Mom and Dad, took up their newly appointed posts as Terran ambassadors to the Ziancan homeworld, she had no choice due to her age but to go with them.

She would have to therefore attend a Ziancan school, and she had already heard how the next season's class was eagerly awaiting her account of what such a voyage was like.

She decided to put in a small appendix where she could explain why it was frowned upon to take youngsters under the age of fourteen (depending on your species) on such long cruises.

Also, to cover that her mother and father had been given a special pass for someone just under nine terran years so that they could undertake an interstellar cruise of a lifetime before taking up their posts.

As a rule, it was a ten terran year appointment so Cherice was well aware that she had no choice and that her final years of 'normal' schooling would be on a strange planet with different customs and indeed rules for her to follow, or was that break, she thought mischievously.

Cherice had already written a huge amount covering almost all of the voyage, based on the original official itinerary of the StarVista 4. However, they had been given extra special permission to travel to the Cantrara system which held a giant planet that had unusual rings, or so the reports said.

Unfortunately, her brother, Danny had been unable to be with the family on the main cruise. Despite initially arranging to be at their final end of cruise stop, Viliak, Spaceport Shalaiq, once it had been announced it was a short stopover and no one could board, Danny had cancelled and instead would await them once they settled in at the ambassador's residence on Zianca.

Although disappointed, Cherice knew that the addition to their trip was special and would add only twelve days at most to the schedule. She could live with that.

Her only regret had been her toys and games luggage had been lost before they'd even begun the voyage, but everyone had helped her forget the lost baggage and she had been given the freedom of the ship, with of course certain safety exceptions, fully understandable.

Indeed, she'd observed so many different professions during the voyage that she now had a bewildering assortment of potential options for when she grew up.

It was a common point of humour between her parents and her best friend on the ship, Lariq, the Alteran, that every day seemed to have a new occupation for her to consider.

Danny thought it hilarious, but privately had confided in his parents that he was slightly envious of how Cherice had been given so many opportunities to explore what she could do for her future employment. Not that he minded being at the Alteran University you understand, it had been his own choice after all.

Cherice closed the report down and swiped the holo diary away as she knew it wasn't going to be long before they reached the Cantrara system.

She'd finish the diary entry to Danny once they were on the way back but now it was time to enjoy the next few days even if she did have a little foreboding about this extra addition to their voyage ...

#

Diary, extended entry:

"Hi Danny, well, we are on final approach to the Tianca system and although many, indeed most of the passengers, are excited about it, I feel a little odd and I think the word is … underwhelmed by it all.

Captain Xaoping Shoo has done a ship wide announcement informing us of the historic nature of the addition to our voyage, so perhaps mom and dad are right when they tell me I don't appreciate such things due to my age.

Piffle!

Sorry for that naughty word but I don't feel the same about it. Xaoping Shoo went on to say, and I quote:

'Please remember that we are privileged in being the first ever commercial passenger ship to be allowed to visit the system. Under normal circumstances, newly discovered worlds orbiting stars on the very edge of the Galactic Arm Association are surveyed extensively before public contact is granted.

However, we have been given special permission due to the wondrous nature of the ring system of Tianca, which if you have consulted the, admittedly limited, details available in your cabins, you will know they are in a unique state of flux.'

The captain went on to remind some passengers they can't buy additional special trips out to the rings as this is a short stay and we are very fortunate, blah, blah, blah! I'm bored already!

The StarVista 4 will be put in the right place to get the best views of the ring system, and all will be invited to specially laid on views on the observation decks with plenty of drinks. Naturally I can't enjoy the adult ones so will have to make the best of things although they do have a great Cantellian fruit juice that is OK for me, and I love it!

I wish you were here with us as I'm sure you'd help me enjoy this more than I expect to!

I have heard rumblings that the captain is not happy about us being given this addition to the itinerary as it seems to break many rules, but she and the crew are under orders to make our additional stay very special.

Apparently new planetary systems are always fully explored and cleared for commercial passenger ships after extensive and exhaustive surveys, yet this seems to have been rushed through.

Someone high up at StarVista head office had pushed this, despite seemingly breaking all the usual protocols. That's made her uneasy and I can understand that.

I'll send this after we've left the system and give you a full report as we're not allowed to send any more personal messages as we are so far away from the usual planetary systems and the hyperchannels have not yet been added to this system which I find odd!

Anyhow, byee for now!"

End: extended diary report.

#

StarVista 4 on final Tianca approach
Helmsman/Comms officer Ryan Carson: Private
log:

An odd thing happened whilst I was off duty in my quarters, having a rest period between duties. As a comms specialist and indeed hobbyist, I occasionally tap into the main comms of the ship and scan for unusual frequencies.

It's a hobby of sorts as sometimes unusual astronomical phenomenon produce noise that could be interesting to monitor. I like to sometimes mix various spurious signals to form music, although those who have heard my compositions usually say it just sounded like noise!

I was sat listening and musing about how little radio static there actually was, when a faint oddly broken up signal caught my attention.

I manipulated the system as best I could but it stayed just too faint for me to clearly make out its origin. My own automated recorder duly took a copy and I thought about it, then tapped for a link to the helm. This is the standard recordings of internal transmissions between officers:

"Delieezas, have we been close to anything artificial in the last few moments?"

Delieezas' face appeared on the monitor, and he did the equivalent of a human shrug.

"Here? Of course not. There's nothing out here but us. We've done a fly past of the largest moon, Zospher and are just passing the innermost small moon Qipf, other than that we have another three hours, ten before we reach the orbital coordinates. Why?"

"Odd, but I could have sworn I picked up some form of signal just now."

"Got to be static as the last official probe to visit here was a decade or so ago and it was a flyby. Most of our info comes from that mission and Cantrara is so far off the mainstream hyperways there can't be anyone else out here. Come to think of it, that probe probably dispersed small recon probes to the various other worlds in the system so perhaps one of those could still be active, perhaps damaged after all this time?"

"Yes, it didn't seem to be a distress call so perhaps I'm making too much of it.

I'll ask the captain if we can maybe take a look when we leave - use it as an excuse to explore the moon to get more data on it to cover us. A bonus to add to the bonus of this detour for the passengers."

"Good idea. For now, you will be needed on the command deck in twenty minutes time ready for our arrival so don't be late!"

"As if!"

I shut off the comms link to Delieezas but am very puzzled so will study it more closely when I have time. For now, nature calls, then duty!

11: STARVISTA 4
2405 AC

Mr Roberts private report #8

Roberts opened his private holo recorder and began to record his report:

"Well, as expected, Captain Xaoping Shoo finally announced the addition of Cantrara and its unusual gas giant planet Tianca to the passengers and crew the day after the Gala and a few days before we reached the final tourist stop of Graylacq Twenty-Nine.

It seems everyone is happy with the addition despite being told it has hardly been explored. As we know, this breaks all the usual protocols the GAA has in place for such worlds and it is highly unusual for anyone, let alone a passenger cruiser, to be allowed to visit before it has been properly examined and certified safe for public traffic.

To this end I have kept up my disguise as a slightly annoying and occasionally drunken passenger asking those I think may have prior information as to why the StarVista 4 will be heading to the Cantrara system, but so far it seems no one has a clue or even cares!

Any passenger that doesn't want to carry on to the Cantrara system can disembark at what should have been the end of voyage and disembarkation star port, Viliak, Spaceport Shalaiq, the last star port before we reach the official edge of GAA space.

I gather no one, not even a single member of the crew is getting off so, as there will be plenty of ship wide announcements informing passengers of our arrival at Viliak I plan to stay in my cabin and act as though I got heavily drunk and slept through the announcements. Due to my personal advantage regarding alcohol, I'm sure barperson Anatonyp will happily vouch for the fact I will have partaken of plenty of it and so help with my alibi.

On another note, my chief suspect re the sabotage attempts, Sicanrinka, has tried a couple more times but now I know she has the tech to go into stealth mode I've been able to stop each one and she has been left quietly fuming. I wish I was a Ziancan gnat on her wall to see if she is sending out any reports to her superiors as she still hasn't figured out who is interfering or what is going wrong with her attempts. Indeed, my impression is that she is no longer trying so perhaps she's resigned herself?

I have found out that she is also behind a small but illegal gambling ring associated with some of the crew and a few passengers; I'm not sure what that is about or why she needed to set it up. Three of her victims are in serious debt to her and one is a crew member, Zalokq , that may be pertinent as blackmail can be a powerful tool.

Of a minor nature but somewhat amusing is that the Richmond's daughter, Cherice, despite being only eight years old shows a remarkable aptitude for espionage. I have caught her several times following Sicanrinka and indeed on a couple of occasions even myself, I am embarrassed to admit. She may well make a fine recruit for the Security ministry when she grows up.

Ahh, we are on final approach to Viliak so I had best attend the bar and create my alibi as it is a short stop now. We know no one is getting off and no one can join the ship. I find that later a little disturbing as I would have expected a few dignitaries to join for this so-called historic event but who am I to question the motives or reasons of others?

Roberts, out."

End of report.

#

A few days after leaving Viliak spaceport Shalaiq Captain Xaoping Shoo log entry:

"We are on our way to this additional stop to our voyage although I still have some misgivings. It is very unusual for anyone to be allowed to visit a planetary system that has not yet been fully explored.

Earlier today I had the misfortune to

encounter the annoying human, Mr Roberts. In my experience on this voyage, he is the only human to have proven to be a nuisance, mainly since the announcement of our addition to our itinerary, Cantrara.

It puzzles my officers and myself as to why he is so annoyed at this wonderful opportunity he has been given. It is free to everyone booked on the cruise, he was given plenty of notice that he could disembark at Viliak, Spaceport Shalaiq eight days ago yet he either slept through the various alarm calls or was so drunk he simply didn't hear them. Who in their right mind would pass up on a chance like this anyway?

Indeed, he was so vocal in public when he accosted me, that several other passengers came to my aid and made clear his views were not popular. The gall to actually expect us to lend him one of our long-distance shuttles to head back was unbelievable and naturally couldn't be done.

He stormed off leaving me to explain to the Ziancans who came to my aid that he had spent the previous twelve hours propping up the bar, slept through five alarm calls we sent to his cabin, and that he really didn't have a leg to stand on.

I am totally confident that if he does indeed complain officially then the company will fully back me.

As I left I was unfortunately ambushed by

the on-board roving reporter from the Haverian news guild, Sicanrinka. She too constantly kept asking questions as to why we were given permission to add the Cantrara system to the end of our voyage, so I gave her the company explanation and left her to it.

I do wonder personally if this addition will really be worth all the trouble!"

End log entry.

#

Captain Xaoping Shoo log entry:

"We are on final approach to the large gas giant planet, Tianca, in the Cantrara system and Mr Delieezas is expertly checking our planned trajectory ahead for any potential dangers such as small uncharted icy moons or anything that may extend further out than the officially known set of rings.

Everything checks out clear and so we are entering orbit. I have made several ship wide announcements on what we can and can't do whilst here as it is only a short stop with no additional excursions allowed due to the timeframe of our visit.

We have been given liberty to the crew to also enjoy the experience and my second in command Graylor is arranging the crew rota as I make this entry.

If I am honest then I do have to say the ring system doesn't seem to be that exceptional to warrant this extra additional stop but then again, no one physically has seen them first hand, so I expect that is why it is so important for the StarVista company."

End report.

#

Timeframe ~ 2405 AC Earth time: Azaline additional report #3

The civilian star cruiser has taken up orbit around the planet Tianca and we are moving closer but at a slow rate due to our damaged systems. We have had a communication from our agent but have advised we are unable to assist in her return to home planet as per our original arrangements, so she is making additional plans for her return.

12: CHERICE'S TIANCA DIARY EXTRA

"Hi Danny, I'm adding this as our encounter with Tianca takes place so you have an idea of what it was like.

Mummy and daddy effectively dragged me to experience the wonder that is the ringed planet of Tianca in the Cantrara system.

For me it really wasn't that special, we have Saturn after all, so I really didn't see what all the fuss was about! I asked if I could stay in my room and watch via the screens but no, I had to be up on the observation deck with them.

Well, to me it was really boring, and I do think that Saturn and even that world, what is it called … Jalthor, is much better! But you'll be pleased to hear that I did stay for a short while. However, I did get bored and eventually Daddy gave in to me and as I'm well known on the ship they let me go back to my room. But I was really naughty. I went to the other side observation port and decided to count stars but there's something odd going on.

They slowly changed. I mean really slowly changed. It was if the ship were moving slightly more than it should have been, so I think the captain knows something more than everyone thinks.

I thought it was odd but then something else

happened so let me tell you what I saw …"

#

Cherice knew how to twist her father into giving in to her pleas. Tears began to form, and Cherice looked so downhearted that Carl's heart broke and he relented, as any father probably would have done.

"OK poppet. Listen, tell you what, we've had a great trip so far. So, as you have at least seen Tianca's rings with us, you can go back to the room. At least you will be able to say that you were on that famous voyage and saw them firsthand for yourself. Off you go then and we will be there soon, I promise. About an hour or perhaps a little more as we do have to mingle with some special people."

Cherice brightened up and so, as she left, she waved at them for several metres, then walked away. Rounding a corner, she started skipping along the vacant corridor. She didn't notice that someone had spotted her leaving and also keeping well back, out of sight.

It was good that everyone was on the observation decks, and it struck Cherice that for a short while, she could explore the starboard side of the ship as everyone seemed to be on the port side for the planet with rings.

Hah! Ringed planet. She had not really been that impressed with Tianca. A bit messy with all those rings and she couldn't understand what all the fuss was about. She reached the travelator and hovered her hand over it which immediately brought a segment to a halt, she stepped on and it carefully manoeuvred itself back into the ever-moving flow.

She loved the ride as the air rushed through her hair and as she passed a few of the crew they recognised her and waved, some with their multiple limbs much to her enjoyment.

As the travelator slowed, she wondered if she would have what was needed to be a captain and for a brief moment, she thought of herself as captain of the StarVista 4 then chuckled again to herself.

"Captain Cherice Richmond at your service," she said out loud and giggled at the thought of being so important.

She arrived close to her room but on a sudden impulse she stepped back onto the travelator to the starboard observation decks and three minutes later she was there. Basically, the same as the port sided except this had one very important difference.

There was no one else around.

She had the deck to herself, much to her pleasure. With that in mind, she ran to the huge clear wall that looked out into space and Cherice had a thought.

"Ship? Dim lights?" she called out, remembering how Lariq had done it on several occasions.

The ship obliged as the deck lighting dimmed and she looked on in awe at the vast span of the galaxy's spiral arm strung out before her. The galactic bulge lay off to the right and she smiled. She knew she wouldn't be able to see Sol from the Cantrara system, but she still looked over in its direction.

She started counting, knowing full well she wouldn't be able to count them all, there had to be tens of thousands visible at the moment. She started at the left side and worked her way up and down, but reached less than a third of the way across the vast view when she had to start again.

Several times she restarted her counts after getting confused. She got up to eleven when something struck her. She again started counting but then noticed there had been a lovely bright orange, supergiant star she remembered Astrophysicist Crayt calling them, it was the first one on the lower left.

But now there were an extra three fainter whiter stars to the orange star's left. She started again and this time hit a thousand and four stars before a small coughing fit put her off.

So, she started again.

There were now five stars to the left of the orange star, so she now started watching intently as a sixth slowly drifted into view.

She blinked then thought about it. They

were moving, very slowly, but still, they were moving the ship slowly. Cherice shook her head, it was probably nothing, and decided to carry on counting. This time she began on the right but decided to skip round the main bulge of the galaxy - too many even for her to count!

She became lost in the task at hand and forgot about the extra stars …

Cherice was almost ready to give up counting when she noticed a few more extra stars then something twinkled and caught her attention.

Puzzled, she fished out her personal holovid flicked it on and held it in front of the view.

"Zoom please"

The holovid responded: what level do you require?

"Half max."

It zoomed in on the twinkle and she frowned.

The largest moon of Tianca, Zospher, was at almost full phase but something seemed to be off to one side of it.

"Full max."

It obeyed and she started, then gasped with glee. Cherice air swiped to capture a quick selection of still images then switched to video record and looked in fascination at the view before ending the recording, folding the screen away and started towards the exit.

She'd never discovered anything before today on her own and she could barely contain her excitement as she imagined announcing her discovery to the captain. She didn't get to the exit however as just then, the reporter, Sicanrinka approached.

Cherice had a bad feeling about her but smiled as sweetly as she could and began to make small talk.

13: SOMETHING AMISS AT TIANCA

Mr Roberts report #9

"A strange situation has developed. My tracking bug on Sicanrinka has stopped working so I no longer know her whereabouts. I headed up to the main observation deck and did spot her for a while with everyone enjoying what I personally think is a fairly unremarkable ringed planet; I don't see what all the fuss is about.

I became distracted by barperson Anatonyp and lost Sicanrinka and as there are so many passengers here it is impossible to quickly check out the whole deck as it is enormous!

I noticed that Cherice was also absent. I did see her earlier with her parents admiring the view but whilst they are still on the observation deck, Cherice is not. I have a bad feeling about this, so returned briefly to my cabin and tried to reset the bug remotely.

Oddly there is a faint signal but it doesn't correspond with any habitable location on the ship and I am at a loss as to where she is. I'm heading back to the main observation deck just in case she or Cherice have returned."

#

Meanwhile on the StarVista 4 command deck:

Xaoping and Graylor were in the captain's cabin when the comm chimed for attention.

"Xaoping, go ahead."

"Delieezas here. Captain, I'm sorry to bother you but we have, well, we've got something odd occurring approximately ten degrees ahead and three chaks closer in towards the closest ring's edge."

"Clarify, something odd?"

"Well, as best as we can make out, gravimetric ripples on a small scale of just a tenth of a chak wide at most, but quite unusual."

"We're on our way. Hold station for now but keep monitoring."

She cut the link. Graylor looked at Xaoping, puzzled, then they both dressed and headed to the command centre.

"Any change? asked Xaoping as she took to her chair.

"No Captain, just small intermittent and quite irregular ripples."

"Graylor, thoughts?" Graylor went over to the science station and along with Officer Calsohn, studied the data. They briefly whispered to each other in consultation, then Graylor nodded and turned to the captain.

"Captain, the phenomenon is highly localised but does not seem to have any origin or anything that could be creating it. We advise continued monitoring and at the first sign of any change suggest we move the ship further out to ensure the safety of the passengers, and of course, crew."

"Agreed. Calsohn, this is not that unusual, that gravity and electromagnetic fields can be in flux is well known, so why is this one an oddity?"

"All known examples, of which there are indeed many, have a source, something that is causing the event or disturbance. But in this case, we can find nothing that is causing or producing the effect. But then again, we're not a fully equipped research ship."

"I can find nothing like a ship at the centre of the ripples which was the first thing I thought of, perhaps a ship in trouble, but scans show no sign of anything artificial at the centre or indeed within twenty-eight light years of us as we are so far off the beaten track," offered Delieezas and Xaoping nodded.

"My thoughts exactly Delieezas, there won't be anyone else out here under the circumstances. Well, it is not often we get a chance to possibly make a discovery of our own and the corporation could benefit from the extra good publicity.

Let us give it another ten minutes and if nothing changes then Delieezas, I want you to slowly drift us in to around a chak from it. If we move slowly then the chances are the passengers won't notice we have moved, and we can study it whilst they continue to enjoy the views of the rings until we have to leave. All agreed?"

Graylor looked thoughtful.

"You don't concur Graylor?"

"Perhaps it would be wiser, as this is a relatively unexplored system, to move away and for now keep our distance from whatever it is we are detecting?"

Xaoping nodded as well as a Gu-alt could.

"Understood, but so far there is no indication of any potential danger, so for now I think we should continue to explore, but carefully.

If we move away that will alert the passengers that something may not be well and could cause alarm and I wish to avoid that. Agreed?"

There was general agreement from the command crew, Graylor nodded in agreement after a little more thought.

"Good. Carson, request Astrophysicist Crayt and Geophysicist Raskaert to perform extra studies of the planet and its rings and come up with possible explanations of what we're seeing. No doubt it will make their careers if this really is something never seen before. I gather they are not the best of friends, but they must put that aside."

Captain Xaoping sat back in her command chair, pondering what they might find over the next hour or so.

#

"No passengers reporting our slow movement so far Captain. I have informed the crew attending them to just comment that we are making slight adjustments to our orbit with the planet to give the best view."

Xaoping noticed something about her second in command. "Something is bothering you, care to share?"

Graylor looked a little uncertain. "Some of the passengers and crew have noticed flashes of light emanating from several of the rings. It may be an electromagnetic effect as Tianca does have a strong ionic flux with its largest moon, Zospher, so it may well be nothing at all."

"Very well. Calsohn, keep an eye out for these flashes with the port sensor array just to be on the safe side. Perhaps we might be witnessing a new phenomenon. It would certainly make this an even more historic voyage and give a boost to the corporation." Xaoping turned to face her trusty helmspilot. "Delieezas, how long until we reach our new position nearer to the anomaly?"

"Just under two Terran minutes Captain."

"Very good, Calsohn, any change in the ripples?"

"No Captain, exactly the same as our first sighting."

Carson looked disturbed.

"May I say something Captain?"

"Yes of course, go ahead."

"I may be letting my imagination run away

with me but, well, it reminds me of a fishing line as it touches the surface of a lake."

"Ahh yes, your species does have a strange idea of capturing live creatures swimming about in Di Hydrogen Monoxide. I'm glad you saw sense and started to use artificial fish instead ..."

Xaoping frowned, thought for a moment then a deep-seated instinct took over. "Delieezas full stop and pull us back a little, around a chak should be enough."

"Aye Captain."

The ship slowed to a halt then started to back away just as a small object headed towards them, suddenly stopped and was pulled out of sight before they could notice it.

The ripples suddenly expanded at this same instant and enhancing the weaker outer ripples, they combined and ensnared the ship with a strange form of space. Everyone momentarily felt space and time shimmer then settle down to normal as if nothing had happened, but warning klaxons sprang to life in response to the brief event.

"Graylor, check with the crew as to any effects and I'll reassure the passengers, Carson, kill the klaxons and patch me into the comms, shipwide, passengers and crew." Carson nodded then indicated the captain was live.

"Attention ladies and gentlemen this is Captain Xaoping Shoo. There is no cause for alarm. We experienced a slight gravitational anomaly but as you can see, we are back to normal. However just as a precaution we will be moving the StarVista 4 to a wider orbit which in turn will give you a slightly different aspect of the multi ringed planet Tianca as a bonus.

Please do feel free to ask the crew anything if you have any concerns, but for now please continue to enjoy the view and our complimentary service."

Xaoping indicated to cut the comms and Carson did so.

"Everyone, report!"

Delieezas: "All flight and control systems normal Sir."

Graylor: "Medical Bay reports no casualties amongst passengers or crew. All systems reporting in as normal, Captain."

Calsohn: "Science station appears to be functional …"

Xaoping shot him a sharp glance.

"What do you mean, it either is or is not, which?"

"Everything appears to be working, however according to the ship's systems sensors, we haven't moved at all. We are instead inside something I can only call an anomaly, based on the readings if they can be trusted."

Silence.

Delieezas looked up. "Captain, our controls appear to be working but I've rechecked and as Officer Calsohn says, we are not moving despite the engines being set at one tenth above station keeping velocity."

"Bring them up gently to a quarter …" Xaoping ordered and Delieezas complied but then looked concerned.

"Nothing, no change in our position. Shall I go to full manoeuvring thrust?"

"No, I don't think it will make a difference and if it did and we suddenly moved, the passengers might start to wonder what's happening. So, for now we are stuck here, well, in this orbital location at least. I want full systems triple checked and close monitoring of our position. Inform me if anything, no matter how slight, changes. I will be in engineering. Graylor, you have command until I return."

"Yes Captain." Graylor replied as Xaoping got up and left knowing full well there was going to be an inquiry if the corporation found out she had ordered them closer to the anomaly against Graylor's recommendation.

Meanwhile Calsohn looked a little glum and deep in thought.

"Spit it out officer Calsohn, what is it?" barked Graylor.

"I just get the feeling Carson is right and we've been hooked …"

#

At the unexpected, strange sensations, Natalie reminded Carl that Cherice was on her own in her cabin and so she headed back to check on her.

Ambassador Richmond and a group of troubled passengers surrounded a hapless waiter as Captain Xaoping Shoo's soothing announcement came over the airwaves. The waiter held up their four arms for quiet.

"There we are, no need for concern and I have been instructed to ensure you have plenty of refreshments and condiments whilst we enjoy our stay here at Tianca."

The various groups around the crew started to disperse and head back closer to the observation screens whilst some took advantage of the refreshments that had appeared from a lower deck via a flurry of waiters. Ambassador Richmond stood for a few moments as his group melted away and the waiter carried on with his duties but then one of the humans approached him.

He now realised it was the awkward Mr Roberts who always seemed a little inebriated, Carl couldn't help but think, *it would be him wouldn't it ...*

Roberts took him by the arm, surprising him with the firmness of the grip and what appeared to be a sudden sobering up.

"Walk with me Mr Ambassador."

As Carl began to protest, Roberts held up his other hand and an identi-card caught the

Ambassadors attention.

"Good grief …" he muttered a little shocked. Roberts smiled and indicated down the corridor.

"Come with me to your suite, it's very important."

Carl nodded. They left the stunning views of the Tianca rings behind for the other passengers to enjoy.

There was more to Mr Roberts than anyone could have guessed.

#

Natalie was both pleased to see Cherice in their room but then consternated at discovering Cherice had been at the starboard observation deck rather than in her own room. Cherice wanted to show her mother what she had discovered, but Natalie was having none of it. Cherice scrolled through the images captured on her holo recorder, but none showed what she had spotted.

She frantically scrolled through what pictures there were left as she couldn't help thinking her memory was a little off, not thinking for one minute that perhaps someone had erased the important images. Then it struck her.

Sicanrinka?

The reporter had briefly 'interviewed' Cherice

at the starboard observation deck and then had left hurriedly.

Natalie, however, took her device from her and placed it in the cabinet drawer.

"Daddy will be here soon when he has found out more about what happened. Now are you sure you are all right? No feeling sick or giddy?" Cherice shook her head and was about to try to explain again when the door chime piped up.

"Open," stated Natalie and the door slid open to reveal not just Carl, but the annoying person she had seen a few times at the bars dotted around the ship; she shot a questioning glance at her husband.

"Natalie, could you do me a favour and take Cherice back to the observations deck. If you see Lariq then ask him to look after Cherice and come back here as soon as you can, OK love? I would like a quiet word with Mr Roberts here. It's official business so has to be private, you understand."

Natalie always knew when Carl was up to something and she looked at Roberts then shook her head, taking Cherice by the hand to go. As they left, Cherice gave Mr Roberts a quizzical look, but he made an ever so slight shake of his head as if to say *not now* …

Carl Richmond was still a little in shock and didn't notice the exchange between his daughter and Mr Roberts.

"OK, tell me everything …" as he turned to

face Mr Roberts.

Captain Xaoping was worried. She knew that once they did manage to get underway again there would have to be questions answered as to her complicity in taking the ship closer to an unusual phenomenon. Pretty much every regulation stated that passenger ships were not to investigate but simply report on what they found if anything unusual occurred on a voyage. A science vessel would then be dispatched to do the real research.

Suddenly she experienced a ripple passing through her and realised that the ship had undergone a second anomaly as the klaxons sounded once again. Quickly Graylor's voice came over the universal tannoy reassuring everyone not to panic and that the situation was under control.

Xaoping felt a sense of foreboding wash over her and she was just about to call Graylor when her comms pinged; she waved a tentacle to open the channel.

"Captain here."

"Captain, Graylor here. I've had an urgent request from Ambassador Richmond to see both of us immediately. I have tried to assuage him of any fears he may have about everyone's safety, but he continues to insist. What do you wish me to do?"

"Very well, I'll meet him in the briefing room of the forward observation deck in say half a terran hour. I'm on my way to you so join me in my anteroom in about ten minutes. If we can put his mind at ease then he will be of help with the rest of the passengers if we remain stuck here for a while."

"Yes Captain." the comms went quiet and Xaoping shook her head as best a Gu-Alt could do. She took stock of where she was before continuing down her present route hoping that no one else would ask for an audience ... for now.

#

Timeframe ~ 2405 AD Earth time: Azaline additional report #4 (Unknown to the sender, never successfully transmitted)

A strange force appears to be all around us, and we can no longer communicate with the Azline Empire. This appears to have occurred shortly after we detected our agent's attempt to return to home planet.

We are unable to establish communications with our home system and may indeed be helpless and unable to defend ourselves. However, our primary purpose has been achieved and the construction of the remainder of the fleet has begun. The transfer station will receive and transfer crews to each ship as they are completed.

Our only solace is that it would appear our plans must still be in place as we have seen no other ships come to the system. One technician who has since been reprimanded severely, claimed to have seen a large ship close to the ring system but we have no other evidence of such a ship.

With no communication and no ability to move we have little choice but to wait whilst our engineers try to solve both problems. We can also only hope our absence has been noted and rescue is on the way from home world.

14: TIME TO COME CLEAN

Mr Roberts stood with Ambassador Richmond facing Captain Xaoping Shoo and first officer Graylor zXanders in the captain's lounge and showed his identi-card to the captain who gave a sharp intake of breath.

"Captain, I have to inform you that I have not been open and honest with you and your crew and for that I apologise. As we seem to be having difficulties with the ship I believe it is time to come clean.

As you can see, I am in fact, Isaac Roberts Malin, Ministry of Security, GAA. I joined under subterfuge when you were at Falaise-c-puc Starport.

One of my little skills is to infiltrate systems and ships to, let's just say, make it look like I have always been on the voyage. I took the place of a passenger, Ignacio Robertz, who has a striking passing resemblance to myself, and I expect is now enjoying a new life on another world. In the meantime, I altered the bioscanners to accept my readings as his.

My mission was to discover why the StarVista 4 had suddenly been given permission to add the Cantrara system to the end of your latest voyage. Considering that it has barely been explored and has not yet been given clearance for public or commercial exploration it puzzled my superiors. I am sorry if I have had to come over as rude, but I wanted to prise out from you what your orders were and why you were sent here.

With my somewhat offbeat methods I felt I was almost there when we felt the unusual gravity ripples affect us. Have you an explanation for what has been going on and for that matter, what were your actual orders?"

Roberts sat back awaiting a reply.

"I'm afraid I must disappoint you Mr Roberts, I am no wiser than you as I have patiently explained ever since you began to harass my chief officers and myself. We received the orders from the Corporation a few days before we arrived at Falaise-c-puc before we headed out to the Falaise Singularities.

The crew and I were informed it was an historic occasion and that we would be given a large bonus and additional holiday if we did not object to the addition of the Cantrara system. I was informed that it had been cleared at the highest level, so I assumed the system had been cleared for public exploration whilst we were already underway on our current voyage.

Naturally none of us refused and we have done as we were instructed. So, as Graylor here will attest to, we were just as surprised as yourself at the late addition. As far as we and the rest of the crew were concerned it was just going to be a minor inconvenience for a few extra days with a very handsome bonus at the end of it. No one was going to refuse that."

Roberts shook his head.

"But none of you wondered why?"

"Why should we? The company is pretty good to us overall and I know that over the last few years it has been requested by various factions. So, as far as I was concerned it was only a matter of time before the Corporation or one of their rivals was given permission. Something like this doesn't come along very often Mr Roberts, so who am I to refuse such an historic chance?"

Roberts nodded. "According to what the ambassador has told me, someone quite high up in the Ziancan administration let the ambassador know that he and his wife were going to be confirmed as the new Terran ambassadors. Ambassador Moore stated she was stepping down and taking early retirement providing the opening for a new ambassador.

That begs the question of what would they gain from letting Carl know about the addition of Cantrara but then swearing him to secrecy? We at GAA security had suspected something might happen as the StarVista 4 was the only peaceful ship that had the potential to be diverted this far out due to its design and long flight capability."

Roberts looked round the small group.

"As I also understand, the ship can't move independently for the time being so I believe we should keep what we know to ourselves for now and hopefully it won't be long before your engineer sorts out the problem and we can head back."

Captain Xaoping was surprised by this revelation.

"How did you know we had problems with the engines? We've not made any public announcement so as to avoid panic."

"Well, I am a GAA operative after all and I have my ways Captain. Don't worry, I understand the importance of keeping this under wraps for the time being and hopefully it won't be long before we are able to leave the system before anyone becomes suspicious.

I do think that we should keep an eye on the reporter Sicanrinka, as we have no information about her prior to just a few months before you began your latest voyage. She refuses any attempt at trying to strike up a normal conversation with her. I don't like it or for that matter her, one bit. What's more, I had a tracking bug on her and recently it showed faint and now has seemingly stopped altogether.

What still intrigues me is what would be gained from coming here? The only thing, apart from the so-called amazing view of the ring system, are the occasional flashes some passengers and crew have reported but that could be nothing.

On the other hand ... the ripples may be the reason we are really here so, was it part of the plan for us to be caught up in them? I don't know but there is a lot to think about whilst we remain stuck here."

Xaoping looked thoughtful as she took in what he'd said.

"If that is all then I believe Mr Roberts you should remain in your guise of a rather annoying passenger, no offence of course, and meanwhile Graylor and I will hopefully get answers from Chief Coaraskk as to when we can get back under way.

Ambassador Richmond, naturally I assume there will be discretion and no talkabout what we know with anyone else, including your daughter, as the last thing we need is wild speculation and possible panic amongst our passengers.

I'm reasonably confident the crew will remain professional whilst we are stuck here and none of them need know anything more unless it affects the ship and our safety.

Contact myself or Graylor however if you notice anything unusual."

Both Carl and Roberts nodded in agreement and left the room going their separate ways, with a lot on their minds.

15: A DEEPENING CRISIS

Cherice opened her holo recorder and began speaking.

"Cherice's extended diaries: Tianca system. I am not sure why, but for some reason we cannot send messages out and we've been told there is a technical fault. I have an uneasy feeling about this as we all thought we would soon be leaving Tianca and the Cantrara system any time now. However, since the unusual ripples that have affected us and the fact I am no longer allowed free range of the ship I am a bit suspicious and a little frightened. I think something has gone wrong, but Daddy and Mummy have tried to reassure me that all will be well.

I can't help but think there is a connection with that strange reporter, Sicanrinka and the odd ship I saw whilst at the observation port when everyone else was looking out on the other side of the ship. I've tried to tell our parents, Danny, but they just shrug it off as no one else can be out here as we're the only ones with permission.

I'm not so sure. I hope I can soon send out my diaries to you and that we'll be on our way back, but something doesn't feel right about the StarVista 4 and I don't know what it is I'm feeling.

Byee Danny.

Captains Report: Cantrara system, Tianca orbit, extended stay. Thirty-six hours since our arrival.

"We have had to announce to the passengers and crew that we have a minor problem with our systems and will be staying for a few days in orbit round Tianca to effect repairs. We have hopefully deflected growing unease that we have not left the Cantrara system for Viliak Spaceport Shalaiq although we are both uneasy at having to 'lie' and cover up what could be a serious situation developing. So far, Chief Coaraskk cannot explain why we are unable to move the ship and are stuck in orbit about the multi ringed giant planet.

I have kept Ambassadors Carl and Natalie Richmond and GAA Security Officer Roberts informed and arranged for the latter and my own Security Chief, Zaclin, to meet so that at least Zaclin is in the know regarding Roberts' true identity.

I have a deep unease about the situation we find ourselves in at present, a trait amongst my kind and a throwback to a time when we were still a superstitious species. Yet, I have often followed ..."

The chimes rang gently sounding an alert that someone wanted to see her. She paused the recorder and checked the security screen. "Yes, enter."

Security Chief Zaclin and GAA Security officer Roberts came through the door and made sure it shut tight behind them.

"Captain, I need a word, it is serious and I'm afraid may well be connected to our current situation." Xaoping stood, intrigued and yet again a sense of deep unease swept over her as several of her tentacles quivered unexpectedly. She indicated for Zaclin to speak.

"I didn't come straight away and report as I felt at the time it was something quite trivial and not to disturb my captain with. However, my discoveries have changed everything. Six hours after we arrived at Tianca and felt the first ripple effect, a maintenance ensign, Zalokq failed to turn up for his shift. He has an exemplary record and so his immediate superior, Yahniz-lq-yin tried his quarters but naturally didn't have clearance to force entry. She came to me and, on entering his quarters along with Dr Sreisse, we found no sign of him, we …"

"Just hold it there please Zaclin. His bioscan readings would clearly ind …"

"Yes sir, but that was the point, I could not find any sensor readings of him on the ship. None. It was as if he had simply vanished. The sensor logs last show him in his quarters but then nothing. What's more there was no alert issued that his bioscans had stopped.

Someone must have tampered with them.

His room was quite neat, and he had slept in his bed at some point prior to our entrapment but otherwise there was nothing. I did check his personal holorecorder but again there was nothing on it to suggest how or why he is missing.

So Yahniz and I systematically checked our systems for unauthorized shuttle or pod launches, airlocks being opened and cargo/baggage docks but there was no indication of anything out of the ordinary. I was at a loss but a short while ago one of my teams physically checking the status of the escape pods discovered that one was indeed missing.

However, the inventory shows it as present and correctly docked in its bay. There are no logs showing it launching."

Zaclin stopped to let the captain take in the news. Xaoping briefly looked at Roberts who nodded and she looked back at Zaclin, square on.

"So, what would possess someone like him to falsify the system and take a pod without authorisation? Where would he go? It doesn't make sense, we're too far from the nearest starport for a pod to make the journey. It might make it to the outer edge of this system at a push but what would it gain him?" she muttered.

"There is more to the puzzle Captain, and you won't like it one bit. Who is the one person you would have expected to be covering, questioning and getting under our skins about the delay in heading back to Viliak? Apart of course from our Mr Roberts here, whose behaviour we now know was an act!"

"Sicanrinka."

More of a statement rather than a question. Xaoping took in a deep breath and exhaled slowly as she answered then continued to listen, her mind beginning to go into overdrive as Zaclin continued.

"The one and only. We've been doing a lot of delving into both of them. Her bioscan is also absent from the ship. Stopped at the same time as Zalokq's. I have discovered she had set up illegal gambling sessions which were cleverly concealed, and I am sorry to report that I failed to find out about until events overtook us today.

My officers have now questioned three other crew and two passengers who took part in them, and all say that Zalokq ended up in heavy debt which was covered by an account I have discovered in Sicanrinka's companies' name. I believe therefore Ensign Zalokq may well have been blackmailed as he would not dare risk his debts coming out in the open and being discovered. May I have access to your holoscreen captain so I can show you something?"

"Indeed, here ..." Xaoping activated it then entered the security pass allowing Zaclin access. He quickly linked into the the security systems.

"I've just received word that my obs' team have found something. Watch the screens for what they are about to show."

They looked on as four multi screens appeared, each with a view of the outside of the ship.

"These are our maintenance systems, and they show nothing out of the ordinary. They have been tampered with and Zalokq does possess the skills to achieve that. Now watch."

A new screen came to life full screen, showing a slightly different angle of the side and rear of the ship. Suddenly a small dot raced away and round the stern of the ship out of sight. The view changed and showed the side of the ship towards the stern but on the side facing the ringed planet of Tianca.

The small dot appeared and streaked away from the ship heading towards the rings but vanished into the distance due to its size. Captain Xaoping looked at Zaclin but he indicated to keep watching the holoscreen.

He manipulated a control and the view zoomed in closer to where the pod appeared to disappear.

"It doesn't vanish but comes to a stop close to the ring particles themselves, but we can barely resolve the pod and certainly not the constituents of the rings. Then the pod suddenly appears to be racing back towards us when …" he stopped talking to let the captain see for herself.

The small pod rushed back almost directly towards the ship but then an incredibly thin pencil of faint light leapt out from inside the rings and the pod was yanked back and vanished. Xaoping began to speak but was hushed by Roberts. As they watched, a ripple in space extended outwards and engulfed the StarVista 4. Xaoping watched with fascination and sheer horror.

"That was when we were caught?"

"Yes Captain. That wasn't the first of the ripples, but they were small until the pod was snatched out of view. We then found the StarVista 4 immobilised and have remained so ever since. The question that worries me is ..."

"Why whatever grabbed the pod hasn't grabbed us and taken us to who knows where?"

"... Yet ..." added Roberts and Zaclin nodded uncomfortably in agreement.

"I do have a thought, if I may? Perhaps we are too large a ship?" offered Roberts.

Zaclin was not finished.

"Dr Sreisse and I took a team to study Sicanrinka's room and it's not good. It had been deliberately cleaned to an incredibly high degree.

It's so spotless that we've not found a shred of organic matter from her. Dr Sreisse says the cleaning has been done to a surgical standard. However, we then examined Zalokq's quarters in greater detail and stuck in the disposal unit almost out of reach was a small bag of equipment that could have enabled him to bypass our security measures. We're not sure at the moment."

"Why not, Chief Coaraskk would know what it's for?"

"I'm afraid not as this equipment is like nothing we've seen before, indeed apart from a modification to connect to the ship, the items look ... alien ..." said Roberts and watched for the reaction.

Captain Xaoping Shoo looked at both of them in shock.

"But ... but are you saying they are from one of the newer sentient species to join the GAA or ..."

"... from outside the GAA." Roberts finished for her.

Zaclin still wasn't done, however.

"One final thing for now Captain. I have done some background research into Sicanrinka along with Mr Roberts' help and we can't find any record of her until she suddenly appeared at the Havaerian news guild two Terran years ago, based on what our onboard library informs us.

Also, as you are aware, our systems are normally directly linked to any number of GAA facilities as a commercial passenger ship and those records are always constantly updated. We've had no contact from the rest of the GAA and they may not have had any further information from us since we became stuck in whatever it is holding us.

If the latter, then with luck there may soon be

a number of ships coming out to find out why we have fallen silent so that could be the one item of good news.

As far as we can ascertain Sicanrinka is a mystery and her actions along with Zalokq's may well have endangered us all. We fear there is more to this system than any of us ever thought possible and I have to now agree with Mr Roberts, someone knew something was not right at Tianca and somehow had enough influence to have us diverted to explore unofficially."

Roberts spoke up now with sombre tone.

"The fact that the GAA Security Ministry went to the trouble of implanting me on the StarVista 4 via a wanted privateer means they must have had a suspicion or been tipped off. However, I doubt anyone there could have suspected we'd become trapped like this, and it is possible that it is simply an accident or an unlucky coincidence."

"Or ..." joined in Xaoping, "Someone needed an excuse to send us in deliberately to see what would happen. If that's the case, then they'll have almost three thousand of us wanting their head or heads and I'll be leading the charge."

"If we can escape ..." Zaclin added ominously and the three stood silently as they contemplated that thought.

#

Timeframe ~ 2405 AD Earth time: Transfer station report to Azaline homeworld and initial infiltration commander.

We are now in place and overseeing the construction of the fleet, but the primary builder ship has vanished as has the civilian cruiser they had detected. We have no explanation and there is no sign of debris, so we are perplexed.

Replacement builder ships have now arrived and as the fleet is being constructed, each ship will be crewed and moved to the nebula known to the GAA as the Qrianlairing nebula, which has too severe conditions for most star ships to operate in. As ours are sufficiently shielded, we can hide our ships there until ready. We have taken up position on the other side of the planet from the original builder ship's coordinates in case others from the GAA arrive.

Additional report:

We were incorrect in our assumption.

A single ship arrived, the GAA defence cruiser 'Cazalee' but after finding nothing they have left. Since then, another single ship, a scout class ship arrived and searched the area of the missing cruise ship and has since been joined by over one hundred other ships, but they too have discovered nothing and we and our operation remain hidden. They have left the system and we are again alone here and can continue with our operation.

Long live the Azaline Empirate!

16: A SURPRISE VISITOR

Security agent Roberts report

"As unease grows amongst not just the passengers but the crew too, the captain has been forced to inform every one of our unusual situation and that everything is being done to enable the ship to leave Tianca. No one is interested anymore in the planet or rings which is no surprise. This should have been just a short stop of a few days at most before heading back to Viliak, spaceport Shalaiq for the end of the voyage.

By now the passengers and some crew would have been making their way home so it is understandable concern is growing.

The ship appears to be surrounded by some form of liquefied or suspended space. I'm no scientist as such but wonder if there is any connection with the damage done to the hypermanifolds after they were damaged by the traitor, Sicanrinka? Security Chief Zaclin and I are convinced both she and the crewperson Zalokq were definitely inside the pod we saw race towards the rings, but it puzzles us that it appeared to attempt to return back to the ship.

Perhaps Zalokq discovered Sicanrinka was not what she seemed and managed to thwart her and turn back but was too late? Astrophysicist

Crayt, Geophysicist Raskaert, Chief Engineer Coaraskk, and I have studied the single monitor view of the pod's short journey out to the rings and its attempt to return, but we still haven't been able to identify the strange pencil of light that seemed to snatch the pod away.

Crayt did suggest that there may be some form of waystation, too deep into the rings for us to see that may have expected to capture the pod, and that this may have been Sicanrinka's plan all along, to get back to her homeworld, wherever it is. Too many *mays* for my liking.

In the meantime, the helmspilot Delieezas, and Security Chief Zaclin attempted to fly a shuttle, his favourite called the 'Trallaac', out of the hanger bay, but they were halfway out when it slowed to a stop and was stuck for a while in mid-flight. Delieezas had a good name for whatever it was they were stuck in, jellified space! Despite varying the engine thrust they could not reverse and eventually managed to escape via the escape hatch on the rear port side which was still inside the hanger bay.

Fortunately, the hanger bay atmosphere couldn't escape either so they returned unharmed whilst the Trallaac remained stuck motionless in you could say mid-air. It took sixteen crew members to manually haul the shuttle back, then just as it was fully inside the hanger, it dropped like a stone on to the deck injuring several of them and damaging the shuttle bay and the Trallaac. Naturally they didn't try to fly out again with a crewed shuttle and a few days later a remotely controlled pod fared no better.

I can see everyone becoming fraught if this situation continues. What puzzles us all is why there doesn't appear to be any signs of rescue ships outside? Technically all commercial and passenger ships send their engineering data back live to a huge range of stations dedicated to monitoring the health and well-being of all ships so they should know we are in trouble.

So where are they?

My own reports, indeed, messages from the passengers and crew don't seem to be getting out as we all would have expected family, loved ones and friends to be asking what we are doing and why haven't we returned. Crayt and Raskaert, almost a comedy act now, have no explanation but Raskaert did suggest the jellified space may be stopping us from sending out and receiving data and messages.

This does raise the question as to why the space we see outside from the observation decks, monitors and every porthole, looks static and unchanging. Even some passengers have noted that the planet Tianca hasn't changed at all, and we've been here several weeks now. Crayt again suggests that we're synced with the planet's rotation anyway so we would see the same side all the time, but here Raskaert disagrees and wonders why he's seen no changes in the atmosphere.

All this is naturally particularly hard for some passengers, and I do know that young Cherice has been upset at not hearing from her brother Danny. However, she has become a mascot and morale spokesperson for the ship, for both passengers and crew.

With her parents' consent, every other night she does a little song and dance routine that she learns from the ship's library. Each appearance is a different song or dance she has learned and along with help from ship's entertainments coordinator, Trionice -pkci and the rest of the ship's official entertainers, she has brought hope and solidarity to the ship.

End of report."

#

Cherice's extended diary:

"Dear Danny, how I, mum and dad miss you as we have been stuck here for months now and cannot understand why no one has come to rescue us. To help with morale, Captain Xaoping Shoo asked my parents if I and some of the other contestants from a few months ago could sing and entertain everyone whilst we try to escape this strange system that has trapped us, but after one of my performances I fell ill and so have been confined to my bed for almost a week.

I do hope we can soon break free and come back to you.

I worry for Captain Xaoping Shoo and first Officer Graylor and the crew. Some passengers and even some of the crew have become angry that we have not been rescued and rumours abound that there is someone aboard who shouldn't be with us and it's making me scared.

I think that something is going on as Mum and Dad sometimes have extra meetings with that odd person Mr Roberts and it makes me wonder about him. They won't tell me who he is, and we've not bumped into each other since we became trapped at Tianca.

Perhaps he is a spy like Sicanrinka said? Which reminds me, she has vanished which has led some to wonder if she is to blame. How could she be, she was only a reporter!

I can no longer roam the ship at will so feel even more trapped and lonely now without any of my toys to keep my mind off things. I am glad you are not with us suffering like this, but I do worry what you think has happened as it is very odd no one has come to save us.

It makes me want to cry.

I'd better go as Mummy is calling for me to eat something, but I don't have much appetite at the moment."

#

Roberts report: additional

"We have had a shocking development occur today. Somehow, someone has managed to board the StarVista 4 despite no signs of any ship or ships in our vicinity. Crew person Pralon was walking along the deck near to docking port three on the starboard side when one of the semi frequent ripples passed through us and to her shock, an Alteran appeared out of the docking port and fell into the arrivals section. The docking port was sealed with no sign of it being opened from the inside.

Security Chief Zaclin tried to access the Alteran's indenti-chip but was shocked to discover it has a design and software that he had not come across before. Pralon also noticed that on dimming the deck lights fine debris could be seen out the portholes either side of the docking port suspended in the jellified space surrounding the StarVista 4. Zaclin suggested and I agree that some form of rescue was attempted but failed drastically, stranding the Alteran inside the docking hatch before he managed to equalise the pressure and attempt entry.

Dr Sreisse has given us a preliminary report on the stowaway, and he cannot explain it.

One moment the person is fine, next they are convulsing in agony and the medical bay instruments cannot detect him. In the rare lucid moments when he can speak, he seems to suggest we are missing. Well that much seems to be obvious but he seems to be suggesting it'sbeen for a very long time.

The other question is: How did he dock with that liquefied space around us if we can't get out through it? Chief Coaraskk has made no progress with either the engine fault or understanding what the 'liquefied space' is that surrounds us. It is all very worrying, and I don't like not having answers.

Roberts, out."

17: A SHOCKING SURPRISE...

Recording: Captains report: Tianca extended stay.

"It has almost been five terran months since we found ourselves unable to leave Tianca and lost all contact with the GAA.

We have made no progress with our unexpected 'guest' and he is confined to medical but appears in no fit state to talk or explain who he is and how he managed to get on board. We have not been able to access his identi chip and Chief Coaraskk is becoming convinced the Alteran is from the future of all things.

I can't have wild speculation at a time like this. In the occasional moments of clarity, the stowaway appears to be saying the StarVista 4 has been missing for decades but he rarely stays conscious for more than a few seconds, so it is extremely frustrating for Dr Sriesse to make headway in understanding what the problem is with the Alteran.

So, for now his presence has been kept from the passengers and the majority of the crew until we can discover more about our unexpected guest."

She continued to file her report then the chimes sounded, and she clicked to receive the call from Graylor.

"Captain, Astrophysicist Crayt and Geophysicist Raskaert wish to see you as soon as convenient?"

"Very well but I doubt they can solve a problem that has vexed Chief Coaraskk and his team all this time in trying to get us free. Send them in now and join us too."

A few moments later both specialists and Graylor stood before Xaoping Shoo who indicated for someone to speak up as the two specialists appeared a little reticent now they had their audience with the captain.

Crayt was the first to speak up.

"Captain, as you are aware, we were tasked with studying the planet and rings in order to see if we could find anything out that may assist Chief Coaraskk in helping the ship break free. There was nothing in our data outwardly to help so after a while in agreement with the chief we stopped our studies."

"So?" Xaoping was a little annoyed that she had not ordered them to stop and that neither the chief nor the two before her had asked for permission to stop. She waved a tentacle roughly to indicate displeasure but to continue.

Raskaert now spoke up.

"We didn't officially stop but decided to allow our various instruments to continue their scans automatically and it was only an hour ago that I had to call Plep, apologies, Astrophysicist Crayt, to say that something had changed."

"It was right in front of all of us but we'd all become bored with it since our entrapment. You see, some of the rings have vanished and in rapid time too."

"And …?" Xaoping didn't like being strung along as if it were a game.

"Well, we can't explain where or what has happened to the rings that have vanished. But the speed of them doing so gives us cause for concern and may explain why we can't communicate or receive anything from the GAA," continued Crayt. Raskaert saw the frustration building on the captain's face and butted in.

"Time for us is moving slower than outside the jellified space. Hence, we see things speeded up. Another thing that is now blindingly obvious is the few subtle storms we detected on approach and initial orbit; they don't exist either."

"Or rather, if we are slow, then outside will appear fast to us and the planets rotation not just on its axis but orbit around Cantrara is so speeded up it has blurred any features." added Crayt before continuing, now with more enthusiasm. "Plus, the time effect must be linked to the orbital period of the planet which is why to us the stars have not changed."

"Barely," chimed in Raskaert.

"Yes, there is a very small shift. So we did a test over the last week and recorded one of the main cloud belts of Tianca at an extreme frame capture rate, then this morning we slowed the accumulated vid right down." Crayt paused, "Captain we've possibly been out here years ..."

"Now look, I have utmost respect for your professions, but this is preposterous. I can't tell everyone we may have been stuck out here for years! We've got growing unease as it is, can you imagine what would happen if the passengers, and indeed some of the crew would do if they thought we'd been out here for such a long time?"

Captain Xaoping Shoo then did something that neither of the specialists had ever witnessed before, she rolled each eye and fixed them both with an eye each in a disconcerting stare. "Does this help us to escape or not?"

Crayt and Raskaert looked at her and shook their heads slowly.

"I thought so. Continue your studies but only report to myself or Graylor and not a word to anyone else at all. Understood? Dismissed. Graylor stay with me for a debrief."

The two scientists departed and as the door closed Xaoping looked at Graylor.

"What do you think?"

"Seems far-fetched but both are experts in their fields and, well now they have mentioned it I can't remember how many rings the planet was supposed to have as there were several main broad rings and tens of thousands of ringlets and small-scale structure. If such features are no longer visible, then at some point someone amongst the passengers may well make the discovery if it is true and then we will be in serious trouble."

"My thoughts too, Graylor. My thoughts too."

#

"This is the captain speaking. This is to advise that there is no concern about our provisions. The StarVista fleet ships can all stay in space for over a Terran year and we have provisions to last longer than that as we always restock at all our primary stop off starports during our voyage.

I emphasise that we can out last anything that this planetary system can hit us with as the last five terran months have shown. We continue to monitor the ripples but have detected a lessening of their strength which we may be able to take as a good sign that the effect on holding the ship will also decrease and so allow us to escape.

We continue to broadcast distress beacons and messages and have no power problems so will continue to honour requests to send messages back to our loved ones. We still have no indication that any of the messages have escaped from the strange form of space that we are trapped in and have no explanation as to why no one has come to our rescue. We must hope that nothing has happened to the Galactic Arm Association whilst we have been entrapped here at Tianca.

We have not been able to find an explanation of why three of Tianca's larger rings have vanished and I urge you to keep a vigilant eye on the remaining rings. Please inform our newly formed science teams if you see anything out of the ordinary, especially if it appears connected with either the ship or the ring system. They will liaise with Astrophysicist Crayt and Geophysicist Raskeart and Chief Engineer Coaraskk.

I have good news about our little 'star' Cherice. As many of you are aware she was taken poorly a week ago after one of her lovely sing songs and she is now back on her feet and determined to give another performance in a few days' time if her parents approve. I'm sure you will all wish her good health, and you will agree with me that she is a shining example of her species, her parents can be very proud of her.

I will give another update either in a few days' time or if our circumstances change then I will immediately inform you.

Captain Xaoping Shoo, out."

Xaoping looked tired and Graylor had to admit that they were all feeling the strain. The captain and she were in engineering with Chief Coaraskk when Ambassador Richmond had sought them out due to a large number of passengers beginning to question if the food supplies would hold out.

Food supplies, she mused. They were the last thing to worry about as they were almost totally self-sufficient. Indeed, the resupply stops were only of some of the more exotic items to ensure they could cater for everyone's and every species particular tastes, but the vast majority of food stuffs were grown and processed in the bowels of the ship with the various hydroponics labs.

Graylor quietly spoke to her.

"Captain, I'm getting very odd reports that some passengers and crew have experienced, well, how to put this, they seem to be having paranormal experiences ..."

"Graylor, this is no time for silly pranks, surely the situation is bad enough without this form of hysteria creeping in."

"Agreed, but the ones reporting the events are quite sober and all describe the same thing. It is as if other people are on board but can only occasionally be seen, heard or in one case felt. Chief Coaraskk here has a theory.

"Well, get to the point Coaraskk." The captain's tone was a clear sign the strain was getting to her.

"It is a long shot, but what if, what if we are truly stranded, caught between our normal space time and some other space time and the ripples indicate we are in flux?"

"You've been talking to Crayt haven't you. Mentioned something similar a few days ago but

I wouldn't hear of it. GAA science has never broken that barrier so why would it happen here of all places?"

"I don't have an answer but if we are slipping between different universes then perhaps the feelings of ghostly occurrences may actually be other people who happen to be in the same place of intersection between them."

The intercom chimed and Xaoping shook her head and clicked to receive.

"Captain, we have another possible ripple starting in the remaining rings." Delieezas stated over the intercom.

"We'll be right there." Xaoping shot a glance at Graylor and they quickly exited and headed back to the command centre bridge. Graylor took up position next to Delieezas as they all braced themselves as Xaoping went over to the comms station and opened a ship wide universal channel.

"Ripple alert, everyone stay safe and keep still that's the advice from our medical team, same as all previous events."

Everything shimmered for the umpteenth time but for some reason things were a little different. It was Officer Calsohn who seemed to sum it up.

"Anybody feel as though things are not real?"

Delieezas turned and nodded.

"My skin is prickling as if everything around us is charged with static."

"No, I just feel cold, but my tips of my tentacles feel a little numb," commented Xaoping.

"I will scan the ship to see if there is anything additional to our circumstances at the moment." Calsohn said and began to operate the console but then lifted his hands up and, frowning, turned to them. "I ... I can't seem to operate anything. Nothing is responding and I can't feel the surface and controls, or at least they don't feel 'real'. My fingers touch the surfaces, but nothing happens."

Captain Xaoping went to open up the ship wide comms again but likewise could not get anything to work.

"Same here, anybody get anything to work?" After a few moments of frantic activity, the crew had to give up as nothing seemed to function. "I don't understand it. If we can't touch the controls, then how can we be still standing? Let alone breathe the air?"

Graylor shook her head and motioned Delieezas to join her but as he stood up, another more violent ripple passed across them and, as they struggled to cope with the pain, five shapes appeared on the bridge out of nowhere accompanied by the most awful screams anyone could experience ...

Coming from the helm station ...

PART 3

2505 AC

Convergence

EXSSV Erebus and StarVista 4

18: COMING TOGETHER

Graylor leapt over to where Delieezas had stood, but now there was a writhing, amorphous mass of flesh with some barely distinguishing features of the officer mixed up with another being. It spasm'd several times quite violently then stopped.

Dead.

The other four strangers were open mouthed and in shock as were the rest of the Command Bridge crew, but Captain Xaoping jumped up and along with Calsohn stood in defiance at the intruders.

Klaxons were sounding and someone was calling the bridge saying there were intruders on the engineering deck.

"Who the hell are you and what's happened to my officer?" Xaoping was incandescent with fury as Graylor joined her and Calsohn as she called for a security detail to the Bridge.

"How, I, I'm …" Andrica Parsons was utterly lost for words as Magda Delfinch motioned to the stricken officers.

"I'm a doctor, let me see what I can do." Xaoping momentarily had doubts but then waved a tentacle for her to attend but indicated the rest to stay put.

"Answer me! How did you appear like that and where are you from? Are you responsible for our entrapment?" bellowed Xaoping as the security detail rushed onto the bridge and took up positions holding the newcomers. Andrica found her voice at last.

"Captain. We're a … a team sent to help you. This is going to be difficult, but you've been missing for a hundred terran years and we've just found you. We thought we were on an empty ship until everything just shimmered and … well … Here we are."

"Damned nonsense, we've been here a few months, not years. Take them to the holding cells and make sure they don't have anything on them that could be used against us. I'll be down shortly, and we will get to the bottom of this."

Andrica tried to protest but along with Magda and the team they were unceremoniously taken off the bridge as Dr Sreisse and two medical orderlies rushed in to attend to Delieezas.

Dr Sreisse scanned the mangled body then shook his head. "I have never seen anything like it. I get two beings in one - it is impossible I tell you. Can't be, yet there's no doubt. Delieezas is somehow merged with this other, what appears to be a Scorion. The combination would have lived just a few seconds." Dr Sreisse's voice trailed off and fell quiet then motioned for the orderlies to deal with, and remove, the body.

Calsohn turned away and concentrated on his instruments trying to put aside the shock and feeling of nausea at seeing his friend and fellow officer die in such a horrible fashion.

"Captain, we are no longer getting reports of any flashes from near the rings of Tianca. They appear to have stopped."

Xaoping was deep in thought but heard him.

"Very well. Continue monitoring and instruct secondary Helms Officer Carson to report to the Bridge. Don't tell him what happened to Delieezas for the time being. Graylor, you have the bridge, and I will go interrogate our unwelcome guests. We will have answers, I swear on Delieezas's honour and memory."

Calsohn had not finished his report, however.

"Sorry Captain but there's more. Tianca has lost another ring!"

Stunned but undaunted, Xaoping stood and left the bridge knowing her officers were professional, but that the situation they were in was now seemingly out of their hands.

#

AJ paced in the cell as Jaal, Hooper and Dryak looked on in a sombre mood. Andrica and Dr Delfinch reported on events on the bridge and the loss of Qhrik. Simonds was sitting in one corner, still in a state of shock at seeing his colleague die in such a horrible way whilst Chelax stood and calmly studied the cell and the guards stationed outside it.

"This makes no sense. I don't understand why the biological components were not in sync with the inanimate aspects of the ship." AJ said out loud trying to understand what had happened.

"You mean the people - they are not just biological components - they are real people so treat them as such," responded Dr Delfinch a little more angrily than she'd intended.

AJ looked at her and nodded deferentially. "Sorry, yes Doctor, you are right. But it doesn't add up. I would have never believed the two could be out of phase like that at the same time. There's never been a single instance recorded of such an event, until now."

"I guess that explains the unusual experiences we all had?" added Andrica as she paced around then stood next to Chelax and stared at the guards stationed outside.

"Definitely. In fact, I had a sighting that I checked with Captain Andersohn shortly after we began our inspection and although they only grabbed a few frames from the drone footage, Liqxal was able to identify her from the passenger logs. The youngest of the passenger manifest, Cherice Richmond, eight-year-old daughter of the newly appointed ambassadors to Zianca, Carl and Natalie Richmond. Odd though as she seemed to be on her own, no parents or anyone at all nearby."

Jaal had been looking thoughtful and now spoke. "I expect it won't be long before they notice a rather large salvage ship docked on their starboard side and I'm sure Captain Andersohn will be having strong words with them as we wait here."

"Yes, that is the consolation, Jaal, so let's keep our spirits up and se ..." AJ didn't finish as the StarVista 4 captain entered the holding station and strode up to the screen to face Andrica and she in turn stepped closer to AJ. AJ still couldn't believe he was seeing the captain of the lost StarVista 4 standing right in front of him.

Alive ...

"I won't brook any nonsense. I've lost a valuable member of my bridge crew and I am not in a good mood, so you had better have an unshakable reason for how you all managed to get aboard this vessel unnoticed and how helmsman Delieezas died from merging with one of your own people?"

AJ stood facing Xaoping and for a brief moment pitied her plight. "If you will open communication with our ship and Captain Andersohn, he will fully confirm what we have tried to tell you."

"Silence. There *IS NO SHIP* anywhere near nor docked with us. So, stop this stupidity and try again. How did you get through the liquefied space? I may not have the liberty of throwing you out the airlocks, but I can assure you that the crimes you have committed already will ensure a very lengthy spell in the system prison on Alteran Seven."

"But, but surely our ship is obvious? It's docked to your docking port 5 on the starboard side." Andrica said as she stepped up closer to the energy barrier. AJ was furiously thinking and searching for possibilities. He looked up at Captain Xaoping.

"Captain. Please believe us, I think I may understand now. If your ship is just inside the anomalous gravity zone and has slipped back into suspended space it may be possible that the Erebus is still attached but we can't see it just like we couldn't see any of you. It's out of phase with us."

"Enough! We have plenty of problems of our own to deal with, so you are confined to this cell until we get underway and back to our official last stop at Viliak Spaceport Shalaiq."

Andrica sucked in breath sharply.

"Of course, you won't know …"

Xaoping looked at her suspiciously. "Know what?" she asked cautiously.

"Shalaiq was dismantled in the 2450's when the Viliak system was rendered uninhabitable from a massive solar flare. The system was evacuated just in time before the star became unstable and collapsed into a neutron star throwing off its outer layers to form a slowly expanding nebula."

"Utter drivel, we only left the system a few months ago, so stop with the play acting. You'll soon change your tune after a few days in this cell."

With that Xaoping turned sharply and left the holding station, still angry but with strange doubts after hearing what the intruders had to say.

"You'd think diplomacy was no longer taught in our time ..." Delfinch said under her breath and AJ shot her a disapproving glance.

"That went well." muttered Simonds.

The feeling was mutual amongst the team.

#

Back on the bridge, Xaoping noticed Graylor was absent. Calshon saw her looking round and replied to her unspoken question.

"Attending to passenger complaints, Captain. The passengers are becoming restless and clearly more worried. In the meantime, Chief Engineer Coaraskk wishes to see you urgently.

"Yes Calsohn, very good. Coaraskk is in my antechamber?" Calsohn nodded and Xaoping briskly walked over and entered the room to see, not just Coaraskk but also Dr Sreisse, both looking exceedingly unhappy.

"Who wants to go first? I guess this is not good news then Chief?"

Coaraskk shook his head and motioned to the table which had an assortment of items scattered on it, all confiscated from the intruders.

"Before I deal with this lot, I have to say I still can't find any way of moving the ship. Even with the help of the passengers we identified as engineers and physicists who were on holiday with us, we are at a loss. Whatever is going on is beyond my experience and all my diagnostics of the ships systems come back with a clean bill of health. There is simply nothing wrong with the ship."

Xaoping slapped down two tentacles hard on to the table giving a loud smack making both officers jump in their skin.

"HOW can you tell me this when we are clearly not going anywhere and somehow, we have unexpected 'guests' on board who make wild claims and have killed one of my most trusted officers?"

Coaraskk bowed his head in deference, then, before he could speak further, Dr Sreisse spoke up, but not with good news.

"Captain, I have some further bad news for you. The stowaway has, well, died."

"Shame but of no consequence under the present circumstances."

Dr Sreisse stood firm though.

"I beg to differ. The manor of his passing is something I have never witnessed or heard of in any medical record or school of thought. Please bear with me and watch the holocast." The doctor activated the holovid and swiped for it to show the scenes recorded in the medical bay. Staff in protective gear were monitoring the stowaway when suddenly, as the most recent ripple, passed through the ship and view, the body simply dissolved into a viscous silver-grey gel like substance that spread over the bed as the orderlies scattered and raced out of the room.

The air was thick with silence as Xaoping took in the possible implications.

"There's, there's nothing we know that can do that to a person?" she asked quietly, knowing the likely answer.

"Nothing we know of."

Xaoping indicated towards the items on the table with her left tentacle. "Chief Coaraskk, these items, what of them?"

Coaraskk stepped forward and picked up a small roundish shaped object.

"This item is a holodrone. Similar in some ways to the ones we launch to check out the exterior of the ship's hull."

But it is a fraction of the size …!" cut in Xaoping.

"Yes sir, in fact we can't download data from it as its dataware is, well, I have to say this captain, it's more advanced …"

"I don't like where you are going with this Coaraskk."

"Neither do I but the new intruders also have indenti-tags but again we can't access them. Similar problem to the one we found on the stowaway."

Xaopings mind went back to the awful view of the body dissolving on the table then shook her head. Dr Sreisse muttered something under his breath then looked at them both in turn.

"Captain, Chief, we may have to think long and hard about what the latest intruders said. 'We may well have been missing for one hundred Terran years."

Xaoping walked round to the intercom and activated it.

"Calsohn, have you managed to contact the GAA yet or our waystation at Viliak?"

"No sir, I still can't get any signal out at all on any standard and even unofficial frequencies." came the reply.

"Bear with me and do me a favour. Use the scanners to look directly at Viliak and let me know what you find." she could sense Calsohn was puzzled as the officer hesitated before replying.

"Very well sir. Anything I should look for in particular?"

"Yes, see what spectral type of star it is." There was a deafening silence over the intercom before Calsohn acknowledged the request.

"Very well sir."

Xaoping turned to her two officers and in

particular to Coaraskk.

"I may find myself apologising Chief. I have a very heavy feeling of foreboding. I can tell you have something else you want to tell us?"

"Yes sir. I have taken one of their devices apart and found something that corroborates their story," he indicated to one of the items which the captain had not noticed was actually several items that she now realised were part of something else.

"And?"

"It has a manufacturer's date stamped on the inside. It reads … 2493 Terran date."

"That's …" stammered Dr Sreisse.

"Eighty-eight earth years after we arrived at Tianca …" finished Xaoping as all three slumped into their seats, stunned. The comms chimed for her attention.

"Captain, I have something of a shock. I have scanned for and located the Viliak system …" Calsohns voice trailed off.

"And?" Xaoping was still in shock but suspected she wouldn't like what she was about to hear.

"I don't know how you knew, it is no longer a blue giant star, but is now a neutron star. There is no evidence that Viliak Spaceport Shalaiq exists …

19: THE TRUTH HURTS

It was a pleasant surprise when they were released and taken to one of the few vacant luxury suites on the StarVista 4 via the crew passageways, as AJ subtly noted the latter. He paced up and down like an impatient tiger in an old wildlife sanctuary and kept shaking his head.

"If they've sent us here then they must know the truth by now. Surely the Erebus is enough proof and if I know her captain, he'll be doing everything he can to sort this mess out."

"Look, pacing like that isn't helping us so don …" Andrica was cut short as the door opened showing the two guards still stationed outside. But now Captain Xaoping Shoo and two others entered the room. Xaoping walked up to AJ, her attitude one of someone in shock.

"Dr Hansone, please accept my sincere apologies for the confusion, but I believe you probably understand how our circumstances, if known outside of our small circle, could cause mass panic."

"So, the Erebus has been in touch then, Captain Andersohn will have been concerned about our sudden absence."

"I'm afraid none of us can find any evidence of another ship either nearby or docked to us. No, it is your equipment, we found several had manufacturers date marks on them which were quite shocking." Xaoping turned and introduced her two companions.

"This is Chief Engineer Coaraskk and our Chief Medical Officer, Dr ..."

"Sreisse, Dr Clispe Sreisse, I know all of you, in a manner of speaking," both officers along with Captain Xaoping looked on puzzled so AJ continued.

"There are two possibilities. Either:

One: My party have been transported back in time and so the Erebus would not be outside, and it is possible we are trapped with you in what we consider the past.

Or ... Two: the effect of being trapped in suspended space has meant that you were suspended in time as well and that we are still in our time frame, and it is yourselves and the StarVista 4 that was out of sync with the rest of the universe.

With the latter I can't explain at this stage why the Erebus is not outside although I'm open to ideas and suggestions."

Xaoping looked quite glum at the thought of both prospects.

"I am sure you understand sir that I and my crew and passengers would much prefer the first option. However, can you fill us in on what the future thinks has happened to us?" Xaoping motioned for them all to sit around the table and AJ began to explain.

"In 2405 Earth standard time, the StarVista

4 with two thousand passengers and seven hundred crew should have ended their eight-month voyage of adventure at Spaceport Shalaiq in the Viliak system. Instead, you received surprising orders to offer the passengers a chance to do something never done before, in other words, add another stop to a relatively unexplored system.

Although the Cantrara system had been discovered decades earlier, it had still not been thoroughly mapped, however, one thing had been discovered that helped make it unusual. It had a gas giant planet, Tianca, with a strange set of muti-inclined rings that were magnificent. Indeed even in our time it ranks as one of the top wonders and mysteries of the GAA, along with your disappearance but is off limits out of respect for the loss of everyone on the ship.

For some reason the StarVista Corporation was granted permission to add Tianca to its itinerary and the passengers were given the option to either disembark as normal at Spaceport Shalaiq or take advantage of the offer of a free few days extra voyage with nothing to pay whatsoever. Naturally no one wanted to miss an opportunity like that, so all the passengers willingly stayed on board."

Xaoping cut in with a little wry chuckle.

"Well, not quite all, Mr Roberts has been what you humans call a pain in the rear until he came forward with his true purpose on the ship."

AJ looked at her puzzled and surprised.

"Mr Roberts? Captain, since a twelve-year-old I have memorised all there is to know about this voyage and there was no one of that name on the manifest or in the crew."

"Surely you can't remember all of them. Two thousand and seven hundred people - impossible." added Dr Sreisse. AJ just looked him straight in the eye.

"All of them. This is my lifelong passion, the fate of the StarVista 4. There was no Mr Roberts listed as missing."

Xaoping tapped her com link.

"Graylor, request Mr Roberts to come to us with immediate effect."

Graylor surprised them.

"Captain, Roberts and Ambassador Richmond are in your anteroom awaiting you. They arrived just before the strangers appeared and wanted to see you urgently."

"Very well. Keep them there and I will call in a few minutes. Xaoping out. Dr Hansone, Mr Roberts came forward and indicated he was a GAA Security Agent almost at the start of our so-called incarceration, so he must have been officially listed. Indeed, I remember he took the place of an Ignacio Robertz, does that ring any bells for you?"

"Ahh, yes, that other name rings a bell now. Odd that the GAA didn't inform me of their agent being on board. I'd best have words with this Mr

Roberts to see what he can add. It may answer why the GAA finally let me come to look for you and the ship.

To continue, for all intents the records show the StarVista 4 arrived at Tianca safely and was moving in towards a synchronous orbit with the planet. Then all contact was lost. I mean ALL.

As you are aware there is a steady stream of engineering data always transmitted by commercial ships, especially the passenger liners but even that stopped dead. No warning or even a gradual change - just stopped. Initially a small fast scout ship was sent out, and when it found nothing, over a hundred ships were dispatched from Spaceport Shalaiq expecting to have to rescue you.

But they found absolutely no trace of your ever having been here.

You were not in the system and a wide field search over five light years found nothing. You had simply vanished.

It was hushed up and an announcement was made that the ship had struck an unknown icy moon and that all hands were lost. That was to cover the fact that no one had a clue as to where you were."

The silence in the room was palpable as Xaoping and her colleagues took in the information. Chief Coaraskk spoke what they were undoubtedly thinking.

"So, everyone thought ... thinks, we are

dead?"

"I'm sorry but, yes."

Silence.

Xaoping straightened her uniform.

"Well, we are not, and I can only hope that your first suggestion is correct so we can still have a life with our friends and relatives."

"There is something else Captain as I haven't quite finished. Tianca was declared dangerous and off limits to everyone. However, in 2430 an Alteran scout ship slipped in and was orbiting close to your last known position when it is claimed your ship appeared for a short while. The scout ship must have docked but was destroyed with no survivors, but I remembered something about the class of ship. It had two crew and only one body was ever found."

Dr Sreisse looked sharply at Xaoping then back at AJ.

"The stowaway? He was an Alteran."

"Quall Elaaf. The captain whose body was recovered was Quall Eliif, she appeared to have died instantly so whatever happened was incredibly quick."

"A male Alteran was discovered on deck seven starboard side, docking port three, after we had one of the more intense ripples pass through us. Crewperson Pralon stated that as she was checking the hull along that section, he just seemed to fall out of the docking port. We couldn't understand him nor get his Identi-chip to work, just like yours we had trouble with it. Now I know why."

"Good, perhaps we can talk to him and see what he can offer us as an extra perspective." suggested AJ thoughtfully. Dr Sreisse shook his head.

"He, he passed away but in a very unexpected and inexplicable manner." Dr Sreisse looked to Xaoping who nodded, and the doctor produced her holivid and threw the view onto the adjacent wall for everyone to see.

"Gosh, I have only ever seen one of these models in a museum," exclaimed Andrica and AJ gave her a stern look.

Undaunted, Dr Sreisse swiped the screen, and it showed the medical bay with Quall Elaaf lying on a bed. Suddenly a ripple passed through the view and then they all saw his body turn to a metallic silver like sludge spread across the bed and onto the floor as the orderlies raced to get out of the room, then sealed it.

"Oh, poor chap. Any thoughts either of you two doctors have on that?"

Magda Delfinch moved and stood next to the taller Dr Sreisse and they watched the screen again. Delfinch shook her head and whispered something to her new colleague and Sreisse did a good impression of a human shrug.

"Captain Xaoping, may I accompany your good doctor to the medical bay so we can look at the data more closely?" Delfinch requested as she looked at AJ and he nodded agreement.

"Yes, but Dr Sreisse, take the crew corridors, I don't want to alarm the passengers or give them cause for concern for the time being until we can come up with a plan of sorts. A new face after all these months will raise too many questions."

Both doctors left in a hurry as Xaoping turned to face AJ and his team.

"I am truly sorry for the loss of one of your crew, we have both lost valuable people and we need to get to the bottom of this."

"Agreed, I think our two chief engineers should take another look at the hyperfield containment manifold in engineering as I had found something just before we made our appearance to you. You OK with that Andrica?"

Andrica was surprised he had used her first name but nodded agreement and with Chief Coaraskk they too now left the room. Xaoping again faced AJ and the remainder of his team.

"If the rest of you don't mind staying here for now, I don't want anyone asking awkward questions if you wander around the ship. So, stay here, in I have to say luxury. I will have my crew provide you with any food you require."

AJ looked thoughtful for a moment.

"I think it wise for now that none of my party partake of any food or drink for the time being until we can ascertain what happened to Quall Elaaf. Agreed?"

"Very well. People, make yourselves as

comfortable as you can, and I am sure Dr Hansone will be back soon to give you a brief on what we've come up with."

The Erebus salvage party murmured agreement and AJ followed Captain Xaoping Shoo out, still in awe that he had met people that he had only read about in the official missing persons list of the StarVista 4's final voyage.

20: REPAIR

"... so, someone tipped off the GAA that the StarVista 4 was being diverted and adding an extra final stop to its voyage. That's when I was assigned to come on board when the ship arrived at Falaise-c-puc Starport."

Mr Roberts and Ambassador Richmond were sitting across from Captain Xaoping, Graylor and AJ. Captain Xaoping leaned forward.

"It still stings my tentacles that somehow you altered the manifest and none of us realised you were an addition.

"That's my so-called expertise. The person in my cabin, Ignacio Robertz, was quite happy to accept a very generous payment for slipping off the ship and allowing me to take over his room. I know it is a bit of an insult to my kind but most of the other cultures do say that every human looks like every other human.

It was easy for me to assume the role and subtly change everything including the ship's logs to look like I'd been on the whole voyage as Ignacio. I even resembled him enough to get away with just light cosmetics for a while until everyone got used to me.

Incidentally there was one person who always gave me an odd look as if she knew something was not right." Mr Roberts turned to Ambassador Richmond and Carl looked at him puzzled.

"Your daughter Cherice, Mr Ambassador, is very smart, smart enough not to say anything but I did have to give her the slip a few times. She would make a fine operative for the GAA if she wanted that career!"

AJ sat deep in thought.

"Interesting that the GAA didn't inform me they had someone lost on the ship. You are not listed in the official records which also begs the question of what became of the person you swapped places with. They would have been listed as one of the missing, presumed dead, yet wasn't," he spoke out loud as he was thinking about the GAA and what their game plan was or had been.

"I guess that shouldn't surprise me. They are ultra careful and may have paid off the person to keep their mouth shut and disappear, start a new life somewhere well away from mainstream life in the GAA. We have been known to do that on the odd occasion. With regards to the change of itinerary, they seemed to think that Captain Xaoping or their officers may well have known the real reason the SV4 had been allowed to come here.

There was no explanation except a vague suggestion that it was time someone paid the Cantrara system a visit. But a passenger ship? Daft if you ask me and under the present circumstances, ultimately quite a foolhardy thing to do."

"Agreed, that was what puzzled me ever since I was a young boy and saw a docudrama about the fateful voyage. It's a mystery why a civilian ship was dispatched, when there are, or were I should say from my perspective, plenty of science vessels that could have been assigned the mission," offered AJ.

"So, I have a question still. Where is your ship Dr Hansone?" asked Xaoping as Graylor nodded in agreement with her and showed the views from the Observation decks with no sign of a large ship outside of the StarVista 4.

"It has mystified Chief Parsons and myself as well. I suspect that we fell into sync with you but that meant we fell out of sync with our own ship, the Erebus. I'd stake everything on her Captain, Eric Andersohn, to be doing everything he can to reconnect with us. I suspect they are still attached but out of phase with us. My bet is that a ship the size of the Erebus is a lot sturdier than the Alteran scout ship otherwise you'd probably be detecting a heck of a lot of debris.

Let's hope we all sync up again soon so we can figure out how to move your ship into normal space from whatever this strange, liquefied space is. Captain, with your permission I would like our equipment back so I can take additional scans of the engineering hypermanifold. I noted something strange there when ..."

AJ was cut off as the intercom buzzed and

Captain Xaoping tapped to accept.

"Go ahead."

"Captain, Coaraskk here. Chief Parsons and I have found something. Can Dr Hansone and yourself come down to engineering?"

"Good timing, we're on our way," she cut the connection and looked at the others. "Let us hope that this is the first good news we have had. Ambassador and Mr Roberts can you do the usual and mingle amongst the passengers. I'd like to hope they haven't yet noticed we have new guests on board as that would raise too many questions and if it looks like we might be getting somewhere then I'll contact you. Agreed?"

"Indeed, you can count on us Captain."

The group collectively looked about with a glimmer of hope that the ordeal could soon be over.

\#

Engineering.

AJ's favourite part of any ship he mused as they entered and saw a small group off towards the hyperfield manifold bulkhead. He was glad that even when the SV4 had been built the engineers of the time had ensured there was enough screening to keep them safe. He caught Andrica's eye and she momentarily smiled before resuming her conversation with Chief Coaraskk.

They all turned to face AJ and Xaoping. The

chief engineer of the StarVista 4 spoke up.

"I commandeered Chief Parsons scanner from security, and we've been scanning the manifolds. Our own instruments show nothing out of the ordinary, however, with Parson's more advanced scanner we've found several incredibly tiny fractures that may be affecting the hyperfield and therefore could be a cause for us to be unable to move. We had a breach here during the normal part of the voyage, between Igrocl and Elac V during one of the longer periods between stops.

Several crew needed medical attention and we sealed the breaches but these micro fractures show they weren't fully repaired. Only your equipment spotted the tiny fractures and fortunately they were not enough to allow any dangerous radiation to leak. I wonder now if these micro fractures are involved with our status? We think, now we know where the fractures are, we can seal them and that may free us. It is still a long shot but it's the only thing we can come up with."

AJ looked at Andrica. "You in agreement, Parsons?"

"Yes sir, everything seems to point to this being the only thing at fault so if we can fix it then, well, it's a chance that we didn't have half an hour ago."

AJ turned to Xaoping and Graylor and Xaoping lifted her left third tentacle.

"Very well, Dr Hansone, let us hope that this works, and we finally get to see which of your hypothesises were right, past, or for us, future. What needs to be done?"

Chief Coaraskk indicated to a holoscreen he'd just started. The schematics of the ship whizzed across the screen then split into two with one zooming in on engineering and the other on a section of the outer hull close to the main hyperdrive engine auxiliary outlet. "There are two micro fractures here in engineering and now we know what we're looking for there is one slightly larger on the aft hyperdrive section exterior which we were unaware of. If Chief Parsons is agreeable, then she will seal the ones here whilst I seal the external fracture."

It sounded a good plan. Too good for Captain Xaoping.

"Chief, are you not forgetting something? We can't leave the ship due to the liquefied space surrounding and trapping us."

"Actually, we think that when Parsons seals the fractures here then it may well allow me to perform the EVA."

"I concur, it's possible that as we seal the fractures then we may begin to regain control and we don't know when or even if it will free the ship fully from the liquefied space, so I agree completely with them captain." added AJ.

"Then, what are you all waiting for? We have two thousand, seven hundred people wanting an end to this ordeal, so we'll be on the bridge awaiting your success." Xaoping indicated to Graylor and they left AJ and the two chiefs to their task.

#

"Chief, are you in position?" Andrica waited for the reply which for a few tantalising moments seemed to take an eternity.

"All set, I'm at the outer hatch looking at that weird form of space. I won't move unless it looks like it has cleared."

"Good luck Chief Coaraskk. I am starting the sealing process, now!" she carefully lifted the large but reasonably lightweight device up and slowly moved it across the area of the first fracture. AJ watched the holoscreen like a hawk but began to relax as he saw the micro fracture begin to seal.

A few minutes later it was sealed but there was no indication anything had changed. Andrica looked at AJ apprehensively. He smiled at her reassuringly.

"It'll work, I've looked over the schematics and my gut tells me we're on the right track and that you are right."

She nodded and tuned back moving the device a couple of metres along the manifold and then began to seal that fracture.

"This one is a little larger than the first but

looks like it too is sealing. Nice work Andri …"

He was cut off as she'd just finished sealing the fracture when the whole ship felt as if it lurched a little and warning klaxons burst into life with alert panels flashing red.

They looked into each other's eyes with alarm but then the klaxons were silenced, Captain Xaoping Shoo's voice came over the intercom.

"Attention everyone, this is the captain speaking. We have had a breakthrough and our engineering team appear to have cleared the liquefied space that surrounded us. We have also been joined by a rescue ship on our starboard side which the liquefied space had prevented us from seeing but for now is on standby if we need further assistance.

Please remain calm and show the universe that we of the StarVista 4 are resolute people in the face of adversity and that our ordeal may soon be over. Thank you for your patience and understanding. Graylor or I will give a further updates once we are able to confirm if the ship can now leave Tianca's orbit and head towards our final port of call."

AJ looked at Andrica.

"I think she is a bit premature on promising we're out of the woods yet." Andrica raised her eyebrows then had a thought.

"Chief, Chief, how's it look from your position?"

Static.

"Chief Coaraskk do you copy me?"

Static.

"Shit!" muttered Andrica as, without another word, both she and AJ rushed towards engineering's exit and together they bolted out into the corridor. AJ tapped the com Xaoping had given him.

"Captain, Chief Coaraskk is not responding we're heading to his airlock now." he got no reply.

On the bridge of the StarVista 4 things were somewhat frantic as they tried to deal with an irate Captain Andersohn on the mian viewscreen. Xaoping Shoo had plenty on her tentacles to worry about at that stage.

Meanwhile, AJ and Andrica passed several startled crew persons then reached the maintenance airlock. AJ brought up the internal display and they gasped as the view showed the outer airlock hatch was still open and in the distance in space was a figure gently tumbling, the right size and shape to be the stricken chief engineer.

AJ tapped a few controls and the outer door shut tight and the airlock re-pressurised. A few moments later they had the green light to get in and on doing so AJ reached for a spare spacesuit but was beaten to it by Andrica. He looked at her and understood as she spoke.

"He's out there - it could have been me so I'm going, no argument." AJ knew it was worthless trying to argue and deep down he knew she had to be the one. He touched her arm gently.

"Be careful, take out the harness and I'll monitor you from here, OK?"

"Yes, any trouble, you can bet your life that I'll soon holler!"

She opened the hatch and stepped inside noting the lack of the liquefied space. At least that was a good sign, she mused.

Andrica had not forgotten her basic training but still found the older style spacesuit a bit simple compared with what they had on the Erebus. She used the suit controls to manoeuvre out towards the stricken chief making sure the extra harness she had attached to her side was still with her and the gap lessened as she approached.

"Chief? Chief? Andrica Parsons here, I'm not sure if your comms are down but I'm coming up behind you. I'm almost there. Almost …" she noticed something. "AJ, can you hear me?"

"Yes Andrica, what is it?"

"The suit doesn't look right … I can grab him now. Ohh."

She held the suit and slowly turned it to face her and looked into the suit visor. She let go and began to breathe fast and deep taking in gulps of air before forcing herself to calm down.

"AJ, it's, it's empty … There's a sort of metallic film on the visor. Oh no …"

"He's liquefied …" AJ finished for her as he

realised what must have happened. "Get back, GET BACK NOW!" he shouted as he looked at the control screen and selected playback to review the footage.

The Chief had been standing looking at the liquefied space then as the ship lurched, he'd been flung out just as the liquefied space vanished. He was caught directly in the flux as it changed. He turned back to live view and watched as Andrica gingerly attached the harness to the lifeless form then she almost whispered for AJ to reel it in.

Ten minutes later with the outer door sealed and the airlock re-pressurised Andrica stepped out and into the arms of AJ who held her as she sobbed uncontrollably.

21: FREEDOM AT LAST?

Meanwhile on the SV4 bridge, over the comms a rather loud and irritated voice was bombarding Xaoping with questions.

"Where the hell did you come from? This is the EXSSV Erebus docked to your starboard docking port five. StarVista 4 respond! Dr Hansone please respond. Chief Parsons, report your status!"

"This is Captain Xaoping Shoo of the StarVista 4, we copy you Erebus, May I take it that you are Captain Eric Andersohn?"

"Whoa! Captain Xaoping Shoo?" there followed a stunned pause … "Err. Affirmative. Are our crew safe and well?"

"Yes, and no. One has been killed along with one of our officers by a fluke accident. I do not know his name, but Dr Hansone will be able to fill you in with the details. It was with his and Chief Parsons help that we have sealed micro fractures in our hyperfield manifold that appears to have brought us back into synchronisation. What is your status?"

"We've been stuck attached to you since we lost contact with our salvage teams. Are you telling me then that everyone on the StarVista 4 is still alive?"

"Yes, by your countenance I suspect I'm not going to like your answer to my next question …

What is your Terran year date?"

There was a long pause and Xaoping began to think contact was lost again when …

"2505, one hundred Terran years after you disappeared."

Captain Xaoping Shoo hung her head low and was pleased she was seated. Graylor stepped over, concerned. Xaoping stood and straightened her tunic and waved a left tentacle to say she was all right.

"Captain Andersohn, we shall have to keep it quiet about the length of our disappearance, you see for us we have been stuck in orbit around Tianca for just over five of Earth's months. I fear the passengers and indeed even the crew will be too shocked if we tell them immediately of the reality of the situation. I su …"

The internal intercom link from Andrica Parson interrupted Xoaping and she saw who it was … "I apologise Captain, but I have your chief engineer Parsons calling urgently. I will be back with you in a moment," she flipped the intercom link to Andrica's channel. "Go ahead …"

Andrica's voice was strained and Xaoping knew deep inside what she was about to hear.

"Captain Xaoping, I regret to have to say that Chief Coaraskk died when the ship came out of liquefied space as he was thrown out of the airlock into the flux of liquefied space as it dissipated. Dr Hansone and I have retrieved him but … his suit is sealed and contains his liquefied remains. I am so sorry. Do you wish us to take the sealed suit to the medical bay?"

Xaoping pondered the loss of yet another trusted friend then she took a deep breath.

"I will send a medical team and Dr Sreisse, I need you and Dr Hansone on the bridge as soon as possible. The ship you have talked about has appeared starboard, is docked and there is a quite irate Captain wishing to talk to you."

She didn't wait for a reply and cut the comms as Graylor made several frantic gestures.

"Captain, reports are coming in from passengers and crew seeing the other ship and I fear another riot is brewing."

"Very well. Calsohn, open up a ship wide passenger and crew comm for me now!"

Calsohn deftly ran over to the comms station and then indicated to the captain she was live.

"Attention everyone of the StarVista 4. I'm happy to report we have a rescue ship that quickly approached us and is ready to give assistance. I am however saddened to report that in helping us become free of the strange space surrounding us and preventing us from leaving, our Chief Engineer, Chief Ahanascal Coaraskk has sacrificed himself for the good of all and we will honour him and another of our colleagues, Helmsperson Delieezas who was also lost in trying to save our ship."

In the ambassadors cabin, a little girl cried out at

*the news that two of her heroes had passed away
and she ran into the arms of her mother in a deluge
of tears.*

The captain continued, unaware. "I hope now that with the rescue ship here we can finally leave Tianca. Please honour our lost comrades by remaining calm and allowing us to prepare to leave orbit. Note that there will be several new faces amongst us from the rescue ship which is called Erebus so there is no need for alarm."

She raised a right third tentacle indicating to Calsohn to cut the comms. "Get me Captain Andersohn again …"

"Connected".

"Apologies Captain, I have just had grave news that our Chief Engineer was lost whilst attempting to help free us. We have lost two fine officers and I am sure we on board the StarVista 4 will only be too glad to get out of this system."

"Understood Captain. I expect you are all going to have a hard time over the coming months. I've just established a comms link with Dr Hansone and will be in touch when I've heard his report."

"Yes, I have asked him and Chief Parsons to come to the bridge if they have finished repairing the fractures. I am sure they will now have a plan of operation as to when we can depart the system. StarVista 4, out."

Xaoping knew deep down they were not

saved yet …

#

AJ and Andrica were on their way to the bridge after handing over the lifeless spacesuit that had been Chief Coaraskk when Eric's voice crackled to life in their ear coms.

"What happened guys? Where have you been all this time?" Eric's impatience was obvious, and AJ just looked at Andrica a little puzzled and replied to the captain.

"Good to hear you too Eric. It's only been a few hours what ar …" he winced at the exclamation on the other end of the link and Andrica did the same as they shared the com link.

"A FEW HOURS? A FEW HOURS? IT'S BEEN THREE BLOODY MONTHS, WISE GUY!"

Both of them stopped dead in their tracks, astonished.

"ERR, what did you say Eric? Repeat that please?"

"Seriously, you are kidding me, right? We've been stuck here in orbit apparently docked to nothing yet something but couldn't move. We were surrounded by some form of odd space for the last three months. The StarVista 4 simply vanished when we lost contact with you. I can't raise the drones that were with you - what's happened over there and how the hell are they all alive?"

"Erm, well, for one thing the drones are in pieces as they didn't believe we were from their future. Look I suspect I know what happened. We'll get to the SV4 bridge and take it up from there as I want to confirm something."

"Good, I've just got hold of Captain Xaoping Shoo, that was a shock I can tell you! Erebus, out." The comms link died, and Andrica was stood with her holoscreen active making calculations. AJ looked at them and began to nod.

"You're right. Ohh sh**!"

They set off again for the bridge.

#

"Ahh, Dr Hansone and Chief Parsons, I have your captain on the comms again and he's somewhat shocked about something you said?" Xaoping Shoo looked tired but was still resolute in command on her bridge.

"Yes. Andrica here has figured it out. Tell them what you found Andrica."

She indicated to Officer Calsohn for her to take the science station and he stepped aside for her.

Andrica deftly tapped in a series of figures and the forward screen came alive with data.

"When we said that from our point of view the StarVista 4 had been missing for just over one hundred earth years, you, captain Xaoping stated that it was impossible as you had been stuck and out of communication with the rest of the GAA for just over five earth months. It didn't click with us that each minute we spent with you was probably a different length of time to the Erebus but now it all fits.

They have indeed been stuck and unable to move because they were physically attached to the StarVista 4, but we all fell out of synchronisation which is why you couldn't see the Erebus and thereby didn't believe us.

According to my quick calculations it would seem that time for the StarVista 4 ran much more slowly than for the rest of the universe whilst you were in what can only be described as liquefied space. If 100 normal terran years equals five months to you then it follows that as it is almost nine hours since we became stuck on your ship, that equates to three months for the Erebus!

I'm afraid it does also confirm that we didn't slip back in time rather we joined your slower time rate until we fixed the micro fractures in the Hyperfield manifold and it brought us back in sync with normal time." Andrica stopped and looked at AJ for confirmation. He simply nodded approval at her logic.

"She's right, we can't travel back in time and I'm afraid it means that you have been missing for a terran century. I'm sorry for this but I fully agree with Chief Parsons conclusions. Eric, you concur?"

Eric's voice came over with a tinge of reflectivity about it as he understood the implications for the captain, crew and passengers of the Star Vista 4.

"I'm afraid so. Ask your comm's officer to re tune general ships outer comms and nav systems to pick up the data links from the GAA as they have changed since your time."

Xaoping looked devestated at the news and shook her head, "Rasquart and Crayt were right after all, they too postulated we had been stuck here for years and likely decades and I couldn't, wouldn't accept it."

She looked over to officer Calsohn and he quickly reconfigured the comms then began to listen intently. He slumped in his chair then looked forlornly over at his captain.

"They are correct, Sir. The ship's chronometers have now adjusted to a new time and date. It's ..." he took a deep breathe. "It's eighteen oh five on October seventh, twenty-five oh five terran calendar.

The silence on the SV4 bridge could be cut with a knife. Then Graylor had a thought.

"The ships chronometer's have been reset. Everyone will know! There'll be mass panic!"

22: SHOCK

There was indeed pandemonium.

Some rioted. Others reverted to prayers to a varied selection of the almost long forgotten gods and deities of each species aboard asking for salvation. Many were just too stunned at the realisation that loved ones, family and friends had passed away and that they had been considered dead for a century.

"CAPTAIN! I'm reading over eighty-five passengers and around twelve crew have barricaded themselves into the shuttle bay. I'm picking up sound, hold on I'm patching us into it." Calsohn tapped away, then sounds of general mutterings and a voice shouting came over the comms.

The bridge crew listened with unfolding horror as, without warning the voice shouted about not being able to carry on, deceit from Captain Xaoping and her crew, lies and conspiracy then there were calls for the shuttle bay doors to be opened. Calsohn didn't need an order and deftly cut control to the shuttle bays to the sound of despair, then anger from those seeking to finish their lives.

Calsohn continued listening to the internal comms and looked pale.

"Captain, I'm getting a report from barman Antonyp that a large gathering is building on the starboard observations deck, both levels. From what I gather it doesn't appear to be unruly, but people are on edge wanting answers to where the time has gone and if it is our fault. There are demands to board the rescue ship to be taken home."

Xaoping turned to Graylor. "You have the bridge Graylor. Dr Hansone you and Chief Parsons come with me. Looks like we have some explaining to do. Calsohn, discreetly arrange for security officer Zaclin and a large security detail to join us. Best be ready for a rough time everyone!"

They headed out as Calsohn also ensured they retained a live link to Captain Andersohn on the Erebus.

#

It was unruly all right. Ambassador Richmond and GAA security officer Roberts were already there trying to calm the assembled crowd, but things were beginning to get heated.

Xaoping muttered something into her comm, and a loud chiming sound rang out and catching everyone's attention but it still took several minutes for them to quiet down. The anger was palpable as the captain and her team made their way through the throng to the front podiums, normally used for pompous occasions.

Captain Xaoping Shoo knew they were at a

crossroads.

"My fellow StarVista 4 passengers and crew. We need your help in order to make our escape from the strange world of Tianca and the Cantrara system. Simply put we need you to trust us for now whils..."

"STOP LYING! WE'VE ONLY BEEN HERE A FEW MONTHS NOT DECADES, WE HAVE FAMILY AND FRIENDS WAITING FOR US BACK HOME SO CUT THE LIES AND GET US BACK!" A deep Ziancan sounding voice rang out defiantly.

Loud cheers rang around the observations deck. And some near the front pushed a little closer. The captain held up her four front tentacles for quiet.

"We have not lied. I too am in shock as is the rest of our gallant crew, we are all in this together. Dr Hansone can explain better than I. He is an expert from the Rescue ship Erebus and he can conf ..."

Another voice rang out.

"RUBBISH, HOW DO WE KNOW THIS IS NOT ALL A SCAM, A CON JOB BY THE STARVISTA CORPORATION? WE NEVER AGREED TO A STAY OF THIS DURATION! WE WERE DUPED!"

Again, loud shouts of agreement rang out and the security team moved in and stood between the Captain, the team and the angry passengers.

AJ stepped forward and linked into the comms.

"I am Dr Hansone and this is Chief Engineer

Patrsons, we're from the Erebus, and I can confirm we are here to help bring you back to your own star systems. We ..."

He was cut short by the first annoyed passenger.

"HOW DO WE KNOW YOU AREN'T PART OF ALL THIS. WE DON'T KNOW YOU, YOU'RE IN ON THIS!"

"Well then you clever person, you've just said it yourself. Do any of you recognise me or my colleague? No of course not because we've only just come on board as part of the rescue team. If we'd been on the ship all the time some of you would have got to know us by now. Am I right or not?"

There was mass murmuring of agreement and now the annoyed passenger sensed he was losing the argument.

"NO, NO, DON'T LISTEN TO HIM HE'S ONE OF THE CREW I TELL YOU!"

It was clear a large portion of the assembled mass were undecided on what to believe and looked like teetering back towards the annoyed passengers' accusations. They began to push forward again, and the security team struggled now, wishing not to harm anyone but time was running out. Suddenly a new voice boomed out over the comms.

"Attention passengers and crew of the StarVista 4. This is Captain Eric Estobahn Andersohn of the Exploration and Space Salvage

Vessel Erebus. Now here this. We are not here on a sight-seeing tour but have come to assist you and return you to your respective home systems where you will be greeted as heroes.

If you are stupid enough to doubt our intentions then I will have no choice but to abandon the StarVista 4 and all hands-on board to your fate and return you to the liquefied space, trapping you for eternity. Is this what you want?"

For a moment again the masses hesitated but the annoyed passenger and now the second person again started shouting out that it was all a conspiracy and stirring the people up.

On his bridge Captain Andersohn shook his head in bewilderment at how seemingly intelligent people could be so swayed by idiotic false statements, but just then something extraordinary happened.

Over the comms came a gentle lilting rendition of one of the most popular songs that had featured in the entertainment theatre. Ambassador Richmond had tears in his eyes as he listened to his little girl calm the passengers over the airwaves.

Cherice Richmond sang her heart out on the bridge of the StarVista 4, a brainchild idea by Graylor and, as she sang in her sweet voice the whole mood changed abruptly with a thunderous applause as she came to the end of her short party piece that everyone had loved just a few months earlier. She coughed and cleared her throat again, then spoke.

"Everyone. I … I am Cherice and I am now aged nine years old, and you all know me and have seen me wandering around the ship during our space trip. I have seen the … the star clocks and I've even chatted to the new Captain on his ship, and it seems I am now a one hundred- and nine-year-old which apparently makes me, and all of you, record breakers.

As for me I am now the oldest, youngest person there has ever been in the galactic, thingy, err, arm association. I trust Captain Xaoping and Captain err … Andersohn and I want you to trust them too as they are here to help us get back home. Please believe me, I so want to go home, and they can do that. Thank you."

The comms from the bridge cut out and although the two annoying passengers tried to get everyone's attention they were met with disdain. Several came forward hesitantly as the rest began to head back to their own cabins or go over and stare at the Erebus from the observation ports. Zaclin motioned to several of his team, and they stood close to the two annoyed troublemakers who finally realised they had lost their chance. They were taken away much to disdainful looks from the remaining passengers who now shouted insults at the two disgraced passengers.

Captain Xaoping Shoo waved aside the rest of

her security team although Zaclin stayed close by her side, and she approached the few that came forward.

One person moved ahead of the rest.

"Captain, I am so sorry. It is easy to think the worst when you are told such harrowing news. It is also easy to forget that you and your crew have also been trapped with us all and so have lost family and friends, homes and livelihoods, indeed, all we may have had, is probably gone."

"It is understandable, it will take all our courage and fortitude to grasp what has befallen us, but I am sure our respective governments will help. After all, we will be celebrities of sorts and have a lot of catching up to do."

The group each shook hands with the captain but still seemed a little wary of AJ and Andrica, but they in turn didn't care. Ambassador Richmond came up to them and looked quite emotional.

"My little girl. Wonderful how she can get everyone to do her bidding. Usually, it's me that gives in to her."

Xaoping smiled at him.

"By the sounds of it she may well make a very good ambassador one day, don't you think?"

"Yes, I guess that was something she didn't think about when she did her diary pieces to Danny. Oh ..."

It dawned on Carl that Danny was now dead and that at some point Cherice would work it out. He hoped he and Natalie would be able to cope themselves when the awful moment of comprehension dawned on Cherice.

AJ was in deep thought.

"Excuse me Mr Ambassador, may I have a word about Cherice?"

"Certainly, she surely can't be in any trouble?"

"Quite the opposite, May I meet with her? Her diary messages to her brother made her famous across the GAA and they have even made films, movies and docudramas about her and her diary extracts. She's quite a celebrity and, well I have to admit it, I too am a fan of hers so to meet her in person would be the unexpected icing on the cake for me."

They turned to leave but suddenly the sound of running footsteps clattered down the corridor and the group braced themselves for a fresh onslaught from bitter passengers, but instead there was a nice surprise.

Trying to keep up with her little girl, Natalie and Cherice came round a slight bend in the connecting corridor. Cherice ran into the arms of her father who lifted her up and swung her round landing her on her feet gently in front of Captain Xaoping, AJ and Andrica.

"Now then my young celebrity. I have some people to introduce to you."

Cherice didn't wait, however.

"You must be Dr Hansone and you must be his girlfriend, Chief Engineer Parsons."

Stunned and a little flustered both AJ and Andrica must have blushed simultaneously as AJ quickly caught his breath.

"Ahh, not girlfriend, colleague, friend, good friend indeed. An excellent engineer too." AJ stuttered. Andrica looked briefly in his direction as discreetly as she could, but it was clear Cherice had not been convinced but just gave them both a knowing look.

"When can we leave Tianca?" she asked Captain Xaoping who smiled then looked at AJ who bent down in front of Cherice.

"That's a good question. We are working on that and I'm hopeful it will be soon. We have a problem still to solve but hopefully it won't be long now."

"I saw a ship out there you know but no one believed me. Now they do but why is it different?" Cherice added and for a moment AJ was perplexed but then it dawned on him.

"Ahh, you did see the scout ship then. I guess that's one mystery solved."

"OK if you say so." Cherice turned to her father who was still beaming with pride whilst Natalie stood at his side, arm in arm and so proud of their little girl. "Daddy, why did you call me a celebritery, err, celebrity?"

"Oh now, according to Dr Hansone as it has been so long since we went missing then your brother ..." Carl Richmond paused, knowing that there was no way Danny could be alive and wondered briefly if he should continue. He decided it was best to be straight with her. "Your brother was convinced we had passed away in a tragedy and according to Dr Hansone, your diary messages were eventually published by Danny and turned into several films and docudramas.

So, you are technically famous."

Cherice's eyes were wide open, stunned then she thought of her long-departed brother.

"I miss Danny. He couldn't be alive as I think he would be one hundred and nineteen now. Am I right?"

Carl looked at AJ pleadingly and AJ didn't know what to say.

"Er, well yes, he has passed but whilst he was alive, he always insisted on the authorities keeping a channel open in case you all suddenly appeared." he couldn't bring himself to tell her the truth for now as even Carl and Natalie didn't know what had become of their son in the intervening years. They looked at him and in their eyes, he could see they were grateful for not giving out any information until they had been informed themselves as to what descendants were still alive, if any.

Cherice had a thought come to her. "Can we visit Xanalorer tric-al-pascer? She is very old, and I want to say goodbye before we all end up going home. She'll be even more famous on her home world!"

"Well, my dear, let us do that once we are

safely on our way from here shall we?" replied Natalie. Cherice took her mother's offered hand and smiled.

"OK, bye bye Dr Hansone and Chief Parsons, thank you for coming to help us and tell your Captain he can do a good impression of you Dr Hansone," she looked squarely and mischievously at AJ as she said the last piece and Andrica chuckled a little knowing she too had spotted Eric mimicking AJ when they were on board the Erebus.

Carl, Natalie and Cherice bade their farewells and headed back towards the passenger decks as AJ turned to Xaoping and Andrica.

"I'll have to have words with the good Captain, can't have him wrecking my reputation. On a more serious note, Captain Xaoping, we still have that final micro fracture to deal with on the outer Hypermanifold but I have a plan to sort it. First, I have something I need to do so if you'll excuse me for an hour or so then I'll come up to the bridge."

Andrica looked at him puzzled but knew from his expression it was best not to ask so she smiled at Xaoping Shoo.

"I've learnt not to ask. Shall we head off?"

"Indeed, Chief Parsons."

"Andrica."

"Protocol Chief Parsons, protocol." Xaoping replied but tried to give her a human wink. It failed but she got the gist of it.

With that they left as AJ headed off to catch up with the Richmonds.

#

AJ sat next to Cherice, Natalie and Carl Richmond in the ambassador's quarters.

"You know, when I was a little boy, I saw a holo-docudrama about the fate of the StarVista 4 and when you were mentioned I was mesmerised by the fact that an eight-year-old was out travelling amongst the stars on such a wonderful sounding voyage. Little did I suspect that I would actually get to meet her!"

"It was one of the conditions we placed on accepting the ambassadorial role for Terra on Zianca. As we were going to have to uproot Cherice from the Earth itself and have her educated on an alien world, we felt that a good way for her to acclimatise to other species was to join us on a voyage to some of the highlights in the GAA.

It is still hard to think of how Danny, our eldest, coped with our disappearance. It is a regret we shall always have that we couldn't persuade him to take a break from his studies at the Alteran Higher Studies University and join us." Natalie smiled but in a sad sort of way and Carl spoke up.

"We've now seen the various transmissions he and his daughter sent. It seems ironic that of all the things he and most of his family would perish on a similar voyage to ours and it was the disaster at the waterfalls of Marlt on the planet Plckendar. Did you know we didn't get to see it - oh, of course you know as you've seen all the transmissions. We understand there were also several films featuring us in various ways."

"Yes, most concentrated on Cherice's story but Danny wasn't keen and managed to stop all films until of course he was killed. After that his daughter Natalie didn't have any qualms about them. She gained a small but significant fee from them so was able to afford the lifestyle she wanted and to do the work she loved.

You know that she came to the Cantrara system and to Tianca in a research ship, the GAA security ship Zal, in 2460?" AJ powered up his holoscreen and selected the relevant data with images and as he did so Cherice gasped.

"I saw that ship!"

They all looked at her astounded but sceptical.

"I did! I was coming back from visiting Chief Engineer Coaraskk and I looked out and for a moment I thought I saw another ship, that's what it looked like."

"You never told us dear, when was it?" Asked Natalie as she looked at Carl wondering if Cherice had been hallucinating.

"I think …" Cherice began as she clearly was thinking hard about it. "I think it was around eighty or so days from when we arrived at the ringed planet and became trapped."

AJ quickly did the maths and looked at Natalie and Carl.

"She's right. According to what we'd worked out for the time duration you were in the anomaly, the year 2460 would be fifty-five or so years since the StarVista 4 vanished and that equates to eighty-two point five days to you on board the ship. There's something I know has never appeared in public records and only a few of us know the un-redacted version, but Danny's daughter Natalie-Cherice stated she thought she saw something the size and shape of the StarVista 4 glimmer momentarily whilst they were near to the supposed location.

No one took her seriously as none of the scanners at the time picked up anything. She said in a private log that for a moment she felt she was looking at 'family' and came over 'warm and fuzzy' as if she knew that you were all right. But again, that part was never made public.

I have something extra to tell you. She and her partner Lariq Siliq are still alive, and she is in her eighty fifth year.

As he is an Alteran, they couldn't have children of their own so adopted three, one human, an Alteran and a Gu-Alt. All three are grown up and have gone their separate ways but occasionally keep in touch with Natalie-Cherice and Lariq."

All three of the Richmond clan looked puzzled. Carl spoke first knowing what Natalie and Cherice were probably thinking.

"Lariq Siliq? But there is a Lariq Siliq on our ship - he looked after Cherice on occasions, and we've become good friends."

AJ smiled and nodded. He pressed a small communicator. "You can come in now Lariq."

The door opened and Lariq entered, somewhat puzzled as nothing had been explained to him when Captain Xaoping had requested, he attend the quarters of the Richmond family. AJ nodded politely to him to take a seat next to Carl who shuffled up as they all exchanged glances whilst Cherice just smiled at Lariq. They'd had a lot of fun when he had to look after her on occasions and was glad, he had come to their room, although she too was puzzled.

AJ continued where he'd left off.

"Yes, Natalie-Cherice's partner is the nephew of you Lariq Siliq and he often mentioned that his uncle had also sent back personal messages during the voyage about Cherice and how much he loved looking after her.

Seems it is a family thing. What is more ..." AJ set up the holoscreen to large format, so it half filled the room. "I have a short while ago after the mini riot, set up a private link with them and they are waiting to talk to you all.

Remember that they are old so it will be quite a shock but they are excited and looking forward to seeing and talking to you. I'm going against the authorities doing this so keep this to yourselves for now. Understood?"

They eagerly nodded with tears in their eyes as AJ confirmed the connection and, as Natalie-Cherice and Lariq appeared on screen, he left them in private as a lost family was reunited.

23: TIME TO FINALLY ESCAPE

Just under an hour later AJ headed up to the Bridge and filled them in on what he had come up with.

"Live link established Captain." Calsohn reported and Xaoping turned to AJ.

"Repeat what you have just told us for Captain Andersohn's benefit."

"Eric, we've only been partially successful. Chief Coaraskk was awaiting our signal for when we'd sealed the micro fractures internally on the hypermanifolds. However, there is a fracture on one of the hyper engines externally and so he was going to seal that one as we expected the liquefied space to begin to dissipate.

We didn't expect the ship to lurch as it did and can only speculate that as the liquefied space vanished it did something to the local space environment causing us to shudder and eject the chief out just as the liquefied space was in flux. What I'm saying is, that we still can't move the ship until the final fracture is sealed. At least that's my best assessment of the situation."

"So what do we do now AJ?" Eric looked at them all from the bridge main monitor.

"I need you to do something for me. There is no way we can risk anyone else going out even if whatever happened to the chief is now over, we can't risk it. I want you to hand over the voice command code to me for the Erebus. I wouldn't ask if it was not that important."

"Sorry, what good will that do?"

"Trust me and do it Eric …"

There was a brief silence then the link with the Erebus went dead. Captain Xaoping looked at AJ in a puzzled way as did everyone on the bridge. Andrica crept closer to AJ and looked at him questioningly but didn't say a word.

The comms crackled briefly as Captain Eric Andersohn's voice came through. "Transfer code Captaincy one complete. Please open a secure channel Dr Hansone and complete the sequence."

AJ looked around and walked to the entrance door and stepped through allowing it to close. Everyone looked around, tension building on the bridge. A few moments later AJ came back onto the bridge.

"Transfer code sent." he looked around as if staring into deep space then. "Erebus, confirm identity, Dr Andrew James Hansone, enable voice confirmation."

A male voice filled the air.

"Confirmation, Dr Andrew James Hansone, CEO, Hansone Industries. Acting GAA Security officer, Special Missions Division. Control systems transferred temporarily from Captain Eric Estobahn Andersohn with immediate effect."

AJ smiled as he knew Eric hated his middle name, especially as it was now known to both bridge crews after his attempt to assuage the passengers earlier. He then realised the ships AI had inadvertently informed the two bridge crews he was also a GAA covert security operative but decided to let it ride and see if anyone broached the subject. They had more pressing matters at hand than in asking him of his connection with the GAA Security Service.

"Erebus, activate subsystem Carmen, one five zero eight."

The voice changed to a female tone.

"Subsystem activated. Hello Dr Hansone, how may I be of help?"

"Hello Carmen, deploy engineering drone B5 equipped with hyperfield scanner and repair systems."

"Preparing.

Deployed.

Destination?"

"Carmen, link with StarVista 4 command and control system data on outer hyperfield engine microfracture. Once completed, transfer drone to shuttle bay ..." AJ turned to Captain Xaoping expectantly and she realised what he meant as she replied.

"Shuttle bay one. You plan to go out there, don't you?" she surmised.

Andrica looked at AJ with a serious expression but knew there would be no arguing with him, but AJ turned to Xaoping.

"Captain, I'm not risking anyone else out there. This has to be me. I have worked on contingency plans since I became an engineer but to be honest, never actually thought I'd end up doing something quite like this."

The bridge was quiet as no one dared speak, all except Andrica. She took a deep breath.

"As the shuttle bays are now operational, I think our salvage team should return to the Erebus. However, as the good Captain Xaoping no longer has a chief engineer then I respectfully request a temporary assignment to the StarVista 4 to help in whatever way I can whilst you do your heroics."

The somewhat blatant sarcasm was not lost on him, but AJ didn't retaliate,

"Very well. Eric, do you concur?"

"Agreed."

"Captain Xaoping?"

"Agreed and with many thanks for the help."

"OK everyone, Erebus salvage team to report to shuttle bay two for transfer to Erebus when we are free of the anomaly, meanwhile I'll head out in the drone to try to fix the microfracture. I expect once it is sealed the StarVista 4 will regain full control and be able to finally leave Tianca." AJ turned and didn't wait for any objections.

#

Outwardly calm and professional, but inwardly somewhat nervous, AJ stood in the ancillary bay waiting for the doors to open and the drone to arrive at the shuttle bay. "Give us some good news Eric, the drone should be almost here in the next few minutes and Captain Xaoping says the natives are getting restless again."

"Good and not so good, I'm afraid concerning our docking tube clamped to the StarVista 4. The seals are literally welded to the SV4, and we can't free them. We're stuck together and I dare not try moving in case the stresses rupture the StarVista 4's hull. We're somewhat bigger than that Alteran scout ship all those years ago."

Andrica had followed AJ down to the bay and mulled this over.

"Erebus, sorry, 'Carmen'. Are you able to interface with the StarVista 4 systems and control both ships?" she inquired as AJ nodded appreciatively at the thought as he figured he knew what she was thinking.

"Affirmative but command codes for the StarVista 4 must be transferred to Erebus in order to do so," replied the AI, Carmen.

Captain Xaoping was linked in and didn't await the request she knew would come next. "Transferring control to the Erebus".

A few moments later the soft tone of 'Carmen' rang out over the comms of both ships.

"Symbiosis complete. StarVista 4 and the EXSSV Erebus connection achieved. Bridge controls of both ships now transferred. Awaiting instructions from Dr Hansone."

"Captain Xaoping, I would like Captain Andersohn to have final authorisation of any actions 'Carmen' and the Erebus suggests, do you concur?"

"I concur."

"Very well, 'Carmen' work with Captain Andersohn, I am transferring control back to him. Code zero black alpha eighty-four over two."

"Transfer complete Dr Hansone." 'Carmen' replied.

Flashing warning lights indicated the shuttle doors were opening and the drone gently glided in and settled on the pad as atmosphere was introduced into the bay and the side entrance opened. AJ was about to head out when Andrica, on impulse, kissed him, taking him aback."

"No heroics …" she said then turned and left for the bridge leaving him a little bemused and shaking his head before climbing into the repair drone.

Sealed in, and on manual control, AJ sent the command for the bay doors to open and piloted the drone gracefully out of the hanger bay as everyone watched on the monitors on both ships' bridges.

"No heroics," he muttered to himself. "I'm on a ship that's been in suspended space and time for a hundred years surrounded by a strange form of liquefied space, we've been stuck on it for apparently three months and there's no guarantee my idea will even work. No heroics indeed."

"What was that AJ, we've got some static interference now you are heading round the other side of the StarVista 4. You will shortly be lost to us from the Erebus as you will be on the far side and towards the rear and too close to the Hyperengines." Eric tried not to sound concerned but he also knew what AJ could be like. He was still bemused that the AI of the Erebus was named after AJ's third ex-wife, Eric's, often annoying, sister.

"Nothing. Will close in on the hypermanifold engine on the port side shortly. Oh …"

"AJ, report?"

"Well, from what I can figure, there must still be a patch of liquefied space still associated with the fracture on the engine. Not sure if it will have an effect but my best guess is it may cause a time delay."

"Roger AJ, be careful out there, we won't be able to see what you're doing as the screen has already gone haywire."

"Now, now mother, don't fret. I'll be a good boy, promise." retorted AJ as he chuckled at Eric's concern. Deep down however he was pleased their friendship had survived AJ's divorce from Eric's sister.

"Just had confirmation the shuttle with the salvage team has docked with the Erebus and

Chief Parsons is with Captain Xaoping on the StarVista 4 bridge monitoring comms."

"OK, has visual gone completely?"

"Yes, voice only now and even that is becoming strangely distorted. Your voice is beginning to sound like some of those old kids programmes we used to watch."

Silence.

"AJ?"

Static.

"AJ? Please copy?"

Static still. Then …

"I'm OK, I'm edging closer to the micro fracture area, but you are becoming distorted. Before this gets too extreme, I will signal one short beep then a long beep then a short beep to indicate the fracture has been sealed. I'm hoping once it is sealed the liquefied space will simply dissipate like the majority surrounding the StarVista 4 did once Andrica sealed the internal micro fractures. Eric? Eric did you copy?" frustrated he looked ahead and took a sharp intake of breath. "Oh shit!"

The signal was too distorted for his voice to get through.

Back on the Erebus, Eric turned to comms officer Liqxal with a questioning look.

"I believe he said something like a beep, long beep then it became too distorted. If there was anything else, then we didn't get it." Liqxal replied as he tried to clear up the signal but to no avail.

"Damn. Wait, that sounds like a really old-fashioned signal used centuries ago, pre catastrophe era. SOS, three dots, three dashes followed by three final dots. If I know Dr Hansone, it's a shortened version of that. But if we can't hear him, how the hell do we know he's succeeded?"

Andrica appeared on the screen with Captain Xaoping with Graylor standing behind them.

"We'll know when the engine responds to commands, so we'll give you the heads up. Captain Andersohn, how about sending a maintenance pod to hover sixty degrees between you, us and Dr Hansone's drone? That way you could at least get a visual on him and it might help the link?"

"Good thinking Andrica." Eric turned to Lieutenant Tracheria. "Tracheria, launch one and place it as Andrica suggests."

A few minutes later a voice came over the intercom whilst the view was strangely distorted. They listened and strained to understand the transmission but all of them had to admit confusion.

"Think, everybody, why is it so deep and drawn out - oh heck, of course!" exclaimed Eric suddenly and turned to Liqxal. "He said a time delay. What if it's his time becoming drawn out, so to him we will sound high pitched and too fast but to us he will be slowed down and low pitch?"

"Understood." Liqxal manipulated his control whilst listening and moving his head in deep concentration almost oblivious to everyone else.

"Wow, here you go."

AJ's still slightly distorted voice now came over.

"... here, almost completed but there is a misshaped 'blob' of I guess liquefied space still close to the engine and it is drifting towards me. If I can ..." the signal broke up.

"Can what?" asked Eric frustratingly.

"Can't help it Captain, we've caught up with his transmission and have to wait for the rest so I can work my magic and bring it up in sync with us."

"So, we're still in the dark." Eric shook his head.

Suddenly 'Carmen's' voice came online.

"Captain, the StarVista 4 engines appear now to be nominal and operational."

Liqxal piped up. "Yes, I think I've got something else from Dr Hansone. It was just a beep and I think he said get moving now. It sounded strained and certainly urgent."

"Very well. Captain Xaoping, Andrica, we're going to see if we can move the ships and I'm handing over control to 'Carmen'. I'm sure when AJ is back on board, he can explain why an illegal AI is installed on a GAA ship. No offence 'Carmen'!"

"None taken, I cannot experience emotion. I

have full control of the Erebus and the StarVista 4 and beginning a low, slow, acceleration within tolerances of the docking tube. Shall I bring in the maintenance pod?"

"We'll have to, but I don't understand why Dr Hansone has not contacted us. He should be clear of the SV4 engines by now."

Tracheria looked round at Eric.

"Dr Hansone's repair drone is no longer in view via the maintenance pod, he slipped behind as we began to move. The static from the StarVista engines prevents communications."

"Where is he then? What's he up to?" Eric flicked the screen to the StarVista 4 link. "Have you got anything from him?"

"No, but the area behind and close to the engines is usually assigned as dangerous to any small craft or pods due to the distortion field of the hypermanifold engines so it's almost unthinkable he would hang around there unless ..."

"Exactly. He's not daft enough to stay put so he must be circling round on our blind side but he's ..."

"CAPTAIN! We have a problem. That distorted space, the liquefied space that Dr Hansone described. Now I know what to look for, I'm able to detect it and it's caught in our hyperwake, being drawn in towards us. It's also expanding in size and closing in."

"'Carmen', options?"

"Captain, I theorize that as there are two ships in close proximity to each other travelling together then the anomaly is caught between our two hyperwakes. If the ships separate and diverge at sixty-three degrees away each side from our course, then the anomaly will be thrown forwards and may well dissipate as the wake collapses between the ships."

"'Carmen', we're still docked together, and the docking tube won't release."

Before the Erebus AI could answer, Andrica's face reappeared on the forward monitor.

"Captain, I believe the maintenance pod could be directed to crash directly at the centre of the tube where it is weakest. There may be some structural damage to both ships, but I believe it won't be significant. Captain Xaoping Shoo has evacuated the starboard sections closest to the docking port and is sealing the bulkheads as a precaution."

"Excellent Andrica keep the link open, now where is AJ? Damn him! We said no heroics."

"LOOK!" shouted Tracheria pointing to the main screen which had switched to an aft view. A tiny dot raced towards the anomaly and struck it as the screen was overwhelmed by the resulting explosion.

"What the ...? 'Carmen', what happened?"

"Captain, I am sorry to report that the repair drone appeared from behind the StarVista 4 and flew at the anomaly, detonating as it entered it.

The anomaly is weakened and is still closing in on us, but it has given us more time."

Silence on both ships bridges as it dawned on them on what had happened ...

AJ had made the ultimate sacrifice to give them a fighting chance ...

24: SACRIFICE ...

"Damn, they'll never hear me in time."

AJ saw the repair had worked and although it was clear the two ships were beginning to move as one, he could see the anomaly was growing and getting closer, being pulled into the wake between the two ships. "If that thing gets caught up with us then we'll all be stuck again and even lost for another hundred damn years!" he knew he was talking to himself but with the comms down and out, it didn't matter to him.

A thought occurred. Risky as he could see the ships appeared to be gaining momentum, but he didn't have the ability to tell them it was going to make things worse unless they could separate. He quickly assessed the options - limited that was for sure but he began manipulating the controls of the drone to rotate it into position and programmed the microwelder for its final act. There was precious little leeway.

OK, he had to admit, there was no leeway for error but that was the nature of the beast.

He finished, then as quickly as he could, he again checked to make sure his hasty calculations and programming were set to do the job at hand. Fastening his helmet and taking a deep breath he swung round and backed to the door, triggered the onboard drone systems to take over. The repair drone swung into alignment with the anomaly, and he blew the hatch, and the rapidly escaping air forced the drone to surge towards the anomaly …

… and AJ hopefully towards the side cooling fins of the StarVista 4 …

#

On board the Erebus and StarVista 4 bridges the shock of what AJ had done suddenly hit them. Captain Eric Andersohn had known AJ since their school days but there was no time to grieve.

"People, I know this is difficult and I'm sure if AJ could have done anything different he would have done so, but we have a job to do so let's get on with it and make sure his sacrifice is not for nothing. Tracheria, have you control of the maintenance pod?"

Traceria looked at him as he contained his grief. "Yes sir."

"Good. 'Carmen', once the pod strikes the docking tube, separate both ships and ensure they follow the course you outlined, monitoring the anomaly. If successful, then bring the ships back into close proximity in case we have to assist the StarVista 4."

"Affirmative."

"Tracheria, bring the pod in."

"On its way Captain."

"Everyone, brace for impact. Captain Xaoping, ready?" Eric said into the comms.

"We're all set here and under your full control." Xaoping replied with just a hint of worry in her voice.

In space, the pod accelerated and swung ahead of both ships then sharply turned back and flew directly between them crashing into the docking tube, disintegrating both on impact. A soundless collision but fine debris scattered everywhere, and emergency klaxons sounded on both ships, but the bulkheads held.

'Carmen' silenced the klaxons and initiated the ships separation effortlessly as they parted company and headed off on their own courses.

Both bridge crews held their breath then 'Carmen' came over the comms.

"Separation successful. Anomaly has been catapulted between and ahead of us and is rapidly dissipating. Indeed, it has just disappeared from scans altogether. There is some structural damage on both ships at the affected docking ports and they will be unusable until the ships can reach the nearest star port, but the bulkheads did their work and both ships integrity have been maintained.

The maintenance pod and repair drone have both been destroyed and I report one loss of life, Dr Andrew James Hansone."

"Thank you for your report 'Carmen'. Please release control of both ships back to their respective captains and stand down."

'Carmen' replied without emotion.

"Lieutenant Tracheria, and Officer Carson now have helm control respectively. Erebus control transferred back to Captain Eric Estobahn Andersohn and StarVista 4 control back to Captain Xaoping Shoo."

'Carmen' went quiet, and Eric looked at his colleagues on the bridge then at the bridge crew of the StarVista 4 on the forward screen.

"We still have a job to do and that is to get the StarVista 4 and all on board her back safely to Star Port Atrica. Remember, it was because of Dr Hansone's single minded determination to find the StarVista 4 that, incredibly, we've not just done that, but we are bringing home all who were onboard her too and I think that should be his legacy.

So let us complete the job and then we can take time to grieve, but also celebrate his achievement."

Andrica was white faced and looked devastated as Captain Xaoping, Graylor and the bridge crew of the StarVista 4 stood and saluted before the screen went blank and reverted to the forward view. Eric lowered his head for a moment in silent tribute to his lost friend but knew AJ would not want them to mope about his demise. Tracheria on the Erebus and Carson on the StarVista 4 coordinated their rendezvous as both ships lined up next to each other.

On board the StarVista 4 the passengers and crew finally began to realise they had been saved and Captain Xaoping Shoo scheduled a celebration and commemoration event for later that day to thank the crew of the Erebus and to remember the lost heroes, Chief Engineer Coaraskk, Helmspilot Delieezas and Dr Andrew James Hansone.

#

Nine hours

#

"Mother, I didn't see Xanalorer tric-al-pascer at the remembrance ceremony, do you think she is all right?" Cherice Richmond had been very sad at the ceremony at the loss of Chief Engineer Coaraskk, Delieezas and to a lesser extent Dr Hansone as the latter she had barely known. But the Chief Engineer and helmspilot, like many of the crew on board, had taken her to heart.

They had been so kind to show her the engineering department and how to fly shuttles so that their loss was all the greater.

But she was a very perceptive young lady and after being stuck with everyone for what they had experienced as just five months but was now known to be over one hundred years, she knew when a familiar face was missing. Her parents stood with her on the travelator as it sped on taking them down several decks and a third of the way to the mid-section.

"I'm sure she is fine my dear, she is quite old you know and very frail, so perhaps she needed to rest up after all the excitement of us being rescued." Natalie looked at Carl for support and he nodded.

"Tell you what, let's head down to her room and say hello. We've still got a couple of weeks on board since the captain said we can't go at our normal speed due to the damage to the starboard side of the ship. I'm sure she will be happy to see you Cherice."

"Oh goody, she'll be a hero when she finally gets back to her home world as she will be the oldest of her people even though she was already the oldest. I guess that is the same for us?" Cherice's mind was working on overdrive at the implications as they stepped off the travelator and moved over to a second one that would take them in the right direction to Xanalorer tric-al-pascer's room.

"Well, in a manner of speaking, yes, although you will of course be the 'oldest, young' person there has ever been, so I gather when we get back to Earth there is to be a special celebration of our return along with the other humans as they reach their respective planets.

I do find it a little sad that we never got to take up our ambassadorial roles on Zianca but that can't be helped." Carl said as he gently held onto the eager Cherice who had shuffled a little too close to the edge of the travelator.

Natalie smiled and knew Cherice wouldn't really get too near the edge but noted they were almost at their destination.

"OK, we're slowing now so we are almost there."

They stepped off and followed the corridor around to the right as Carl looked at the various cabin name tags.

"Here we go." he held his hand over the control panel to signal there were visitors and waited.

Cherice shuffled impatiently, then had a thought.

"She might be out, perhaps she did go after all but was on the other side of where we were at the ceremony?"

"Could be, tell you what, hold on a moment." Natalie pressed the panel and brought up the menu for the nearest steward and clicked for communication.

The steward's face appeared for that particular deck, it was an Alteran and they immediately recognised Lariq.

"Oh, hello Lariq, thought I didn't see you at the ceremony, I expect you had enough work to do so couldn't attend?"

"Ahh, my dear friends, yes, indeed work never stops for us. Tell me what I can do for you?"

"We wanted to say hello to Xanalorer tric-al-pascer but she doesn't appear to be in her room.

Can you either let us know where she is or give her a message that Cherice would like to say hello."

"Not in her room you say. That's odd as her biosigns show …" Lariq suddenly went quiet. "The last status update shows her in her room but for some reason the bioscan appears to have failed. Let me have a word with her and I'll ask if you can enter."

With that the small holo screen went blank and they stood patiently waiting until …

"Erm, Ambassadors, this is very odd. I can't raise her and the bioscan last readings showed she was indeed in her room, but they stopped a short while ago. I gather Dr Sreisse and a medical team are already on the way, but the odd thing is that the bioscan didn't fade away. It just stopped."

As Lariq explained this, Dr Sreisse appeared with the team and the doctor from the Erebus. Natalie and Carl took a puzzled Cherice by the hand and led her to one side as Dr Sreisse used her security clearance to gain access. The door slid open, and they entered but to gasps which caught Cherice's attention and she managed to pull free and look in through the open door.

Her high-pitched scream was ear shattering as she went into a full-blown panic attack at the sight she could see …

#

Eight hours twelve minutes

Captain Xaoping, Graylor, Dr Sreisse and Dr Delfinch stood in the medical observation room looking at the 'in cabin' medical monitoring footage that only the doctors were normally allowed to see due to privacy concerns.

"So, our little girl, Cherice, saw everything?" asked a deeply worried Xaoping. Dr Sreisse nodded as they watched the monitor and she indicated to the time stamp for them all to pay close attention.

Xanalorer tric-al-pascer was frail which was no surprise given her age, but she wandered unsteadily towards her bed and lay down, shivered then the onlookers gasped as she turned instantly to a silver liquid that flowed over her bed and dripped onto the floor leaving her garments covered and limp on the bed.

Dr Magda Delfinch took a deep breath and sighed slightly.

"We've set up the system to continuously monitor everyone on the ship. We already have three more examples of the same thing. Dr Sreisse?" she looked at the official chief medical office of the StarVista 4 and Sreisse looked pale.

"Although it is early in our investigation, there seems to be one common element to the occurrences. All, regardless of species are, or rather were, old. Just like astrophysicists we use what is termed a 'standard candle' to compare ages amongst the species of the GAA and there is no doubt that all four were close to the same equivalent age. Some species don't look their age, so it was only Xanalorer tric-al-pascer who actually did look very old and of course she was regarded as a celebrity.

She was the oldest of her kind by a long way even before events overtook us."

"But is it an infection? Can you predict who might be infected? Isn't this the same as the Alteran who tried to board us and died in the same manner? Chief Corrask went the same way - neither of them were old?" the questions came thick and fast as Captain Xaopling Shoo grasped the potential disaster that could be before them.

"Captain, we simply don't have answers and we ca ..." an orderly came into the room ashen faced and handed a holoscreen to Dr Sreisse.

The doctor looked even paler than before.

"Another case. Looking at this data, slightly younger than the first casualties. Captain, we will need to keep this under wraps for the time being if we can so we have time to try to figure something out and see what we can do. But for now, Dr Delfinch and I have no answers."

Graylor looked at Xaoping. "This is going to be almost impossible. Everyone knows each other so well since our extended stay at Tianca. Word will get out. I think we also need to inform Captain Andersohn on the Erebus as protocol requires for us to become quarantined until we have an answer and hopefully a remedy."

"Agreed. As the ship was safe despite the loss of the starboard docking port the passengers are not expecting to disembark to any other ships until we reached a star port so let us keep calm and for now play down any problem unless things escalate out of hand, agreed?"

They all nodded just as word came through that, yet another passenger had 'liquefied'.

#

Seven hours one minute.

#

Eric Andersohn sat in silence in his quarters as Magda Delfinch concluded her medical report on events taking place on the StarVista 4.

"So, for now, you both have to stay on the StarVista 4 until you can confirm if you are not affected? What about the original salvage party that have returned?"

"Andrica and I will have to stay here, and you will need to quarantine the salvage party until we know more about what causes the effect." Magda replied with a heavy heart.

"You realise that technically that leaves the Erebus without her medical officer or her chief engineer …" Eric said as he grappled with the news.

"I'm sorry Captain but we have no choice. I will level with you; I don't have a clue as to what is going on but can only think it is associated with the trapping of the StarVista 4 in the liquefied space all those years ago. Perhaps in our cases, we might not be affected as we have only been on the ship for a few months whilst they were trapped for a hundred years, and Dr Sreisse and I are working along those lines.

But to be frank, we're no nearer understanding what is going on than when the first people started to liquefy. There's been another five cases, but it does seem consistent with how old the person is, so that's the angle we're exploring without anything else to go on.

"Oh well, I guess in AJ's case it is just as well he's no longer with us. He'd be heartbroken if he thought by rescuing the passengers, he might instead have doomed them."

"Thanks for that cheerful note, Captain! But I guess you are right. Talking of Dr Hansone, Andrica has been exceptionally quiet since his death and has buried herself in her work ensuring the StarVista 4 engines are working at peak performance. I'm concerned for her."

"Well, keep an eye on her. I do know she was quite a fan of his work and was somewhat enamoured with him, but wouldn't admit it to his face or officially to me either. Make sure she is OK, won't you?"

"Will do. Delfinch, out."

The comms died and Eric sat contemplating the probable sad fate of the passengers and crew of the rescued ship they accompanied. Due to the damage to the docking ports, and the admittedly slight possibility of a more serious structural issue, both ships had to travel at sub hyper speeds and so it would still take over a couple of weeks to reach the nearest star port.

The GAA Security Ministry had already imposed a news blackout which had rattled some of the passengers and crew of the StarVista 4 but for the moment they simply didn't want news media racing out to intercept them.

And now this.

He prepared his report and sent it to the GAA Security Ministry knowing full well they would quarantine both ships and that it was highly unlikely they would be allowed to go near a commercial, public space port.

Eric took a breath and sighed at how things had turned out then flicked the light sensor to off to allow him to sleep.

It was a troubled few sleepless hours ahead for him.

#

Two hours twenty minutes

#

Eric awoke to a gentle alarm and realised he was still shattered but had to ignore his fatigue so got up, showered, dressed then headed up to the bridge.

Comms officer, Liqxal along with Chief salvage officer Craysol were in discussion as he entered and Liqxal turned to address Eric.

"Captain, I've had a reply back from the GAA Security Council. You're not going to like it however …

They have directed that under the extenuating circumstances, the StarVista 4 is to carry on to Alteran, a three-month flight at present speed and a special facility is being set up for them with no one to leave the StarVista 4 unless specifically cleared by the medical team on board."

Eric nodded as he thought that was going to be the likely outcome, but Liqxal wasn't finished.

"We are also to be quarantined and accompany the StarVista 4 to the Alteran facility …"

"Oh. I guess I shouldn't be surprised. I did make it clear that our studies so far show no effect on our salvage party. I suspected they would lump us in with the StarVista 4. Captain Xaoping is not going to be very happy either."

Liqxal was still not finished, however.

"The GAA Security Ministry is sending a military escort which should reach us in the next twenty hours and they have instructions to escort us. However, they also have instructions to shoot any escape pod if any of the passengers or crew of either ship try to escape the quarantine."

Liqxal fell silent but Eric just shook his head and took up his place in the command chair.

"We don't have a choice then. I'll inform Captain Xaoping shortly. Craysol, how are things coming along with repairs to the docking ports on both ships?"

Craysol came over and stood close to Eric.

"We've secured and made safe the damaged areas on the Erebus, Andrica has been coordinating the work on the StarVista 4. I can't for certain say that there is no other structural damage so for now we will have to continue sub hyper velocity as a precaution."

"Very well. Worth launching a couple of maintenance pods to check round both ships for anything obvious?" Eric suggested and Craysol smiled.

"Thought you'd say that, so I have three of them ready to go." Craysol turned to Tracheria at the helm. "Ok Trachy, launch the pods. Send them round both ships, the Erebus first."

"Launched and beginning scans." Tracheria had anticipated the request and smiled with satisfaction as both pods raced away then began to circle the Erebus looking for potential damage.

#

Forty-six minutes

#

Cherice looked out from the port observation deck and spotted two small lights moving up and past the front of the StarVista 4. She didn't much care what they were as she ran through in her mind what she'd seen at Xanalorer tric-al-pascer's room.

She shuddered and her father put his arm around her for comfort.

"I don't like this ship anymore Daddy," she exclaimed in a soft, sad voice.

Carl Richmond really wanted to agree with his daughter but knew that they all had to keep positive.

"Well, it won't be too long now Cherice, after the main voyage then the five months it seemed to us at Tianca, the next few weeks will surely fly by. You could always ask the captain if you could sing again for everyone. I'm sure that will lift their spirits?"

"I suppose so," something caught her eye as she watched one of the lights do a sudden sharp turn then head towards the rear of their ship. "I think they've found something wrong with the engines as one of those thingy's has just rushed towards the back. Oh, I hope it doesn't make us stay even longer on this ship. I'm really fed up now. I want my toys."

Cherice had never forgotten her luggage full of her favourite toys had become lost right of the start of their voyage - it still bounced crazily around her mind that it had been a hundred years ago. Now she knew how long they had been stuck at Tianca, she briefly wondered if her toys had ever been found and were in some sort of museum.

That actually made her smile as she saw the light reappear from the rear and instead of heading back around the StarVista 4 it raced away towards the other ship, the Erebus that was flying alongside the StarVista 4.

"That seems to be in a bit of a hurry. Oh, it's changed course again, coming back to us!" she exclaimed and Carl stood with her as they watched the maintenance pod streak past and they both gasped as they saw what was in the robotic arms …

25: A CLOSE CALL

Tracheria brought Maintenance Pod 3 round and proceeded with a spiral orbit about StarVista 4, checking the scans as it continued its flight. Initial scans confirmed that only the Starboard docking port was severely damaged but structural integrity was not compromised and the bulkheads had done their designated job.

He noted M-P 2 had completed its scans of the Erebus and smiled as it returned similar readings, Dr Hansone had certainly designed a good ship he mused as he glanced back at M-P 3's latest 'orbit' and was about to look away when something odd caught his multifaceted eye.

Organic matter.

Close to the rear of the StarVista 4 and not far from …

He jolted upright and took manual control of the pod changing its direction abruptly and it raced towards the rear where the hyperengine manifold fins were located as he stared in disbelief.

Carefully Tracheria manoeuvred the pod closer as his three hearts began to race as the pod made a connection with the suit electronics.

#

One minute seven seconds.

No time to lose but he shouted to the rest of the bridge as he deftly manipulated the pod grapples as carefully and delicately as he could then turned the pod round and raced at full speed towards, firstly the Erebus then realising there was no time, the nearest StarVista 4 shuttle bay.

"Captain, It's Dr Hansone! He's barely alive and I'm taking him to the secondary shuttle bay on the StarVista 4, he has just seconds of life support left so no time to bring him here."

Eric wasted no time as Liqxal opened a ship-to-ship channel. "Captain Xaoping, Medical emergency. Incredibly we've found Dr Hansone and he's in a bad way. Bringing him to your shuttle bay two. Open the bay and get a medical team there and just hope we're in time!"

#

Suit Failure.
Life support out of allocated time.
Life signs: zero.

#

M-P 3 swung into shuttle bay two and settled down with its precious cargo. Dr Sriesse, Madga, Andrica and the medical team stood trying to hurry up the re compression even though it was mere seconds and, as the green light flickered on, Andrica had the door opened and the team raced across to the lifeless form held limply in the pod's articulated arms.

Seeing his face through the tightly fitting suit helmet Andrica didn't have time for a sigh of relief and ignoring protocol, they tore the suit off him, and she could barely look at the badly burned face. Between the four of them they heaved AJ into the medical intensive unit and sealed him in as it began to work on his vital signs. A weak pulse sprang back into life and Magda nodded as she noted a very shallow but discernible rise in his chest as the damaged lungs clawed at dragging in oxygen to fill them.

Magda indicated to the team, and they set the unit to take the quickest route to the medical bay as Dr Sriesse quickly filled Captain Xaoping in with AJ's status.

Up on the bridge Xaoping looked over to officer Calsohn who opened comms to the Erebus.

"Erebus? Xaoping to Andersohn?"

Connected.

"Captain, we have him, and they've just placed him in intensive care and he has been partially revived. Doctors' Delfinch and Sreisse are in attendance and Chief Parsons is in the medical bay and will be in touch with more details when she has them."

"Partially revived?" Eric didn't like the sound of that as he looked at the screen.

"He is alive but has severe hyperburns, severe damaged to his lower body and legs and is in a coma. Ahh, I believe Dr Delfinch wishes to give us an update."

The link became three way, then four way as Andrica joined them.

"Captain Andersohn. It's not good. The StarVista 4 medical bay is not as modern as ours on the Erebus. We have to transfer him if he has any chance of survival."

"I was thinking that, however, both ships are quarantined, an official directive from the GAA." he replied deep in thought.

"So?" butted in Andrica who was stunned at her Captain's response. "We sent the original salvage team back to the Erebus so there's no reason not to also transfer AJ, I mean Dr Hansone. This is a medical emergency after all."

"Chief Engineer Parsons, I appreciate the lecture, but the salvage team returned before we had any idea passengers on the StarVista 4 would start to liquefy."

Andrica stared back with a stern look on her face, deep down she knew he was right but before she could say any more, Eric continued.

"But it is extenuating circumstances after all, he's my former brother-in-law but what's more I think the GAA public would be aghast if we let the person who pushed to find the StarVista 4, die due to a directive that had not anticipated such an event. Captain Xaoping, may I send over one of our shuttles to collect Dr Hansone and Dr Delfinch?"

"Of course, I concur with your assessment considering the unusual circumstances."

"Good, you might already have noticed a shuttle is already nearing your shuttle bay one in anticipation of your cooperation."

Captain Xaoping smiled, knowing she'd have done exactly the same thing and indicated to Calsohn off screen. The bay doors opened, and the shuttle headed in to land.

Eric turned his attention to Magda Delfinch.

"He's in your hands Magda, I just hope we got to him in time." Eric addressed the fourth screen. "Andrica, I know you'd want to come over, but your place is on the StarVista 4 and that is your job, I'm sure you understand?"

"Yes sir. No problem. As long as Magda does everything, she can ..." replied Andrica, although deep down she really wanted to fly back over to the Erebus, but her professionalism held sway. "Magda, he's a hero, do everything you can, yes?"

"No worries, but no promises either, we're heading to the shuttle bay even as I speak. I'll do what I can, and I do think there is a chance of recovery once he's aboard the Erebus." Magda flicked off her wrist com and just three screens remained active. Andrica was about to sign off too when Eric indicated to her and Xaoping he had something else to say.

"A couple of things. Firstly, Andrica, how did he do it? We saw the pod race towards, and be destroyed, by the anomaly. It had to be piloted so how did he manage to control the pod and get out and somehow attach himself to the StarVista 4?"

"I should have guessed he would come up with something. It did seem controlled, and I should have realised he wouldn't give up without some sort of plan. My only thoughts are that he managed to re program the pod then the only way he could get out would be to initiate the pod engines as he blew the rear hatch.

That would have sucked him out and back to the StarVista 4 and it would then be a matter of luck if he could hold onto the ship."

"Hmm, he's damned lucky if you ask me.

Secondly for both of you, for your information for the time being, but the GAA Security Ministry is sending an armed escort with four ships to accompany us. We have been directed to fly to Alteran so I'm afraid we have around a three-month trip ahead of us but Tracheria is of the belief from the maintenance pods scans of both ships that there should be no reason why we can't go to Hyperspeed so as soon as it is confirmed I expect the trip to be just a week.

My crew have been informed and naturally they are not happy, but I suspect you will have your hands full captain. We will have to go public with what we know regarding the passenger deaths so far and I expect it might get a bit ugly for you."

"I appreciate your concerns," said Captain Xaoping, "Just for the record, we now have six crew members also perished. They were the oldest of the crew and people are beginning to notice the trend." Xaoping looked worried, at least as worried as a Gu-Alt could look. Eric understood what now lay heavy on Captain Xaoping's shoulders and could feel empathy for her.

"We're all in this together now so we will do whatever we can to assist."

"Thank you, Captain. StarVista 4 out."

All the screens went blank and on the StarVista 4 Captain Xaoping Shoo contemplated what to announce in order to try to allay fears.

But if Dr Sriesse's recent report was right, all on board the StarVista 4 who were part of the original voyage were effectively doomed … including herself. Graylor looked on, knowing full well the implications and could only wonder at how her Captain was holding up.

#

Ships log: EXSSV Erebus. Captains' additional notes:

It took a week of intensive care and hyper radiation treatment before Dr Hansone finally responded. Dr Delfinch has kept him deliberately in a coma during this time, so that gradually the skin burns healed, and the doctor could begin to relax as the patient's vital signs returned to normal.

However, Dr Hansone has lost his legs due to the intense exposure and will have to be kept sedated until we can get him to a star port medical facility. Dr Delfinch is confident that at the proper facility his legs will be regrown, but it generally takes a several months and even up to a year of intensive treatment. For now, he has artificial limbs being attached so may well be allowed up and about with help in the near future.

Our engineering team discovered there was slightly more damage to both ships than anticipated so we are still moving at sub hypervelocity and have been joined by the four escort ships.

In the meantime, on the StarVista 4 the passengers and crew have taken the news badly and the liquefied body count has risen to eighty-three.

Sadly, seventeen of them crew members as of this additional note.

Dr Sreisse has liaised with Magda via a dedicated com link but as they had more data, read deaths, it was quite clear that the effect is age related and likely linked to the length of stay within the anomaly. There is as yet no indication that the members of the Erebus salvage team who boarded the StarVista 4 so many months ago are in danger but there is so little to go on it can't be ruled out entirely.

Andersohn, out.

#

In the Erebus medical facility, Magda looked at the readout and linked up with the StarVista 4 medical bay once again.

Dr Sreisse looked worn out.

"I've checked the figures too many times to count. You're correct in your assessment and formula. If this really is right, then the next to pass will be passenger Cranlo-fixt, she's the next oldest if records are right. It could also be any time …"

"Yes, I didn't want confirmation, but her bioscan signs stopped abruptly ten minutes ago. The team is well prepared now and know what to do so we are collecting the liquefied remains and keeping them safe in one of our now spare refrigeration bays. I never would have imagined that instead of provisions, we'd be storing such a thing as the passengers.

You know what this means?"

Magda closed her eyes, shut them tight then

opened them hoping she'd stifled the tears.

"Yes, you have at my best guess just eighteen hours left to live."

"Seventeen hours and nine minutes to be more accurate. Yes, I too had reached that conclusion. I will continue to work on our studies of this phenomenon, but I have arranged for my final moments to be in one of our recuperation chambers so that all my liquefied remains can be kept in pristine condition for you to study."

"How can you be so calm about this. You literally know when you are going to die!" she asked, her voice trembling a little.

"We Ziancan's are renowned for being very practical when it comes to our passing. If we are not in touch again, may I say it has been a pleasure to work with you Dr Delfinch, Magda, and that I have the utmost trust in you to make some good out of our misfortune. I have no family to speak of as my podding partner, well, she passed away many years ago before the final voyage of the StarVista 4.

So, in some small way my life will have come to its end with no, how is it you say? No loose ends. Just promise me you will find out how this occurred and ensure it doesn't happen to any other ship in the future."

"You have my word, Clispe, you have my word as a doctor and a friend."

Dr Clispe Sreisse smiled at her mention of his

first name and bowed his head slightly before cutting the com link. He then sat back and began to cry, knowing his fate was sealed …

26: THE RAMIFICATIONS

"So, Mr Roberts, your favourite tipple then?" barman Anatonyp smiled as Roberts strolled into the Starboard Observation Decks favourite and only bar.

"Yes, indeed, anything to blot out thoughts of things to come."

Anatonyp nodded as best a Ziancan could. "I for one have longer I gather than you and I think that makes it worse. By my own estimate, over three quarters of us will have gone by the time it is my turn and I don't relish looking out to see who else no longer treads the travelators of this ship."

He leaned over the counter and taking the hint, Roberts leaned in wondering what Anatonyp was going to do or say.

"You know that in my culture, the number you know as 'four' is considered bad luck. I believe you humans had a culture who believed the same?"

"Yes, the Chinese didn't like the number when it was spoken as it was very similar to their word for 'death'. If I remember rightly, thirteen and nine were also unlucky for some parts of the Earth too. I seem to think that the Alterans try to avoid fifty-seven as well as it is supposed to translate into one of their earliest languages as 'they who walk the cold and empty path' or put another way they haven't got long to live. About sums up our situation then doesn't it!"

"I only bring it up as it implies this ship was doomed from the start. When it was launched several Ziancan dignitaries refused to attend as it was the fourth designated ship.

For the first few weeks of its shake down voyage it lived up to the superstition as the hanger doors malfunctioned, the hyperdrives failed to start on first try, something unheard of apparently and the first captain had to be quietly removed and committed suicide after her first voyage. All that was hushed up so as not to upset the passengers and of course the various commercial interests at the time."

"Charming, you would have to tell me now! Hang on, I thought that this ship was originally supposed to be the fifth?" Roberts looked at Anatonyp and tried to look perturbed.

"Yes, it originally was the fifth to be built, but all that went wrong happened after it had been officially confirmed as the fourth to be operational. Something stronger then to take away the thoughts and memories?"

Anatonyp didn't wait for a reply as he moved over, reached down and picked up a very dark ruby red coloured bottle with a layer of dust on it.

Roberts was now amused and inquisitive as he looked at the bottle and nodded for a glass of its contents.

"I don't think I have ever seen any dust on this ship until now." he said as he accepted the drink and was about to take a slurp.

"Best take a sip at a time. This is almost a thousand of your years old and one of the most potent concoctions ever created. It's from Coriqz and is illegal across most of the GAA. But you knew that didn't you?"

"Yeah, unmistakable and deadly. I need a drop in a large glass of water otherwise it really would bring a premature end to me! So, we're heading for Alteran. I wonder what the facility is like that they are preparing for us?"

"Prison more like, we will have no freedom to leave and let's face it we are all doomed." muttered Anatonyp who looked down at the glass of ruby red liquid and took another careful sip.

"You heard about the breakout?" Roberts looked around as he asked and Anatonyp shook for no. "Eight crew and fifteen passengers tried to commandeer a shuttle but although they managed to get past the captain's security team, as they launched, they were flanked by four fighters from the nearest escort cruiser and were given no doubt that if they continued, they'd be destroyed. Shook them up and now they're in the brig on level four dash two."

"I can't seem to blame them. We have no life now to speak of. Nothing to look forward to. Makes you wonder if that Dr Hansone should have stayed away and forgot about us. At least we'd probably still all have some sort of life even if it was stuck on this ship."

Roberts couldn't help but think the same.

"Tell my Anatonyp, how long did you know?"

"Know what exactly?"

"That I was not Ignacio Robertz."

"I suspected something a day or so after our stop at Falaise-c-puc star port but couldn't quite, how do you say ... put my finger on it. It was a good disguise, that and almost looking like Mr Robertz which, I assume is why you were chosen. Remember we checked you as you signed for your first transaction here at this very bar and I noticed the slight difference in your surname, so I called for Security Chief Zaclin to say 'hello'."

"Ahh yes, I remember. You both accepted my explanation."

"True, especially as both our systems miraculously changed to reflect your new identity. Clever but left me suspicious enough to inform the captain. Incidentally I also found myself a little suspicious of that reporter too, Sicanrinka. So, she was definitely up to no good?"

"The fact she disappeared at roughly the same time we became ensnared would seem to suggest so. There is no record of her existence except for about two years working as an Haverian Newsguild reporter.

Definitely up to no good but I can't see how she could have been the one to get us stuck in that strange form of space. Something for the boffins I reckon. Hard to believe we've been lost for a hundred Terran years, and everyone thought we were dead. I do wonder what story was given to my brother and his family.

"I didn't know you had family. I guess in your profession they expect the worst."

"Problem is my dear Anatonyp, they didn't know what I did for work. Caused a bit of a rift, especially when my parents passed as I was away on a mission and couldn't attend their funeral. My brother, David, didn't take my absence too well and we haven't talked since. Or at least up until the StarVista 4 was announced as lost and ironically he wouldn't know I was on it."

"But surviving family will now be told?" Anatonyp suggested trying to raise Roberts spirit.

"No idea, unlike almost everyone else, I have heard nothing. Still, it will be interesting to find out if David was ever told by the security ministry where I was.

"Thanks to our heroes finding us we may find out soon."

"Indeed, in fact, let's drink to our rescuers."

"I'll drink to that!" they raised their glasses and carefully took a sip from them.

#

Andrica Parsons received the communiqué from

Captain Xaoping and was relieved. Dr Hansone showed signs of being well enough for Magda to bring him out of his coma and Xaoping and Eric had given permission with clearance from the escort commander for her to take a maintenance pod over to the Erebus to be there when AJ regained consciousness.

A few hours later after she felt she could trust the temporary engineer to take charge of the StarVista 4 engines and systems with Captain Xaoping's approval she was now waiting to go inside the Erebus medical bay. Eric joined her, then Madga Delfinch remotely allowed them both into the intensive care bay.

AJ stood with the aid of artificial legs, still a little wobbly after so long recovering but he had a grim look about him.

"I have condemned them, condemned them all," he paced awkwardly around the bay shaking his head at Eric, Andrica and Magda from the holoscreen. Magda Delfinch had returned to the StarVista 4 medical bay since Dr Sreisse's passing.

They looked on knowing full well he wouldn't take the news of the fate of the people on board the StarVista 4 very well.

Captain Andersohn was having none of it.

"That's enough self-pity, mister! None of us could have even imagined we were going to find anybody alive let alone even find the ship. You said yourself there was no guarantee of even finding it, only you had a better idea of where to look compared with all the other attempts. How could we have possibly known?"

Andrica chimed in. "AJ, we all pretty much thought it was a fool's errand and that after a few hours or at most a day or so you'd have given in and that would have been that. Imagine it. We found them because of you, and you gave them hope of being rescued even when they realised it had been a hundred years and not a few months. They were still happy to be rescued when all was said and done."

"Andrica is right, Captain Xaoping Shoo informs me that although there have been some escape and even suicide attempts, most passengers now accept their fate, and no one has actually laid the blame on you. In fact, there is a movement afoot to have their voice heard so that you are recognised as their saviour." Magda added from her remote station.

"That's all very well, but, but you've confirmed it now, they will ALL die, even little Cherice ... two years, six months - that's all she has got?"

Magda lowered her head and tried not to look broken hearted at her failure to find any form of a cure or even anything to slow the process.

"Yes, I expect her parents who are of a similar age to each other to pass in the next eight months. By then over half of the passengers and crew will have perished. I'm at my wits end and just hope this new facility they are hastily constructing and adapting will give us some answers and maybe even stop it in its tracks.

But I'm not hopeful," she trailed off looking glum.

"So, all in all, despite what any of you have said, if we'd not found them they would have probably continued to survive in the anomaly at least until they could no longer produce food. Water should have been no problem and my basic estimate is that they might have had at least a few more years. Instead ..."

The room was quiet. The air thick with misgivings and regret but Andrica was not having it.

"I think that you should go aboard the StarVista 4 now that Magda appears to have confirmed it isn't something that can be caught. I'm sure Eric can assuage any concerns from the GAA. You will be surprised at how much you are loved and, in some cases, revered."

"I don't want to be revered like some old-fashioned god. Don't they understand that by finding them I've doomed them all?"

Eric looked at him in despair. "Yes, you knucklehead. But at least they all now know what happened and that each of their worlds had honoured their memories. The GAA has been passing on millions of messages to the ship from the general public from all parts of the GAA and it has done wonders to lift their spirits.

You should be proud and not keep up this self-pity lark. I agree with Andrica, go aboard the StarVista 4 and meet with the passengers and crew. It will change you, I'm sure of it."

AJ looked down at his artificial feet then round at his friends and nodded, resigned to the moment.

#

Four hours later, with the Richmond family, Captain Xaoping Shoo, Captain Eric Andersohn, Andrica and a security team from the SV4 keeping watch over them AJ began a tour of the passenger observation decks.

As the group approached the ceremonial area of the forward observation deck a large crowd gathered ahead of them and a familiar person stepped forward on behalf of the passengers and crew. GAA Security Officer Roberts smiled as he greeted AJ.

"Dr Hansone. We know that considering the unfortunate circumstances since our rescue you feel responsible for the passing of so many and that none of the people of the StarVista 4 will have the chance to grow to an old age.

Nevertheless, we were lost and have been found.

All due to you.

We would have continued for a few more years in our trapped time as centuries would have passed by with no one knowing our true fate.

That changed.

All due to you.

None of us can change our past or future but we all feel a great debt of gratitude to you for finding and saving us from what could have been a violent and awful end.

I'm sure that at some point, things would have got out of hand if we had still been trapped. Instead, we have come to accept our fate.

The amazing and emotional messages from our loved ones at the time we were lost, up to the present day when millions of GAA residents have sent messages of love and sympathy, and the knowledge that our memories were honoured so highly and not forgotten, means a great deal to us.

We thank you and the crew of the EXSSV Erebus for coming to our aid and not leaving us and we appreciate the personal sacrifice you yourself made so that both ships could escape the Tianca planet.

We salute you sir and as we approach the new Alteran medical orbital facility all we ask is that no one ever again suffers the same fate as we did and that Tianca and the Cantrara system remain off limits.

Mr Roberts stepped back and saluted again as AJ raised his right hand to salute in reply, overcome with emotion and lost for words.

#

Seven weeks later

Now with a small fleet of ships, StarVista 4, EXXSV Erebus, four Defense class GAA ships plus a flotilla of smaller ships from all across the Galactic Arm Association press corp finally reached Alteran.

The new, hastily adapted, but highly sophisticated medical facility orbited Colspe, a small moon of Alteran so that it was well away from the main Star Port Atrica.

Severe quarantine restrictions were put in place with only properly identified and certified distant relatives of the remaining passengers and surviving crew allowed to visit and then under strict supervision.

The press were kept away although several made attempts to infiltrate the facility but they were quickly arrested and imprisoned at the facility as a stark warning to others not to try anything.

Dr Magda DelFinch became the de facto medical expert and was assigned as overall chief medical advisor as the medical staff began continuous monitoring of the remaining passengers and crew. As each passed away, their liquefied remains were carefully stored although no one knew what could be done, if anything.

Mission over, the Erebus and its crew was allowed to quietly slip away to an unknown destination for them to recover from the harrowing experience. Captain Andersohn and the bridge officers, along with Dr AJ Hansone and Chief Engineer Andrica Parsons were interviewed, some say interrogated, about the events surrounding the discovery/recovery of the StarVista 4 but all were released.

Dr Hansone reported to the GAA Security ministry for debriefing and Chief Parsons joined a small engineering task force to better understand fine fractures in the hyper drives to discover if such an event could again happen.

The GAA Council voted unanimously to set up a memorial to the crew and passengers of the ill-fated StarVista 4 to compliment the original memorial and update it with the recovery and sad loss of all lives aboard. However, the relocation of the memorial was still not resolved as the GAA Security Ministry insisted that the Cantrara system remain off limits and only to be investigated by an upcoming science mission, so the site would have to be somewhere that everyone could visit.

27: TO SLEEP, DEAR CHERICE AND DREAM NO MORE…

Two years later

Standing at the podium giving his summary to officials of the prime worlds of the GAA via hyperlink and to the honoured selected dignitaries in the auditorium, AJ continued his address.

"So, the failure to identify and repair even the tiniest micro fracture inadvertently contributed to the trapping of the StarVista 4 close to the strange ring system of Tianca. However, we should not be harsh in our criticism of Captain Xaoping Shoo, second in command, First Officer Graylor zXanders or Chief Engineer Ahanascal Coaraskk, as it was only with our more sophisticated scanning equipment that the micro fractures in the hyper-manifolds on the StarVista 4 could be found.

Therefore, from that perspective, with the equipment at their disposal and bearing in mind it was one hundred years old compared with ours, they didn't stand a chance of discovering the incredibly tiny micro fractures that contributed to their plight.

We can only speculate about the

strange character, the so-called news reporter Sicanrinka. It is clear from the onboard security agent Isaac Roberts that he stumbled upon her trying to undertake acts of sabotage in various parts of the StarVista 4 and the original so-called accident in engineering was more likely her first attempt to prevent the ship continuing its voyage. As to why she coerced ensign Zalokq into stealing an escape pod and taking it into the rings of Tianca, we still have only theories.

We do know that he was heavily in debt to her, but that she had somehow orchestrated it from the start. Perhaps she wanted what all news hounds chase after: an exclusive. A close look at the rings would have indeed been a scoop for the Havaerian news guild but it doesn't explain the mystery of where Sicanrinka was before she joined them as a roving reporter.

Her past still remains a mystery to the authorities for there is no record of her anywhere in the GAA population data base and she is the subject of an ongoing investigation by the GAA Security Ministry.

All we do know is that something made them turn back to the StarVista 4 from the rings and perhaps by interacting with those rings they created a distortion in space-time that ensnared them, pulling them back to whatever fate befell them.

That event in effect, as far as we can ascertain, caused a ripple effect which rapidly expanded and somehow linked up with the microfractures in the hyper-manifolds of the StarVista 4 engines, creating conditions we have never experienced before, trapping the StarVista 4 in a form of liquefied space where time ran differently for them.

So, for Captain Xaoping Shoo, her passengers and crew, where to them only minutes, hours and days passed by, for the rest of the universe, days, months and indeed years passed. Their experience of five months seemingly trapped orbiting Tianca meant that in reality, one hundred years passed of our Terran referenced time, so it is understandable that once we entered the ship and synced up by accident, it was quite a shock to them to discover the truth.

What none of us knew but discovered quite horrifyingly was that they were in effect doomed. To this day I wonder if we, or indeed I, did the right thing in rescuing them. It will remain forevermore on my conscience. I refer of course to the awful anomaly of each of them succumbing to a terrible effect whereby their bodies liquefied depending on their age, once we were no longer in the liquefied state of space. I and the salvage/rescue team will have to live with what we've done now that we approach the last few days of the very last passenger of the StarVista 4.

Young Cherice Richmond.

In theory she should never have been on

the StarVista 4 in the first place and I suppose you could call it fate. With her parents joint promotion becoming ambassadors to Zianca, it was understandable that before they took up their post, which was for at least a ten year position, Natalie and Carl, along with eight year old Cherice, would enjoy a final holiday before taking on official duties on Zianca."

Something caught AJ's attention off to one side.

"Ahh, I see that my colleague has arrived and so I must now take my leave of you but please make sure you follow events over the next few days and I hope you will take a moment out of your busy schedules to spare a few thoughts for Cherice and indeed the rest of the passengers and crew of the ill-fated StarVista 4. I will see you in a few weeks' time after I return to update and conclude this seminar.

Thank you for your time."

AJ stood for a moment as the muted applause died down and faded the hyperlink to the audience scattered across the GAA worlds. He looked over at Andrica, standing there in her own quiet contemplation, smiled faintly and stood up, walked across the stage and gently embraced her before letting go.

"So, it's time then?" he asked quietly and she nodded.

"Yes, I have a medium range transport to ferry us into orbit then a flight to rendezvous with Eric and the Erebus out orbiting Saturn. It should take the Erebus, five days at full speed to reach Alteran and the research medical facility."

AJ thought about how the worlds of the GAA had quickly pulled together and funded the adaptation of a hurriedly commandeered cargo/transport station hub into a first-class medical research centre where the survivors of the StarVista 4 spent their final time once the enormity of their fate had hit home.

Andrica broke in on his train of thought. "I've hardly seen you since we parted at Star Port Atrica?"

AJ looked down at his feet. "The official investigation by the GAA security ministry effectively meant I had little time for socialising. Even whilst I was undergoing the regeneration of my legs. I assume they had you in for a debriefing at some point?"

"Yes, I must have said the right things as I've not been called back. It will be good to be back on the Erebus again. Get to see the captain and crew even if it is for a sad occasion."

"Yes, it'll be hard after all this time to finally reach the end of life for Cherice," he saw her odd look.

"Oh?" AJ was a little puzzled as something she had said hit home.

"I've transferred to the 'Trl'l'pic' research vessel as their expert engineer for the Tianca system. The ship is Ziancan owned and has just been sent out to Tianca to thoroughly study the rings and see if they can replicate conditions that trapped the StarVista 4.

Your advice to the GAA council must have worked but it did take them until just a few months back to get their act together. I've been given leave from the Trl'l'pic', under the circumstances, to attend the final moments of Cherice but once it's over I'm to rejoin them at Tianca as quick as I can."

"You're a natural choice given your experience as an engineer and our own experiences regarding the StarVista 4. Apprehensive?"

"A little, yes, but I feel there is more to what happened than we had time to discover. Anyhow, we must go otherwise we'll miss the connecting flight up to orbit."

"OK, lead on and I trust you have the required documents?"

"Of course ..."

#

It had been a strange couple of years since she had arrived at the medical centre. Cherice Richmond's somewhat simple life of fun and education prior to, even on, that fateful and last voyage of the StarVista 4 felt like a distant memory now. She was no longer a happy go lucky child. Who could be with the loss of all she had known on board the StarVista 4 …

Indeed, who could be after seeing their parents pass away, or rather liquefy in an instant? She had been allowed a few final moments to say goodbye on both occasions but had been taken from the room roughly an hour before her father, then a couple of weeks later, her mother, were taken from her forever.

With the discovery that her brother, Danny, had suffered a tragic death along with most of his family decades earlier, it felt as if the universe had something against them. His daughter and her husband, Natalie-Cherice and Lariq, had initially visited but it was clear there was no true family bond, and it didn't take long for the visits to subside.

Cherice had begged her parents to let her attend Captain Xaoping Shoo's final moments and indeed that of all the prominent crew members who she'd developed a bond with. They had relented as long as she was not present at the very end of each of those lives. It had proven harrowing, especially the Captain's and indeed Lariq's but she had persevered as she knew they all were doomed to the same fate. A fate that then took her parents and since, the rest of the passengers and crew.

And now it was her moment. The final member of that tragic voyage and she knew the time was drawing near.

The door chimed and Nurse Caliqr along with

Doctor Magda Delfinch entered. She smiled at them both feebly knowing that she had only a matter of a day or so before she succumbed to the still unknown condition caused by being trapped for one hundred years on the ship in that strange space.

Cherice had grown fond of both Caliqr and Magda. Magda Delfinch had worked tirelessly alongside Dr Sreisse on the way back from Tianca on the StarVista 4 and together they were able to confirm the condition was not contagious. Both doctors had been instrumental in pushing for a special medical facility in which to both care for and study the remaining survivors.

Once Dr Sreisse succumbed to the condition whilst still en route, Magda Delfinch had become the de facto chief medical officer of the complex on their arrival.

Magda looked at her holoscreen notes then smiled at Cherice. "How are you feeling Cherice?"

"The same, boringly the same."

"I understand. It has been almost three years since we found you at Tianca. I will be honest with you, and I know that you are fully aware of the situation and I ..."

"I know. I'll be dead in two day's time. Mom and Dad's passing was quick. Are the others here now?"

Magda looked at Caliqr with a knowing look. "You mean Dr Hansone and the Erebus crew?"

Cherice looked at them in puzzlement then

realised it had sounded as if she thought her mother and father were the ones she'd meant. She nodded and smiled for the first time in many months. "Yes."

"I thought so, Caliqr, please bring in Cherice's guests." Caliqr barely nodded and left the room.

"Will it be painful Magda? The end …"

"As far as we can ascertain, no. Cherice, are you afraid?"

"Strangely, no. I thought I would be, but mother always told me that the end is just another beginning. Although of what, she never said. They looked peaceful when they passed. I'm glad you let me see the holovid of their passing. They looked asleep. Will I be asleep when it's my time?"

"That is why I am here now. We offer everyone who was on the StarVista 4 two options. One is to stay awake until the end, the other is to take a sleeping agent. Your parents took the latter."

"Why?"

"Cherice. Some people can cope with the idea of their impending passing whilst others were more, shall we say unsure they wanted to experience the end. It is quite understandable, especially when we are approaching something unknown and, well, so final. Very few chose to stay awake until the very end."

"What happened to those who stayed awake? You've never let me see anyone else's recording of their passing."

"They just felt very sleepy then it happened. There appeared to be no pain and our recorders just stopped picking up any life signs. It was a request from your parents that we not show you any recordings and I had to honour their wishes."

"I guess they were right. What did Captain Xaoping Shoo choose?"

"She remained awake until the end with her companion, Graylor standing nearby but not allowed to touch."

"Then I will be strong like the captain and not go to sleep."

"You are a very brave young lady, dear Cherice. Your parents would have been proud; indeed, they were proud of how you coped all through the entrapment, then the subsequent rescue of the ship."

At that moment Caliqr entered with someone and Cherice's face lit up.

"Well, hello there our young twelve year, oh sorry, one hundred and twelve year old young lady," said AJ as he, Andrica and Eric entered with Alteran civerian flowers, Earth lilies and an assortment of exotic sweets.

AJ bent over the specially designed bed and kissed Cherice on the cheek as Andrica handed Caliqr the flowers who took them out to find a vase for them. AJ stepped back as Andrica, then Eric, also gave Cherice a light kiss on her cheek and she welled up with emotion.

"Hey there, no worries, we always have that effect on people, isn't that right Dr Hansone?" Andrica said and winked at Cherice who broke out into a smile again.

"Cherice, don't listen to the old grumpy doc there, you are only twelve and a very brave young lady as well," offered Eric as AJ play acted as if he was hurt by Eric's comment.

"You are funny AJ. I'm the oldest, youngest person in our galaxy so there!" Cherice pouted her lips at AJ, and he stuck his tongue out at her and they both giggled. Andrica and Magda just shook their heads as Caliqr looked on in bewilderment at the humans. As a Scorion, she knew she would never understand the human species, but they did add a little extra colour to the many worlds of the GAA.

Cherice looked up at AJ and then at Andrica.

"Have you two married yet?"

Caught off guard, stunned and amused at the same time by her forthrightness, Andrica just smiled.

"Oh no, we're much too busy and we're not really a couple." Andrica bent low and whispered something into her ear and Cherice nodded mischievously as she noted AJ was bemused at their antics.

"So, have you been keeping Dr Delfinch here busy and not being naughty?" asked Eric, changing the topic.

"I'm a good girl. But it is a bit boring. Magda can always cheer me up however, so it's not been too bad."

AJ took her hand. "Have you heard the latest? There are several new movies been proposed and even filmed whilst we speak so there will be another boring film about the StarVista 4 starlet and her antics!"

Cherice playfully slapped his hand.

"They will be boring, and I bet they can't find anyone decent to play me. I saw several of the older films and they were rubbish! The actresses didn't look a bit like me!"

AJ nodded then let Andrica sit next to Cherice as he slipped off to one side with the Magda. She knew what he was going to ask so beat him to it by carefully motioning to a small side monitor, just out of view from Cherice's bed.

Two hours, fourteen minutes, the screen read.

"That's our best estimate based on what happened to everyone else." she whispered. "Cherice may be different due to her very young age compared with the rest of the passengers and crew of the StarVista 4, but our best guess is it will be minutes, perhaps an hour either side of that. We have misdirected Cherice into thinking she has a couple more days so as to not become to upset, hence contacting you all so you could be here in time. Are you staying?" Magda asked quietly.

He knew exactly what she meant and nodded.

"Good. I know you all have been present at most of the 'passings' but, well, this one is probably the most poignant. I assume the news media are outside?"

"Yes, Cherice asked me some months back via holocast if I would do something as she was fully with it and knew the GAA media would be here for the end. The end of a rather difficult and still enigmatic period. We are still no nearer to understanding fully what caused the tragedy. Perhaps we never will."

Andrica came over to them. "Cherice says she has something she wants to ask of us. She won't say anything without AJ."

They wandered back over to her bed. It was designed with a ten-centimetre lip all around, needed to prevent Cherice's liquefied state spilling onto the floor once she passed. It would then allow the liquid to drain into a special container which would in turn be stored separately with the remains of the rest of the passengers and crew of the StarVista 4 in the central storage facility of the orbiting complex.

"Dr Hansone, AJ, I have something to tell you all. On board the StarVista 4 whilst we were still on our normal voyage, I was given a solid holo recorder instead of the ship's holo recorder to help me record the trip and also for when I sent my messages to Danny. But when we were first at Tianca, whilst everyone was marvelling about the rings, I was bored so my parents allowed me to leave the port observation deck and I was supposed to have gone back to our room.

However, on the way I decided to go to the starboard observation deck and count the stars. I saw something, a ship, just before we had the odd ripples hit us. I recorded it but as the ripples hit us several times my parents had too much to think about and took the recorder away and stored it during the emergency. I forgot about it when we became trapped until a short while ago.

I didn't know the ship. I only remembered when I asked Magda to bring some of the things my parents had left me a few weeks back and the recorder was one of those items. I know I haven't much time now but I'm sure that ship is not from our peoples. I'm giving it to you so you can take a look and decide what to do. I'm sure that just before my mum took it away I tried to show her the pictures of the ship, but they weren't there.

I'd been met by that reporter, Sicanrinka at the time I took the pictures and I think she deleted them. I'm not sure if you can find them again but if you can, you may know what it is, and I may be being silly, but it would mean a lot to me knowing you will look into it when I'm gone."

AJ leaned forward and held her hand and shook it gently.

"You have my word Cherice, in front of our friends here, that I will take a look at it. I suspect it was probably the Alteran Scout Ship that was lost when it tried to dock with the StarVista 4 but I will check for you when I take a look at it. I assume Magda knows where it is stored?"

Magda smiled and nodded but also looked at him still holding Cherice's hand and he carefully let go so that he did not give away anything.

"Thank you. It probably was that ship as I didn't get chance to look at the database here but at least I know someone will take a look and I'd prefer that it be you," she smiled but seemed a little tired. "Will you come back tomorrow before, well, you know, before the end and let me know if you have found anything?" She suddenly yawned and AJ shot a glance at Magda who just shook her head, not sure herself.

"Of course, you must have a lot of faith in me as I haven't got it yet, but I will do my best for you."

Andrica moved forward sensing something was amiss. "We'll make sure he looks into it for you Cherice, I'll make sure he does."

Cherice looked up and glanced at AJ then Andrica. "You two really should be together you know. I can see it in your eyes … I feel tired. Magda, can you turn the heating up, it's quite cold in here an …"

She didn't finish as her body turned to silvery liquid and flowed neatly filling the specialised bed as it was contained as intended.

Despite all the times AJ, Andrica and Eric

had witnessed the effect, this one was the most harrowing. Andrica hurriedly left the room in tears with AJ quickly following her, putting his arms around her as they left. Captain Eric Estobahn Andersohn stood to attention and quietly saluted as he too tried to keep the tears back. Magda and Caliqr carefully sealed the bed and switched off the monitoring equipment which all now showed flatlines.

Cherice Richmond, the youngest member of the ill-fated last voyage of the StarVista 4, after all she had been through with the loss of her friends and family, was herself finally at peace.

28: TROUBLE AHEAD?

An hour later they convened at the nearest restaurant at AJ's request for a small ceremonial drink to toast the passengers and crew of the StarVista 4 and their final passenger, Cherice. As they gathered, they were joined by Tracheria who due to his customs had not wanted to be there at the end of Cherice's life. As they made small talk, it was clear to Andrica that AJ had something on his mind and looked troubled.

"OK, I know that look, something is bothering you AJ so come on, what's up?" she looked round the group as they sat at a large hexagonal table as the Erebus bridge crew looked instinctively at AJ for a reply.

He sat, clearly in deep thought for a few moments then realised they were all looking at him.

"It's something Cherice said about seeing a strange spaceship. I assumed she was talking about the Alteran scout ship that tried to dock, you know, the one where one of their crew managed to board the StarVista 4 but eventually perished just like everyone else would much later on."

"So?" Andrica was puzzled as she remembered Cherice saying she thought it was the scout ship.

"But she was incredibly intelligent for her

age, and apparently knew a lot about the various ship configurations. The logs show that sometimes she and Lariq would spend time on the observation decks when it was quiet and watched for ships when they were following or close to the hyper lanes.

She actually said she didn't recognise the ship at all. It keeps bugging me, that's all, and I'm not sure why."

"Do you think you are letting it get to you now she has passed? It might well have been nothing after all," offered Eric.

AJ sighed.

"I don't know. Perhaps I am. However, she said it was when everyone else was looking at the rings of Tianca and she got bored so went off to count stars, but something doesn't feel right."

Andrica shrugged but then saw the look on Tracheria's face. "You feeling all right Trachy?"

"Dr Hansone. You are right. It doesn't fit because she saw something before they were ensnared in the liquefied space. She spotted it during the initial first encounter, well before they were trapped. There were no other ships at the Cantrara system as it was so far from the edge of standard GAA systems. The Alteran scout ship event took place *after* they were caught in the liquefied space."

"Magda, where is Cherice's holo recorder?" AJ asked as his mind raced.

"We had all her belongings packed knowing

she was close to the end. They have been sent on to be added to the memorial museum for the StarVista 4 over at Star port Atrica. I'd guess they'll be there in the next couple of days.

AJ turned to his colleagues, a worried look on his face. "Tracheria is right. We need to get hold of that holo recorder and see what she spotted. Eric, the Erebus is undergoing maintenance at star port Trels, the next system to Atrica, what say you if I suggested I rehire you again?"

"We're not scheduled for any mission for the time being so I can't see that being a problem. Jaal is overseeing the work, now that of course Andrica here has up and left us."

"Hey, that's not fair. I was asked by the science council to join the Trl'l'pic once we'd had time off to mourn Cherice, but they are already underway so perhaps if there is a lift in the offering to get me to Atrica it would be appreciated."

"That depends on his lordship here, what say you AJ?"

"Fine by me. First let's get the flights sorted to get back to the Erebus then on to Star Port Atrica and see if we can commandeer that holorecorder."

They raised their glasses, paid the bill and headed out to their respective lodgings to grab their belongings before rendezvousing to head back to the Erebus.

Three days later, AJ entered the briefing room of the EXSSV Erebus, noting everyone present was standing ,uncannily, in the same places as the first time he had boarded the ship. That was a few years earlier just as they had embarked on their quest to find the StarVista 4. It now felt like an eternity ago, he mused, as Eric saw him, walked over and warmly shook his hand. AJ noted ensign Jaal now sported the insignia of Chief Engineer of the Erebus and he smiled in approval.

"Congratulations Jaal, I said you would make a fine chief engineer for the ship."

"Thank you, Dr Hansone. I have a lot to live up to, but I hope to make Chief Parsons, the Captain and yourself proud of me."

Andrica smiled at him but stood to one side and appeared hesitant.

Eric went over to her.

"Glad to have you on board Parsons, even if it is just as a passenger. We'll drop you off at Star Port Atrica soon enough but for now, you are a guest. It is only a short hop from Trels but we have a few basic maintenance routines to perform before we leave, as you will be aware."

"Thank you Captain it is appreciated. The Trl'l'pic should be at the Cantrara system in two weeks by my reckoning, so I'll be soon out of your hands and off on a fast long-distance transport to join them."

"Indeed. We'll miss you but I'm sure Jaal is up to the job." Eric turned back to AJ. "The cargo hold team says that Cherice Richmond's items have been retrieved and the holorecorder is being taken to your room, so no doubt we'll hardly see you over the next day or so?"

"You know me Eric, you can get on with running this fine ship of yours and I'll stay out of the way. So, if there is nothing else then may I take my leave, Captain?"

"Permission granted and don't cause any more trouble do you hear?" Eric smiled at AJ and they both grinned.

"Moi?" he replied then looked over at Andrica.

"Dr Parsons, it seems odd calling you that but now you are no longer under the strict thumb of the harsh captain of this motley ship, I'd like your opinion and advice so if you'd care to join me, we'll take a look at that holo-corder."

Eric scowled at his old school mate as the other officers held their tongues at the cheeky insult, but Andrica turned to AJ.

"Indeed, I will, but don't you go talking about my former colleagues and captain like that or I'll have to chuck you out the nearest airlock - I'm sure none here would object if someone went missing!"

"Point taken."

With that AJ winked at the others, turned and set off as Andrica just shook her head, looked at the others as well, shrugged her shoulders and set off to catch up with him. It felt like déjà vu for a moment as she did so, remembering their first meeting, first official meeting that is. She'd never fully admitted that she really had been a fan of Dr Hansone for some years but now she had a true and genuine working relationship with him and so, in her head, bygones were bygones.

Meanwhile Eric dismissed the remaining officers and with Tracheria and Liqxal set off for the bridge to ready for departure.

#

Tired and frustrated, AJ and Andrica turned off the holocorder having discovered nothing unusual to show for the last three hours.

"Do you think Cherice was mistaken?" Andrica asked as she got up and fetched them both a drink of water from the food dispenser.

"For her age she was pretty intelligent. She did spot the Alteran scout ship whilst they were trapped in the anomaly even if no one took any notice of her. That's why I was puzzled when she asked us to find the ship. I thought she meant the Alteran scout ship, but it came to me later that the timeline was wrong."

"Erm, you mean Tracheria worked that out a few days ago at the restaurant. Yes, she saw something before they became trapped. But she must have been mistaken as there's no image of a ship as she said. Unless of course if it was deliberately deleted."

AJ looked at her and blinked as his expression changed to one of enlightenment.

"The simplest answer is almost always the right one." Andrica quickly sat next to him as AJ reactivated the holocorder and this time tapped the options tab then the deleted folder.

They looked in fascination at the folder of over a hundred deleted stored images, the earliest from the time when Cherice had said she'd seen the ship.

They both instinctively gasped at the third image.

A ship. Andrica activated the zoom function and homed in on it. Large, ungainly, somewhat complex and completely unknown to any civilisation in the GAA.

"She was right," muttered AJ under his breath.

"This is serious. We could be looking at some form of spy ship from somewhere beyond the range of the GAA. We may be in danger."

"But why was the image deleted, look there are several more as she zoomed in on it."

AJ began to scroll through them until he reached the closest view of the set. The ship was intricately designed with an outer latticework surrounding an inner bulkier ship. Something that looked like a work horse, not a star cruiser. Something on similar lines perhaps to the

Erebus.

"But if Cherice thought it was important, why delete the images?"

AJ zoomed out to browser mode, then noticed a video file just after the last image of the alien ship. He clicked on it to play.

The view showed the observation deck on the left-hand side of the ship as it zoomed in then out again from the alien ship and they could hear Cherice chatting away about making a new discovery, she was as excited as an eight-year-old could get. Then the view swung round, and AJ and Andrica gasped in astonishment.

News reporter Sicanrinka approached Cherice and exchanged pleasantries before asking what Cherice had seen. Cherice excitedly announced her discovery of a new ship and asked if Sicanrinka would take a look. The video stopped and the browser came back up. There was another video file and Andrica reached forward and touched it to begin.

This time Sicanrinka appeared to be doing an interview with Cherice who had apparently discovered a new ship. Then as they watched AJ realised something and paused the video.

"Notice that holocorders record everything, including the screen if you haven't swapped to full screen mode. Look there down the right-side icons."

They watched as each icon appeared to have been passed over until the image folder icon was activated, a fly out menu listed the images and very quickly Sicanrinka deleted the images showing the alien ship, little realising her actions were also being recorded. The first video was also deleted then the one being taken at the time became highlighted and a small delete timer appeared next to it indicating it would be deleted after a pause of five minutes from the recording ending.

All the while Cherice chatted away about how she had got bored with the Tianca Rings and came away supposedly to her room, but had decided to go and count stars from the starboard observation deck when she made her discovery. She had not noticed Sicanrinka doing more with the recorder than taking the vid.

Sicanrinka finished off by thanking her and stating she had forwarded the video to her own system so she could edit it and prepare it for publication. The video stopped with Cherice looking pleased and begining to reach out for the holocorder.

"The sneaky so and so. She deliberately deleted the evidence," Andrica exclaimed. "But why would she do that unless …"

"I always said there was more to Sicanrinka. There is no record of her at all ever being born or living a normal life anywhere in the GAA. That leaves just one possibility. She's linked to that alien ship."

"A spy!"

"Why else would she destroy evidence - but why didn't Cherice tell us about meeting Sicanrinka?"

Andrica looked thoughtful then her eyes lit up.

"Have you got all the StarVista 4 data now, I seem to remember you asking Captain Xaoping Shoo about it before we arrived at Alteran."

"Yes, why?"

"The internal security may have picked something up."

"Good thinking." AJ tuned to his room's console and punched in details. It took several minutes before he had access to his full archive from the StarVista 4. Looking back at the time code for Cherice's holorecorder he started an algorithm to search the security data.

They waited, begining to think it was a forlorn gesture when his console pinged, and a video stream sprung into life. It showed a distant view of Cherice arriving and beginning to count stars. Several times she appeared to get flustered and begin again.

First, she appeared to start counting from one side, then after several attempts she swapped and seemed to be preoccupied with the view looking forwards. They could just hear her excited chattering then another figure came into view and walked up to Cherice.

Sicanrinka.

They appeared to be in discussion quite

amicably. Cherice handed the holocorder over and they saw Sicanrinka using it to record the little girl as she chatted on about making her discovery. Then they noticed Sicanrinka also using the controls more than she needed, without Cherice suspecting anything.

Their conversation was muted due to the distance and AJ began to manipulate the various options until they could finally hear what was being said and they listened intently to what followed:

Cherice:

"I've seen you around. You've interviewed many people but not me. I am the youngest on the ship and I thought you might want to talk to me during our voyage."
Sicanrinka:

"I thought I needed permission from your parents and with how busy I've been I didn't get to ask them. I've seen you watching me from a distance. You are a very clever young human. Can I let you into a secret?"

Cherice looked intrigued and nodded.
Sicanrinka:

"I am actually a spy!"

Cherice's eyes went wide.
Cherice:

"I knew it! I kept seeing you and thinking you were ideal for a spy. But why?"
Sicanrinka:

"My bosses think someone on the ship isn't who they say they are. So, I have to discover who they really are and find out what they are doing. Do you think that's exciting?"

Cherice nodded.

Sicanrinka:

"Isn't it! But it is also dangerous. That ship may be the key, so this is really important Miss Cherice. We must keep quiet about what we've seen until I can unmask this person and find out what is going on. Can I trust you?"

Cherice:

"Ohh yes. I can be your other eyes and I will keep a look out for anyone being odd. Ooo what about that strange man, Mr Roberts, he's always being odd!"

Sicanrinka:

"He's on my watch list but you keep quiet for now and if I need you, I will contact you. Is that a deal - I think that's what you humans say?"

Cherice:

"Yes, deal!"

Sicanrinka handed back the holo-recorder and left Cherice as the little girl stood looking back out at the stars as Sicanrinka walked towards and below, out of sight of the camera sensors. AJ and Andrica watched as the timestamp carried on for another thirty minutes, then the whole view shook and wobbled and the feed died.

AJ was thoughtful.

"That was when the first disturbance struck and the StarVista 4 became ensnared."

They watched as Cherice left and headed back to her room.

"And now we know she had been sworn to secrecy by Sicanrinka. No wonder she didn't mention it to anybody. Poor Cherice, she never realised she was probably helping the wrong person." Andrica sat back; something was bothering her in the back of her mind.

AJ said it first.

"Sicanrinka must be an alien spy from outside the GAA and she's linked to that ship. But why didn't the StarVista 4 detect it?"

Together they ran through the StarVista 4 data digging deeper and it became clear Sicanrinka had been busy covering her tracks. A cold feeling came over AJ and Andrica was just as troubled as they contacted Eric for a meeting.

#

"So, what are you suggesting?" Eric pretty much knew where the conversation was heading.

"Although the Cantrara system is still off limits, I can see if I can pull a few strings we have no real proof there is still another ship out there at Tianca," AJ said as Andrica looked thoughtful.

"The thing is ..." she began, "... whilst we were there, we didn't see or detect any other ship once the StarVista 4 was freed from the jellified space."

"True, and even whilst we were stuck for three months docked with it when it vanished we were careful not to alert the authorities until we knew what was going on. Only when we were heading back did we officially inform the authorities of our success at finding and saving the StarVista 4."

AJ stood and paced the room. "We're missing something obvious ..."

"Care to elaborate?" muttered Eric and AJ shook his head at him.

"I think the term 'missing' is clear." AJ shot back a little more harshly than he'd intended.

"What if ... what if that other ship was also caught up in the jellified space? What if when we fixed the problem, and it dissipated it also released them as well?"

"Yes, yes, that's possible Andrica, good thought. We were so preoccupied saving the StarVista 4 that we weren't really on the lookout for anyone else as no one else should have been there."

"But we're forgetting something. If they had been caught up like the StarVista 4 then their crew may well be dead by now," suggested Eric as he remembered the harrowing ends of the passengers and crew they had saved.

AJ stopped pacing. "But the ship may well be on automatic and still be there. Worth seeing what the Trl'l'pic finds when they get there. I doubt there is any danger if the crew have perished. Might just find a lot of silver slime all over the insides."

"Yuk!" Andrica wasn't impressed with AJ's humour.

"Do we inform the authorities? The security ministry, seeing that you are an agent for them!" Eric still found it somewhat amusing that AJ was part of the security of the GAA.

"No, not for now. Let's face it, all we have to go on is a few images taken on a holo recorder by a young girl aged eight and a half to suggest there could be someone out there with an agenda. It wouldn't stand up legally.

I say we head back out and on the way Andrica and I can study Cherice's extended diaries and the StarVista 4 security data now we have access to it and go into them deeper. There may be something we've missed. Agreed?"

AJ looked at his companions, nay friends, as they nodded in agreement. "Looks like we'll be taking you after all to join up with the Trl'l'pic, Andrica."

She smiled thinking of the extra time she would have on board with AJ as Eric turned to Liqxal. "Is Dr Delfinch on board yet?"

"Yes, she was resuming her post on the ship now all of the StarVista 4 people have passed. The medical facility is no longer a priority and the remains of the StarVista 4 passengers and crew will be kept in storage with the team Dr Delfinch trained up for the task."

AJ stood next to Eric. "Glad she's back on board. Tracheria, set course at maximum speed for the Cantrara system. Liqxal, monitor communications and keep a continuous scan for ships following us or heading on an intercept path. I sort of have a bad feeling about this and I'm not sure why.

Ladies and gentlemen …

we're going back to Tianca to discover the truth …"

EPILOGUE

He turned to his second in command.

"Has the fleet made contact yet?"

"Yes General, they are almost in position to strike right across the prime systems of the GAA."

"Good, dispatch …" General B'lac'tric paused. "Dispatch the Zenyrion to intercept and, if need be, destroy the Erebus. Inform them the Erebus has been discovered to have being taken over and that they are a part of an alien strike force giving away strategic information on the defences of the GAA. They are an extreme danger to the GAA and must be stopped at all costs."

"Yes General."

"Also give me our prime commander's connection on our secure line. Ready?"

The second in command signalled she was ready. General B'lac'tric switched to his native tongue.

(Translated from the Azline language for the benefit of the poor human species reading this transcript.)

"Prime Commander of the Azline Fleet. Apart from a minor problem at Tianca, you are cleared to begin offensive phase one to take out the main defensive GAA cruisers that have been redirected to your positions on a false premise. We have lured them into a trap, and they are completely unaware of our presence. Manitain silent operations until otherwise authorised.

Once completed, phase two will commence immediately with the annihilation of the primary worlds of the GAA. The secondary worlds are expected to crumble soon afterwards.

To the success of the Azline Empirate.

Begin!

COMING NEXT IN: THE LEGACY OF THE STARVISTA 4

Book 3 of the
StarVista 4 saga

The mystery deepens as AJ, Andrica, Eric and the EXSSV Erebus head out back to the Cantrara system only to find themselves following up clues left behind from Cherice's extended diaries and from an unexpected source ...

The long dead explorer, Sir Harley Ryker-Smyth, yes, he of the - well you get the drift ...

Meanwhile the Azaline forces assemble, and the GAA comes under attack from their long-forgotten foe ...

Will this be the end of the Galactic Arm Association ...?

Will it be the Legacy of the StarVista 4 ..?

AUTHORS NOTE

The author has always had a love of science fiction via books by Arthur C Clarke, Edmund Cooper or Ian Banks and Greg Bear amongst many others. Since a child, stories have formed in his head, but he always struggled to get them down or complete any of them which was naturally frustrating.

Having a vague sceptical interest in ghostly goings on, he surprised himself by writing and completing his first full novel: 'A Ghostly Diversion' which for a month was an Amazon teen and young adult bestseller to his surprise and delight. Even more of a delight was the fact that at last he'd broken through a barrier and actually completed a full-scale novel and tied up its loose ends; before long a sequel was produced, 'Secrets of Grasceby Manor'. Three more Ghost novels now form the five book 'James Hansone Ghost Mysteries' series with more books on the way.

However, this also spurred on the revival of interest in writing science fiction and work began on the StarVista 4 Saga. 'The Last Voyage of StarVista 4' was the first novel to take place in the Galactic Arm Association (GAA) Universe which was published in November 2021. This novel, 'The Fate of StarVista 4', is the sequel and will be followed by 'The Legacy of the StarVista 4'.

In the meantime, a short novel: 'The Fragility of Existence' was published in early 2019 and is more of an apocalyptic style novel along the lines of H.G. Wells famous classic 'The War of the Worlds'. This will now be a 4-book series with the overall title of 'Fragility ...' and book 2: Fragility of Survival was published August 2023.

An omnibus of the first five Ghost Mysteries was published in early Sepetmber 2023 so do check out the Astrospace web site for more details!

https://www.astrospace.co.uk/Fiction/

ASTROSPACE FICTION NEWSLETTER

To keep up to date with the novels written by Paul Money under the Astrospace Fiction banner, then why not sign up to the newsletter.

Those signing up will receive a *free* mini novel: "Lord Shabernackles of Grasceby Manor".

So, if you want to know more about the James Hansone Ghost Mysteries or the science fiction novels from Astrospace Fiction, such as how to purchase them and where, or when the next book in each series will be released, then simply sign up and you'll be the first to be informed. There will also be occasional competitions or give-aways so it's worth subscribing to see what may be on offer soon. Note your information will not be passed on to third parties.

Just head on over to the following link where you can enter your email to be added to the newsletter list.

Note I will not share your email with anybody, it is only for keeping up to date with Astrospace Fiction books.

https://mailchi.mp/1c69765ddf7a/
jameshansonegm-signup
Best wishes and see you soon: Paul M

THE FRAGILITY OF EXISTENCE

A Sci-Fi/Apocalyptic tale

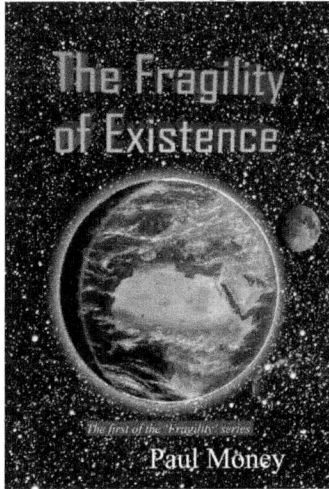

The extermination of our species was probably inevitable when you look back with hindsight.
Every advanced civilisation has almost always wiped out the resident less advanced occupants whenever they came into contact.
So it was the same for us, Homo Sapiens.
   But it wasn't supposed to have happened.

   We were not to know that though.
      Perhaps that is a good thing.
         For the Universe...

Matt and Simone stared out at the devastation and knew it could only mean one thing... Humanity was about to become extinct.

Could they escape the fate they had seen befall others in their small village of 'Woldsfield'?

They were not going to wait around to find out...

Available on Amazon UK as Kindle, POD and Kindle Unlimited.

First of the 'Fragility' series

THE FRAGILITY
OF SURVIVAL
Book 2 of the 'Fragility' series

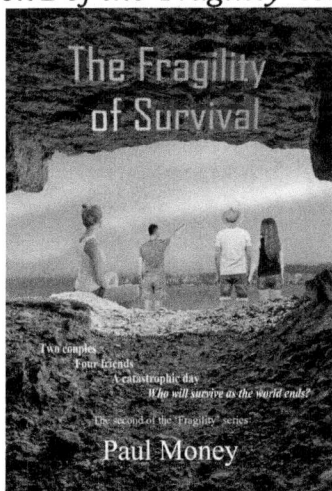

Holidaying in the Algarve region of Portugal was the norm for Scott, Katrina, Danny and Robyn.

Sun, sea, sand and well, yes, sex, all played a part in their plans, but not necessarily in that order.

And all was going well until the world ended and two of the foursome became trapped in a local cave system, unaware of what was happening to their friends and indeed the world at large.

As they emerge into a desolate landscape, the fight for survival begins...

Now available as Kindle, POD and Kindle Unlimited.

THE JAMES HANSONE GHOST MYSTERIES

It all started with a simple unplanned diversion, '*A Ghostly Diversion*'.

James Hansone is a computer and IT specialist and a complete sceptic when it came to all things paranormal. Until *that* diversion. It changes everything once he becomes intrigued with a ghostly face at a broken window of a rundown cottage, deep in the Lincolnshire countryside. Little did he know that he would go on to uncover the mystery of a missing girl that would change his life forever.

Now with four sequels, James Hansone unwittingly becomes a ghost hunter roped in to explore further mysteries with more books planned in the series.

A Ghostly Diversion
Secrets of Grasceby Manor
Return to De Grasceby Manor
James and the Air of Tragedy
The Haunting of Grasceby Rectory

All available as Kindle, print on demand and Kindle Unlimited from Amazon.

THE JAMES HANSONE
GHOST MYSTERIES
OMNIBUS VOL 1

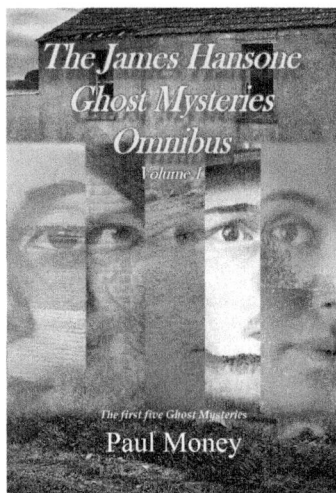

The first five ghost mysteries all in one book.

Check out Paul's Amazon author page:
https://www.amazon.co.uk/Paul-L.-Money/e/
B003VNGE1M

ABOUT THE AUTHOR

Paul L Money is an astronomy, writer, public speaker, publisher and occasional broadcaster. He is also the Reviews Editor for the BBC Sky at Night magazine and for eight years until 2013 he was one of three astronomers on the Omega Holidays Northern Lights Flights.

He is married to Lorraine whose hobby/ interest is genealogy/ family history. As an astronomer Paul has been giving talks across the UK for over thirty years and was awarded the Eric Zuker award for services to astronomy in 2002 by the Federation of Astronomical Societies. In October 2012 he was awarded the 'Sir Arthur Clarke Lifetime Achievement Award, 2012' for his 'tireless promotion of astronomy and space to the public'.

His first novels were ghost stories: 'A Ghostly Diversion' followed by the sequel, 'Secrets of Grasceby Manor', then 'Return to De Grasceby Manor' followed in 2019 with 'James and the Air of Tragedy' in 2020 and 'The Haunting of

Grasceby Rectory' in 2022 with at least two more planned in the series.

A first foray into the realms of sci fi saw the publication of a shorter novel, 'The Fragility of Existence' in early 2019, a version of the 'end of the world' stories that seem popular. 'Fragility of Survival' was published in August 2023 and is a standalone novel with two more in the 'Fragility' series in development.

'The *Last* Voyage of the StarVista 4' was the first novel to take place in the Galactic Arm Association (GAA) Universe published in 2021 and now this book, the sequel, 'The Fate of the StarVista 4' is here whilst a third, 'The Legacy of the StarVista 4' will follow in due course.

Another novel almost fully written ('*This New Horizon*') will be the first of another trilogy whose story will eventually link up with the saga begun with 'The *Last* Voyage of StarVista 4'.

More info can be found at the Astrospace web site:

Astrospace/ Astrospace publications
https://www.astrospace.co.uk/Fiction/

November 2023

Printed in Great Britain
by Amazon

46944585R00202